PARTNERS IN CRIME

-A Singapore Murder Mystery-

*For Celia,
Best Wishes!
Shamini
2005*

This book is a work of fiction. Any resemblance
to actual events, locales or persons,
living or dead, is entirely coincidental.

Published by Heliconia Press
(An Imprint)

ISBN No: 981-05-4628-9

All rights reserved.
No part of this book may be reproduced or
transmitted in any form or by any means, electronic
or mechanical, including photocopying, recording, or
by any information storage and retrieval system,
without the written permission of the Publisher,
except where permitted by law.

Copyright © 2005 by S Mahadevan Flint

Cover photography by Lizard on the Wall

Printed in Singapore

acknowledgements

This book could not have been completed without the assistance of friends and relatives. With special thanks to Georgie Campus and Kristine Kraabel for brainstorming and proofreading as well as my lawyer mother for her comments and criticism including, "But the book is a slur on lawyers!"

For my husband –
principal supporter and critic

'No man is an island, entire of itself...
any man's death diminishes me,
because I am involved in mankind;
and therefore never send to know
for whom the bell tolls;
it tolls for thee.'

John Donne, Meditation XVII

-prologue-

'Whereas by Article II of the Treaty of the 2nd day of August 1824 made between the Honourable the English East India Company on the one side and Their Highnesses the Sultan and Tumungong of Johore on the other. Their said Highnesses did cede in full sovereignty and property to the said Company, their heirs and successors for ever, the Island of Singapore together with certain adjacent seas, straits and islets…'
Straits Settlements And Johore Territorial Waters (Agreement) Act 1928

-one-

'Singapore shall be forever a sovereign democratic and independent nation, founded upon the principles of liberty and justice and ever seeking the welfare and happiness of her people in a more just and equal society.'
Independence of Singapore Agreement 1965

Dust motes danced in the frugal ray of light sneaking in between the heavy drapes. The light solidified the darkness around it. A slender hand snaked out and gently turned on a bedside lamp. The half-light illuminated a woman lying stiffly on a bed, covers drawn up to her throat. She slipped out of bed and started to dress from a pile of clothes neatly folded on a chair. The woman had the quick, surreptitious manner of a nocturnal animal. Once dressed, she padded silently to the entrance, slipping on her heels when her hand was on the door. Only then did she glance back at the bed. Lying in deep sleep, mouth hanging open, large belly silhouetted against the crisp white sheets, the prone figure looked like the famous silhouette of Alfred Hitchcock. It ran through the woman's mind that an apple in the mouth would render the sleeper fit to be the main dish at a Chinese wedding banquet.

A shudder ran through her slight frame. She slipped out of the room, closed the door gently behind her and hurried down the corridor.

At the lift, she kept her eyes firmly on the ground and allowed a thick wave of hair to fall across her face. She ignored the cheerful salutation of a passing bellboy. Only when she was out on the pavement and across the road from the luxury hotel she had left behind did she straighten up and compose her features into the pleasant mask with which her acquaintances were familiar.

•

A plane banked sharply left and descended to a thousand metres above sea level. It flew in low over a sea that appeared as smooth as a plate of glass on which sat beautifully-detailed miniature ships. The coastline, dotted with high-rise office towers and apartment blocks, was clearly visible to the passengers who had their noses pressed up against the windows. Annie, a nervous flyer, had her eyes fixed on the Asian Wall Street Journal. There was the sudden shudder of the undercarriage descending and a few minutes later the plane touched down in the January sunshine.

Annie disembarked and hurried towards the arrival hall, ignoring the headache-inducing blend of fluorescent lights, patterned carpets and busy shop windows. She did not notice the mass of humanity hurrying to and fro, corralled into waiting areas, watching television screens with slack mouths or hunting for homecoming presents. She cleared immigration in fifteen minutes, flashing her green card at the indifferent officer, a middle-aged Malay woman with tired eyes and a forced smile, and walked to the taxi rank, bypassing baggage reclaim. A wheelie bag with briefcase strapped on and laptop bag over one shoulder constituted her luggage. Climbing into a taxi and leaning back, Annie sighed with relief. She was pleased to be back in Singapore - happy not to have to stop by the office at the end of a long working day spent in Kuala Lumpur.

The taxi swung out onto the Pan Island Expressway and then the East Coast Parkway. As Annie travelled the curve of the six-lane elevated highway running parallel to the coast, the view, which she had refused to admire from the plane, sent a wave of pleasure through her. Turquoise waters dotted with ships - tankers, cruise ships, yachts - spread out to the left. A couple of grey warships with gun turrets and antenna protruding looked like so many silver pincushions. In the hazy distance, a thin strip of muddy brown, a sliver of the Indonesian archipelago, formed part of the horizon. Directly ahead, dappled with the sunshine peeping through the leafy trees planted along the central embankment, the road undulated. In the middle distance, the city of Singapore gleamed and twinkled as the setting sun reflected off the glassy skyscrapers. As the car swept over the crest of a hill, the driver slowed down for a speed camera. All around the cars did likewise, creating a rhythmic ebb and flow in the traffic, as they sped up again once beyond range of the camera.

The cityscape she was gazing at never failed to awake within Annie an ambitious spirit - a desire to compete with the people in the gleaming towers. She smiled to herself at the mercenary nature this revealed. A trip around Hong Kong harbour in a junk had provoked similar transient emotions. There, too, dominated by the jagged stroke of lightning that was the Bank of China building, the 'blind skyscrapers' thrust upwards. Annie enjoyed the brief sensation that she, a junior partner in the international law firm of Hutchinson & Rice, was a small but necessary cog in a massive capitalist wheel; facilitating the flow of money and goods to every corner of the globe. From the car, she could see the rows and rows of cranes of Singapore's massive port facilities, looking like long-necked metal birds peering anxiously out to sea. The same cranes could be seen from her office windows on the sixty-eighth floor of Raffles Tower. But while at work, she sat with her back to the view, poring over her documents.

•

Across town, in those same offices, Mark Thompson, senior partner at the firm of Hutchinson & Rice, sat in silence and in semi-darkness. Only his desktop monitor cast its blue light, throwing his angular face into sharp relief and leaving his curly mass of prematurely white hair, receding from a high forehead and curling round his ears, looking as if it was blue-rinsed. His shaggy moustache, by contrast still youthfully brown, encroached on his upper lip like an untrimmed hedge. Australian by birth, English by adoption and Singaporean by residence, he looked like the popular image of a successful attorney in the American South. He would have looked a natural in cream linen and a bow tie. Instead, he wore a dark suit and a heavily embroidered silk necktie, the knot carelessly loosened. His hand reached for the telephone and then hesitated. Instead, he pulled open the bottom drawer of his desk and took out a hip flask. A long swig settled his nervousness. Mark Thompson squared his shoulders, bracing himself for the ordeal ahead. He picked up the telephone.

-two-

'...culpable homicide is murder...if the act by which the death is caused is done with the intention of causing death...'
Section 300, Penal Code, Chapter 224

A slim, brown youth sat cross-legged on a bed. The doorbell rang and he grinned, enhancing the elvish cast of his features.

'That is the pizza. Just on time!'

His companion nodded languidly, 'Why don't you get it?'

'I got no money,' he answered sheepishly.

The other man nodded and clambered to his feet, wrapping a towel around himself. He reached over to his suit jacket tossed over the back of a chair and rummaged for his wallet, absently scratching the rug of curly black hair on his chest. A phone began to ring. Extracting a wad of cash, he tossed it on the bed and nodded to the youth who grabbed it and made for the door. The big man held the slim phone in a large hand and said, 'Good evening, Mark.'

Annie walked slowly up her driveway, through a green tunnel, the branches of the trees firmly entwined overhead. The white walls of her single-storey bungalow glowed pink, reflecting the dying embers of the sun. There was a warm moist smell in the air. It was the scent of freshly cut grass, mingled with that of frangipani blossoms. Some members of her extended family had been dismayed to find that she had a white frangipani tree in the garden. It was considered an unlucky tree, always found at graveyards. They spared no energy in trying to persuade her to chop the tree down. Annie was either amused, or annoyed, depending on her mood, by what she considered superstitious nonsense.

She kicked off her shoes and headed barefoot for the kitchen. She walked through the living and dining rooms, past the seasoned wood furniture. She could smell the musky, spicy odour of teakwood - an aroma as invigorating as fresh coffee. The kitchen was bright, modern and filled with the latest in kitchen gadgetry. Annie was hopeless in the kitchen, unable to cook and unwilling to clean, but she could never resist a new bread maker, coffee machine or microwave and her kitchen was a shrine to the latest in kitchen technology. She mixed herself a stiff gin and tonic, took the drink out to the veranda and collapsed into the solitary cushioned easy chair.

The strident note of a telephone ringing penetrated her doze. Annie struggled to resume her state of blissful oblivion but failed to shut out the insistent sound. She fished her mobile out of her bag.

'Hello.'

A gruff voice said, 'Annie, is that you?'

Her reply, 'Yes, Pa,' was drowned out by a paroxysm of coughing. Her father had been a three packet a day man for thirty-five years and there were days when he was too hoarse to speak. But he would still light up.

'Pa, can you hear me? How are you?'

'Good, things going well. Nothing new. How are you?'

'Fine, Pa. Tough day at work.'

'You work too hard. When are they going to make you a partner?'

'They have. Six months ago. I called you and told you!'

'Well done!'

Another bout of coughing. Annie waited for the inevitable.

'Annie, I need a small favour, just to tide me over…'

'Pa, I told you that I was not going to lend you any more money the last time.'

'Yes, but this time it's different. A really good deal. I just need a few thousand. You know I hate to ask!'

'Hate to ask? You manage to overcome your reluctance every time!'

'Look, I'll pay you back. I really mean it. This is my chance to make it big. I'm not getting any younger. But I know I have one more deal in me.'

Annie's grip on the phone was so tight her palm was starting to sweat. How could he do it? Come to her time and again for money. Without embarrassment. Always convinced it was for the last time. His eternal optimism was too hard for her to fathom. She sighed. She was tired. Her back ached. She gave in.

'How much do you need?'

'Fourteen thousand…'

'I'll send it tomorrow.'

'Thank you, I will pay you back this time. I've worked everything out…'

Annie hung up. Her father did not call back. He had what he wanted.

The phone rang again. Annie shook her head. What

was going on? She groaned at the phone number flashing on the screen. It was the office. She picked up the phone.

'Yes?' she asked curtly.

'Annie, is that you?'

This time her groan was heartfelt but silent.

'Yes, it is. What's up?'

She injected a measure of politeness into her voice for Mark Thompson. He was after all the senior partner at the Singapore office of Hutchinson & Rice, the firm where Annie had recently reached the giddy heights of junior partner. This success had not been achieved by her being unpleasant to those who had power in the firm.

'I want to see you. Are you back in Singapore?' he asked.

'Just got in,' she replied, and then kicked herself for wasting a gilt-edged opportunity to pretend she was out of town.

'Can you come into the office? I'm trying to set up a meeting for half past eight,' Mark continued, unconscious of her reluctance or ignoring it.

'What's it about, Mark? Who's the meeting with?'

A reasonable question. There was no answer.

'See you then,' he said and hung up.

Annie stared at her phone. Mark, for all his faults, was unfailingly polite. Something must have annoyed him considerably. Searching her own conscience, she could find no cause for his abrupt manner.

Annie decided not to compound Mark's irritation by being late. Twenty minutes after reluctantly setting out from home, she pulled into her reserved parking lot in the basement of Raffles Tower. She drew up next to the four-wheel drive of her colleague, Julian Holbrooke. He was just climbing out of his car, looking somewhat harassed. He was a man of medium height, with mousy hair speckled with grey and a pair of pale blue, protuberant, watery eyes. Even features and expensive spectacles, non-reflective, high index and trendy, allowed him to be pleasant looking without being handsome. He was dressed casually in dark blue shorts and a Ralph Lauren polo collared t-shirt - the tropical yuppie's uniform. Julian usually did his best to avoid wearing anything that did not have a designer logo, his discreet badge of success. There was a well-known chain of stores in Singapore, 'Why Pay More?', which appealed to the thrifty natives. It was a recurrent joke among his friends that Julian would have shopped at 'Why Pay Less?' if it had existed.

'What are you doing here?' she asked him in surprise.
Julian was notorious for never allowing work to interfere with his Friday night pub-crawls.
'Summons from above. Not by choice,' he replied.
'I got a call too. From Mark. Do you know what it's about?'
'Haven't the foggiest. He was insistent though.'
Annie nodded her agreement.
They made their way to the lift lobby together. She walked with long even strides. He matched her pace but had a curious rolling gait with his feet splayed, which seemed more appropriate for a ship deck. In the lobby, Julian looked for his swipe card.
'Damn, can't find my card, do you have yours?' Julian asked.
Annie hunted in her handbag and found her card. They started up to the sixty-eighth floor. Beating her to the main entrance, Julian typed in his four digit personal code and they walked into the reception area. Annie fumbled for the light switches just inside the door and a few discreet lights in the ceiling and a standing lamp behind the reception desk came on.

The décor in the reception area was intentionally muted. It was designed to suggest both tradition and discretion. Dark wood bookshelves filled with leather bound law reports lined one wall. On the opposite wall hung three Oriental paintings, fine brush strokes depicting caged songbirds. The firm handled no criminal work so it was not feared that the cage motif would offend any potential clients. On the floor an intricately designed cream and red, hand-knotted Persian Tabriz carpet muffled footsteps. A door on the left of the reception led to a large meeting room that could be sub-divided into smaller rooms by discreet sliding panel doors. The room had large clear windows which could be rendered opaque, and thus ensure privacy, at the touch of a button.

So late on a Friday evening, the office was silent and deserted. There was no cacophony of shouted instructions, secretaries typing or phones ringing. A few doors were open. A few rooms had their lights on. It did not indicate that someone was at work. Many of the lawyers did not switch off their lights on the way out in the evenings - a practice developed to suggest to inquisitive partners that work was still being done long after the lawyer had left for the day. It was a deception that Annie had adopted in her own days as an assistant. Now she smiled to see that the ploy was still in use.

At the end of the corridor was the office of Mark Thompson, Senior Partner. His door was closed.
'You go ahead, I'll just check my email,' said Julian, disappearing into one of the rooms, his own office.
Annie nodded absently and carried on towards Mark's room. A quick tap on the door was met with silence. She knocked again, this time louder and again received no response. Annie shrugged and tried the handle. The door opened easily and she stepped into the room.

Julian heard her scream, a muffled sound through the heavy doors. He stood stock still, the hairs on his arms standing on end. Then he left his room at a run and burst into the room at the far end - Mark's room. He found Annie standing by Mark's desk, her hands cupped around her mouth. Mark was sitting in his chair apparently oblivious to the entrance of the two lawyers. His head was resting against the table. His eyes were shut. He might have been asleep at his desk - except it would have been impossible to sleep through Annie's screams. Then as Annie turned and rushed past him, Julian saw what she had seen - a dark rivulet of blood, matting Mark's hair and turning it almost black, running from a gash on his head down the side of his face. Taking a deep breath, Julian edged up to him trying not to look at the wound. He could not bring himself to feel for a pulse on the bloodied neck but walked round the desk and gingerly put his hand to Mark's wrist on the other side. He could not feel even the faintest murmur of life.

Julian heard a sound behind him and swung round in fright. Annie had come back into the room. She looked pale and shocked but was no longer hysterical.
'I've called an ambulance and the police,' she said. 'Is he dead?' she continued less steadily.
'I think so.'
His voice cracked, like a boy on the cusp of adolescence.
'I can't find a pulse,' he continued, unconsciously rubbing his hands against the sides of his trousers, trying to erase the lingering feel of death.
Annie nodded.
'Maybe we should go outside. The police won't want us in here.'
She left unspoken that it was the last place she wanted to be, closeted in a room with a dead man, as the blood dripped from his head to the floor like water from a leaky faucet.
Julian led the way out. Here inspiration left her and they both stood outside the door like undisciplined sentries. Neither wishing to be separated, both unwilling to say so.

'Good evening, you two, am I late?' a cheerful high-pitched voice, betraying its Indian origins, struck a discordant note. A lumbering bear of a man, with thinning curly hair and a cherubic face framing soulful Hush Puppy eyes, wandered towards them.

'What's going on? You two look like you've seen a ghost!'

Julian winced at his choice of words, and to her embarrassment, Annie felt hot tears roll down her cheeks.

'What's happened? What is it?' Rahul was worried now. He came towards them and patted Annie awkwardly on the shoulder. A big man, well meaning, but clumsy.

'Mark's in there, we think he's dead,' Julian answered.

Rahul Gandhi looked disbelieving.

'You're pulling my leg, right? That's just not funny, chaps!' Rahul's accent, more pronounced in times of stress, contrasted oddly with his public school idioms.

'Jesus, you're serious aren't you?' he continued, taking in their expressions and Annie's tears. 'Heart attack, you think? He always looked like a pretty fit old boy. Just goes to show, doesn't it?'

What exactly Rahul thought it showed was never to become clear because Annie interrupted him to say, 'He's been murdered!'

It was out in the open. The unbelievable, yet undeniable.

'Don't be daft,' was Rahul's immediate response. 'What do you mean? You think someone's killed Mark?'

'What the hell do you think she means? Which bit didn't you understand?' Julian knew that he had no reason to lash out at Rahul. His patent disbelief was not unreasonable. But he needed an outlet for his stress.

Rahul pushed past them, raised his hand as if to knock, thought better of it and pushed Mark's door open. Neither of the others tried to stop him. Despite knowing what had happened, they welcomed independent corroboration. Rahul stopped short just inside the door. There was no need for him to go any further. Moving to stand beside him, Annie wondered how, as she had first done, she had thought Mark asleep. With the benefit of prior knowledge, it was clear from the unnatural position and absolute stillness of the body that they stood in the presence of death.

'My God!' Rahul looked from one to the other. 'What happened?'

'We don't know. We just found him,' Julian said.

He too was calm now. Rahul's presence and confirmation were a relief to him.

'When did you find him? Do you think whoever did it is still here?'

The others looked at Rahul in horror.

'I suppose he could be. Mark can't have been dead for long. He called me less than an hour ago,' Julian said doubtfully. 'Should we look around?'

Annie noticed that he was already turning to Rahul for guidance. Although all three were about the same age, in their early thirties, Rahul seemed older, calmer; able to deal with the unusual situation they found themselves in. Perhaps his sheer physical presence made him seem a bulwark.

'I'm not looking for a murderer,' Annie said decisively. 'Let's wait for the police.' In response to Rahul's enquiring gaze, she said, 'Yes, we called them, I guess they should be here soon.'

On cue, there was a loud knocking on the front door. At the same moment, a phone began to ring.

Rahul said, breaking the tension, 'You two get the door, I'll get the phone.'

Again, he assumed command. The division of responsibilities was also a tacit acknowledgement that he, of the three of them, would be safest on his own. Julian and Annie headed for the door hearing the familiar, 'Hutchinson & Rice, can I help you?' from Rahul as he picked up the phone. Annie wondered how he could sound so normal. The purpose of a rote greeting she supposed.

-three-

'...the Police Force shall have the following functions throughout Singapore:
(a) to maintain law and order;
(b) to preserve public peace;
(c) to prevent and detect crimes;
(d) to apprehend offenders...'
Section 4, Police Force Act 2004, Act 24 of 2004

At the entrance, Annie and Julian found a short, rotund Sikh man who flashed a badge at them. He was followed by a number of uniformed personnel. They led the policeman into the office. Rahul was still on the phone.

'Who is this?' asked the Sikh curtly.

'One of our colleagues, Rahul Gandhi,' answered Annie promptly.

He said, 'Mr. Gandhi, please do not communicate the situation here to anyone,' and then, assuming compliance, he asked, 'where is the victim?'

He addressed his question to Annie. She silently indicated Mark's closed door, and the turbaned man, using a handkerchief, pushed the door open and went in.

Rahul, who had fallen silent during this exchange, now spoke into the phone again. 'Ai Leen, it's me. Yes, I think you'd better come in and bring Reggie as well. Come as soon as you can.' A pause and then, 'No, it had better wait until you get here. I'll explain then.'

What could he explain? Your senior partner is dead. Murdered. Easy to express, difficult to explain. Men might have turned to murder since Cain killed his brother but Annie could not comprehend it. Powerful emotions were not unknown in the corporate world she inhabited; but expressions of such emotion had always been confined to verbal exchanges.

'Who's the towel-head?' demanded Rahul, hanging up.

Julian silently handed over a card.

Rahul read out loud, 'Inspector Jagjit Singh, CID, Central Police Division.'

The policeman stepped out of Mark's room. Annie wondered if he had heard Rahul. He gave no sign of having done so. His fleshy face remained expressionless. Annie looked at the policeman with interest. He had a suspiciously black, full but neatly trimmed moustache and beard that hedged a wide mouth. A full pink lower lip suggested a pout. The Inspector wore a dark turban and a white shirt with a slightly sagging breast pocket that contained more pens than could reasonably be required of one person, however prolific a writer. His dark trousers were worn over rather than under his stomach. The trousers were held in place with an old leather belt that showed the creases of his slimmer days. And on his feet were snowy white sneakers.

The policeman ignored Annie's scrutiny, beckoned to his men and gave a few quick instructions. Two of them set off down the corridor and started looking in individual rooms. They opened each door and peered in. A third took up a position outside Mark's door.

'Is there anywhere these men can wait?' Inspector Singh asked, gesturing at the two men in white. 'Ambulance personnel. We won't need them for a while.'

Annie led them to the pantry and, as an afterthought, invited them to sit down and help themselves to anything in the fridge. Correct social behaviour in a changed landscape. Rahul and Julian trailed in her wake, unsure of what to do and glad of a temporary purpose.

'Wait here all of you. I will need to ask you questions later.' Inspector Singh issued commands with the calm certainty of one accustomed to being obeyed.

'Where are you going now?' asked Rahul as the Inspector headed for the door. He had a big man's disdain for figures in authority and was the only one of the three who was not quietly intimidated by the presence of the policeman.

'To wait for the pathologist and secure the crime scene,' was the Inspector's brusque reply.

'A couple of colleagues may be here shortly, Inspector. The ones who called,' Rahul continued, aware that he had overstepped the policeman's instructions.

The Inspector nodded.

'What about his family? Should we notify them?' This time it was Julian with the question.

'You have not called them yet?' asked the Inspector.

'No,' said Annie, wondering why they had not done so. That should have been their first instinct, to notify the bereaved. What had held them back? The reluctance to be the bearer of bad news? The others felt that the omission warranted explanation as well.

'We haven't had time, we were waiting for you,' Julian clarified. It was a plausible explanation but not accurate. They had had the time if they wished. But individually and collectively, consciously or unconsciously, they had chosen to ignore the immediately bereaved.

Inspector Singh did not cavil at their explanation. He merely nodded. A man of few words apparently. 'I will see to it then. Please give me the address and phone number. There is a wife?'

'And two kids, both in school in England. They're away now. His address is #15-04, Tanglin Vista Apartments,' Rahul told him and gave him the telephone number from memory as well. Rahul had a phenomenal memory that assisted his performance as an outstanding commercial lawyer. Behind his back, those less fortunate said that he did not just look like an elephant.

'She's his second wife,' blurted out Annie. The others looked at her in surprise. The Inspector gave no sign of having heard the interjection. He did not inquire further and left the room.

'Why'd you tell him that?' asked Rahul.

Annie shrugged.

'Prepare him for the surprise, I guess.'

The next few hours took on the unreal quality of a waking nightmare for Annie; one of those dreams where the circumstances are too unlikely to be real, and there is a measure of subconscious skepticism. But there was to be no relief upon awakening. White-coated men wandered up and down the corridor. Blue-uniformed personnel stood around. There were sharp barks of command. Light bulbs flashed as photos were taken. Voices were heard on the telephones. Strips of yellow tape were used to cordon off parts of the office.

'They really do dust for fingerprints!' exclaimed Rahul at one point, poking his head round the door. Later, 'They're moving the body.'

Even later were the interviews; telling Inspector Singh everything they knew over and over again. Each time she repeated her story, Annie found she was adding layer upon layer of detail. To her mind, the minutiae were irrelevant, but the Inspector appeared keen to picture each unfolding scene in glorious technicolour. It had begun with getting the phone calls. Mark had called each of them in for a meeting that evening. No, it was not the usual practice. In fact, it had never happened before. Mark had been insistent on the phone, demanding that they present themselves at the office. But he had been calm. His voice had been a bit tired perhaps. Annie contributed this information. The other two had not noticed.

There had been no hint as to what it was about. Coming into the office, finding the body. Had they been together? No, Annie had gone ahead. Called for Julian when she found the body. She omitted to mention the screaming. No, they hadn't touched anything, except to check for a pulse. Who had done that? Julian. Annie's involuntary shudder at the suggestion that she had handled the body spoke volumes. Were they sure that nothing had been touched? Yes, but they were in and out of the room often during the working day. That day as well? Not Annie. She had been travelling. It was so long ago now. Like a childhood memory, half remembered, half imagined. Here, too, the boundary between the past and the present was marked by innocence lost. She explained that she had come home from an all day meeting in Kuala Lumpur. The others had been in the office. Mark had been alright. Perhaps quieter than normal? Difficult to tell. Even with the benefit of hindsight.

No, he had no enemies that they were aware of. Business rivalries. But nobody really disliked him, as far as they knew. No one hated him. Not enough to kill him. No one they knew about anyway. Except his first wife. That last remained unsaid. Sarah Thompson was not in the country. There was nothing to be gained from dragging her into it. That was the unspoken consensus. Already, the lawyers were closing ranks against the police. Protecting one of their own. After all, Mark had been a good enough boss. Arrogant and demanding, but there was nothing unusual in that. He didn't suffer fools gladly. The rumours that he was being replaced, that the alcoholism was taking its toll, were left unsaid. Annie knew, and she was sure that the others did too, that these omissions would hinder the policeman in forming an accurate picture of the dead man. But she could not bring herself to speak ill of the dead. Nor could the others. Perhaps the social caveat against doing so was rooted in a natural reticence and not intended to prevent an outpouring of enmity towards the dead. As Rahul said later to the others, justifying their instinctive omissions, nothing about Mark's life was that out of the ordinary. A successful, clever man. Mid-life crisis. Failed marriage. Social drinking getting out of hand. Perhaps serious drinking showing up socially. He was hardly the first. Just the first to be found dead in their offices.

Once, Annie wondered aloud why Reggie and Ai Leen had not turned up. Or for that matter any of the other partners if they too had been called by Mark to the mysterious meeting.

'Some of them are here, in another room,' was Inspector Singh's impassive response.

That was a bad moment for all of them. The first time it had become apparent that the flow of information was all in one direction. Annie thought that, short of clapping them in irons, Inspector Singh could not have emphasised his authority over them more clearly. He was the policeman. Information was in his gift, to be distributed or withheld at his discretion.

'Why are you keeping them away from us? Are we suspects? Are they?' asked Annie, her tone betraying her dawning fear that this murder was going to embroil them all in an experience going well beyond the immediate horror of sudden death.

She did not get a response from the taciturn policeman.

The worst moment for Annie was explaining the

security system, that after eight in the evening, the lifts could not be operated except with a swipe card or by filling in a visitors' book and being escorted by a security guard to the correct floor.

'Who has a card?' asked the Inspector immediately, not slow to see the implications of what she was saying.

'Only the partners,' confessed Annie reluctantly.

The other two looked as if they wished they could contradict her but it was the simple truth.

'Where is the visitors' book kept?' asked the Inspector, unaware of, or feigning a lack of interest in, the undercurrents of tension and dismay in the room.

'In the lobby, with the security guards.'

This piece of information provoked a whispered instruction to a uniformed policeman who scurried off to do the Inspector's bidding. It was not difficult to guess that the young policeman had been sent to retrieve the book and corral the security guards. Annie desperately hoped that some light would be shed on the murder by the guards or the book. Already her own concern, and she suspected that of the others, had shifted from the fate of Mark to the consequences for themselves. The survival instinct was quick to show itself, she thought bitterly, leaving the dead ignored and unmourned when the living felt threatened.

Finally, Inspector Singh said as midnight approached, 'You can go now. But don't speak to the press. I will need your passports. Bring them in to the station by lunchtime tomorrow. The address is on my card.'

The minute he left the room, a babble of voices broke out. 'Can he do that? Take our passports?'

'Doesn't he need a court order?'

'What's to stop us absconding now?'

'They got Nick Leeson back quick enough.'

All of them remembered the rogue trader who had brought Barings Bank to its knees and then fled. He had travelled through Malaysia, Borneo and reached Germany.

But the Singapore authorities had tracked him down and arranged his extradition. He had served time in Changi prison.

'Well, I'm not going anywhere except to bed. We haven't done anything so we have nothing to be afraid of. There'll be some explanation for all this in the morning.' This was Rahul being pragmatic. He continued in the same practical vein, 'We should all meet tomorrow. We'll need to take stock. Tell HQ. Support the grieving widow.' This last was said with a wry smile.

'We need to find out about the others as well,' Annie added. 'It looks like Mark called most of the partners in for this meeting…one of the others might have a clue why.'

'Where shall we meet? Will we be allowed back in here?' asked Julian, looking questioningly at the other two.

Julian's eyes were bloodshot and red rimmed from the tension of the last few hours. Every few moments he would shut his eyes, in an action somewhere between a blink and a conscious action. It could just be his contact lenses thought Annie but it came across as a nervous tic and made her feel jumpy. Rahul on the other hand was bearing up well, at least physically, looking no more bemused and tired than if he had stayed up a couple of hours watching a cricket game on television. He demonstrated again that he was as yet unfazed by events by immediately making a decision.

'Good point. We might not be allowed back in here. Let's meet here anyway at nine and if we can't get in, then at Starbuck's.'

'Alright,' said Annie and Julian nodded his head. They stood there, the three of them, looking at one another uncertainly. And then Rahul gave Annie a quick hug, Julian a pat on the arm and turned on his heel and left. The other two followed more slowly.

-four-

'domestic worker' means any house, stable or garden servant or motor car driver, employed in or in connection with the domestic services of any private premises.' *Interpretation, Employment Act, Chapter 91*

Maria Thompson sat half upright, half lying on a red velvet couch. A less poised figure would have been slouching. She wore a silk kimono dressing gown with a dragon embroidered on the sleeves and back. Smooth, unblemished legs with almost child-like bare arched feet were hooked over a sofa arm. Maria's almond shaped eyes were fixed on the flickering images on a wide screen television. The sound was turned down to the point of inaudibility. Her oval face, with its smooth flat planes of cheek, was expressionless, mesmerised by the silent, moving figures on the screen.

On a side table, a few silver-framed photographs of Maria, and a smiling white haired man, at least thirty years older, were neatly arranged. In one, the couple stood side by side formally, not touching. In another, he was smiling down at her in a close-up of their faces. The photos had all been taken on the same occasion. The clothes, an elegant body-hugging white satin gown and a black tuxedo, were the same in each. If the woman in the room had not been the one in the photos, a stranger might have assumed the pictures had come with the frames.

Someone pressed the doorbell and she heard the chiming of electronic bells. Maria Thompson stirred instinctively, then remembered herself and lay back. The clicking heels of sensible shoes marked the progress of the uniformed Filipina maid as she walked down the hallway to the main door. She returned a minute later.

'Ma'am, there is a visitor to see you.'

'Who is it?'

'He does not tell me, ma'am. He says he is from police.'

The maid's expression betrayed the concern she felt.

'Why is he come here, Ma'am? I have not done something wrong, I swear it!'

The Filipina maid voiced her fears, although her papers were in order and she did not supplement her income by working in more than one home or moonlighting as a prostitute. The mistress of the house, who had done both before marrying, went out to meet the police.

A Sikh man said, 'I am Inspector Singh of the Singapore police. Are you Mrs. Mark Thompson?'
She nodded.

'I'm afraid I have some bad news, Mrs. Thompson.'

Formulaic words, understood by everyone to be a herald of death.

'My family?'

Her voice was trembling, emotion-charged, the face starting to crumble. A mannequin coming to life.

It was the Inspector's turn to nod.

'What has happened to them? Tell me, please. Oh God! Tell me!'

'It's your husband, Mrs. Thompson. I am sorry to have to tell you that he is dead.'

'My husband?' she repeated after him blankly.

Then the second wife of the dead man fell to her knees, as if in prayer. The police officer could not make out the words she was saying over and over again as she rocked back and forth. Then he heard her. The words were indeed in the manner of a prayer. She was on her knees repeating, 'Thank God!' The face of the policeman betrayed his surprise.

Ten minutes later, Mrs. Mark Thompson was again on the velvet couch, this time sitting bolt upright, kimono folded decorously over both knees and clutching a mug of hot chocolate close to her breast - for comfort or to give her hands something to do. The Inspector sat across from her, stiff backed in a stiff-backed chair, at a slight angle so that the woman had to turn to look at him directly. For a while they did not speak. His eyes took in the genuine antique Chinese rosewood furniture, buffed to gleaming and the brushstroke paintings of mountains, fields and blossoms. A highly polished grand piano stood in the corner, lid down. Two large vases filled with green bamboo shoots stood on either side of a gilt-framed mirror. The room had all the passion of a shop display.

Finally, Maria, her face blotchy with crying, but defiant said, 'You must understand Mr. Singh, I thought you bring me bad news of my children. I have one boy and one girl, six years old and eight years old … from a … another marriage. For a long time I have not seen them.'

He missed neither the heartbeat of hesitation before the word 'marriage' nor the absence of photos of the children from the side table.

She must have seen his gaze stray to the photos because she said, 'Mark said that I would be happier without reminders of my past in the house.'

'And were you happier?' He was not afraid to ask the

unexpected.

'I miss my children!' she snapped.

He did not repond but instead sipped the tea that the maid had brought him. The flash of spirit died as suddenly as it had appeared.

'What happened to my husband? Was it a car accident? Mark is very careless driver sometimes.'

Watching her face, framed with the long straight black hair, the Inspector said, 'He was murdered. Hit repeatedly on the head with the paperweight he kept on his desk.'

She dropped her steaming mug, both hands going to cover her mouth. They both watched the cocoa stain spread dark across the cream carpet like blood from a wound.

'Who did it?' A whispered question. A brilliant actress or a woman almost prostrate with shock.

'At present, we do not know.'

'It was her. I know it! She hates…hated him. And me also.'

Each word said with rising hysteria.

'Who did, Mrs. Thompson?'

'His wife!'

'I thought you were his wife.'

'His first wife…his ex-wife. He left her to come to me. She threatened him … and me. I tell you she killed him. She will come for me next. You must stop her. Oh God! What will happen to my children?'

The Inspector interrupted her, 'I understood the ex-Mrs. Thompson to be out of the country.'

'You are wrong. She is here right now.'

-five-

'All persons are equal before the law and entitled to the equal protection of the law.'
Section 12, Constitution of the Republic of Singapore

All the partners of the Singapore office of Hutchinson & Rice, bar one, were gathered together at the penthouse club of their office tower block. The absent partner lay in a chilled steel drawer at the morgue of a Singapore hospital, naked except for the small plastic identification tag tied to his left toe. Their law offices were still out of bounds, with strips of tape across all the entrances. A cheerful yellow that the television-age had taught everyone to identify as a police barricade. Two uniformed policemen had politely ushered the lawyers away as unwanted visitors to the scene of a crime. Starbucks had been vetoed in favour of the privacy of a private room at the club.

The session functioned as combination group therapy and council of war. They all sat now, around the table, ignoring or oblivious to the panoramic view of turquoise seas and blue skies visible through the ceiling to ground windows.

In addition to Annie, Rahul Gandhi, and Julian Holbrooke, there were Lim Ai Leen and Reggie Peters, who had also been in the office the previous evening, Stephen Thwaites, most senior partner after Mark Thompson, and Sophie King. Each had taken turns to update the group on the events of the previous evening. Reggie and Ai Leen had each received a call from Mark. Reggie had offered to pick Ai Leen up on his way into the office. They had been running late, hence the call to the office that Rahul had answered. When they had finally got there, Mr. Singh had incarcerated them in an office and refused to answer their agitated queries except to tell them that Mark had been murdered and then to ask them endless questions.

Reggie was sweating despite the cool of the room, droplets of moisture on his forehead and upper lip. His thinning hair was clinging damply to his flushed scalp and there was a speck of saliva in the corner of his mouth.

He said now, 'He was extremely rude. I've a good mind to complain to his superiors. How dare he treat us like that? As if we were common criminals.'

Annie wondered what an uncommon criminal was. Was it the nature of the crime or the criminal that attracted the sobriquet?

'We weren't even allowed to make any phone calls... and we were in my office!'

Reggie reached an even greater pitch of self-righteous anger. Annie could not see how being in his office made a difference but Reggie saw this as the last straw. Bad enough to be subjected to the authority of some local policeman, but to have that happen in his own domain, that was adding insult to injury. She thought that he was not dealing well with the situation. A red-faced man, getting redder with his annoyance. Reggie was very conscious of his own dignity. He lost his temper with subordinates over imaginary slights. His condescension towards the locals was neo-colonial. Annie, with her mixed parentage, usually found him offensive.

Today she felt sorry for him. It was perfectly apparent that Reggie's contempt for the Singapore officialdom had not been displayed the previous evening.

Rahul intervened unexpectedly in defence of the policeman. 'I thought he was competent enough. It's early days yet. Anyway, we're here in Singapore and will just have to make the best of it.'

Ai Leen had hardly uttered a word although she had been with him the previous evening, leaving Reggie to describe his version of events.

Now she said in her quiet firm tone, 'He did not appear rude to me.'

Reggie, who had been on the verge of disagreeing vehemently with Rahul, subsided at this contradiction from an unlikely source. Ai Leen, her contribution to the conversation over, reverted to stony-faced silence. Unlike the rest who were dressed casually, Ai Leen had arrived for their meeting dressed for a day at the office. She was wearing a powder blue twin-set with a string of pearls around her neck. Her face was carefully made up, eyebrows recently plucked into a fine, inquiring line, as if she was about to meet an important client, rather than discuss the murder of Mark Thompson. Annie had to admire her sang froid although she could not help but feel mildly disturbed by her almost unnatural calm in the circumstances.

'Well, I had a message from Mark on my answer phone when I got out of the shower. I came straight to the office but was too late to see him. The Inspector had me incarcerated in my office,' said Sophie King, weeping quietly. 'I still can't believe it. Who would do something like that? Why? Was it a robbery?'

Annie remembered that Sophie and Mark had known each other for many years, qualifying as solicitors in the same year. Idle gossip in the office had suggested that there had been a relationship between them. Sophie had never married, choosing instead to devote herself to her job, coming out to Singapore a couple of years after Mark, when the opportunity had presented itself. She was a quiet, intense woman with great legal ability, much respected by her colleagues and clients. She was a role model for some of the younger women in the office, including Annie, having been one of the first women in the firm to crack the glass ceiling, although hardly shattering it. Now she sat at the table peering at each of them through spectacles that made her eyes loom large and tearful. A successful professional crumpled into an elderly, defeated woman.

Stephen put his arm round Sophie's shoulder and she leaned towards him, a comforting presence. He said briskly, in the plummy baritone that would have ensured a successful career at the Bar, 'We'll let the police worry about who did it and why…'

Reggie interrupted, 'Well, you haven't presented us with your alibi yet.'

Stephen ignored the jibe. 'Unfortunately, I was home in bed with a headache and did not pick up any messages from Mark until this morning.' He continued, 'Our immediate concern must be to reassure clients and staff that this had nothing to do with any matters he was dealing with for the firm.'

'But how can we know that?' Annie asked.

Stephen shrugged off the question irritably, '*I* know it and anyway it's hardly relevant. Our first priority must be to avoid a scandal. For the sake of his family, and the firm. For our sakes! Some passing madman is not going to destroy this office.'

'It's what Mark would have wanted,' murmured Reggie.

Annie itched to slap him, belatedly co-operating when the issues were spelt out in terms of his own self-interest. Reggie's attitude was too much for Sophie as well.

'Listen to yourself, you sanctimonious bastard,' Sophie said, getting to her feet and pushing Stephen's arm away. 'You don't know what Mark would have wanted and you don't give a damn either. Mark was a decent man…a good man. He made a few mistakes, we all do. He didn't deserve this. He didn't deserve to be the subject of a damage limitation exercise!'

'Well, that's what he was in life, why should his death change anything?' asked Reggie angrily. 'Drinking, pissing off clients, screwing the maid. In death as in life. The final scandal!'

'Alright everyone. Let's take a step back here,' said Rahul, always the conciliator. 'We're all upset but Stephen's right. We need to stick together. I think we ought to issue a press statement…and close the office for a few days as a mark of respect. We should get in touch with the widow as well. Help arrange the funeral. God knows what Maria will do if we leave it to her.'

There were nods of agreement around the table and even Sophie lapsed into a bitter silence. The business of living must go on, thought Annie. The dead become a dead weight and are left behind.

'We should contact Sarah Thompson as well,' said Julian. 'If we leave it to that woman, God knows what she will say and do.'

'Joan will handle that,' said Stephen, looking embarrassed.

Joan was his wife who had been a close friend of the ex-Mrs. Thompson before she had fled back to the relative anonymity of the United Kingdom six months ago after the collapse of her marriage to Mark and the accompanying scandal. Again, there were nods. It seemed appropriate.

'There was nothing in the papers this morning. It may be a good idea to draft a statement now. Make sure when the story does break, we have a response,' said Rahul, ever practical.

'I suppose someone *would* have told Maria? We are assuming that she knows,' asked Julian doubtfully.

'Yes, she would have been told by now,' said Annie. 'The Inspector said he was going to stop by there last night and tell her.'

'If you'll excuse me. I don't think you need my help to draft the press release,' said Sophie coldly, getting to her feet and walking to the door. Nobody tried to stop her leaving. As the person with the most personal feeling for Mark, her grief was too immediate.

The others leaned forward. Stephen fished a writing pad out of his briefcase and a carefully sharpened pencil. Annie wondered whether the pencil was an affectation, a step up from quill and ink. Perhaps it indicated that, despite a job whose stock was words, he distrusted the permanency of the written word. He was an interesting man, Stephen - overweight and jowly, with a spidery scrawl of broken veins on a prominent nose. His bushy, tufted eyebrows overshadowed dark observant eyes. Usually bluff and hearty, he had a sensitive streak that was not far from the surface, as his comforting of Sophie had shown.

Now he said, 'The partners of Hutchinson & Rice regret to announce the sudden death…or demise?' he looked round enquiringly.

'Demise, I think,' said Reggie, unaffected by their macabre task. The others remained silent.

'Demise, then,' said Stephen and continued to write in his firm hand. He was not destined to finish. The door was flung open and Sophie marched back into the room. She slapped a newspaper on the table. The others looked at her in surprise and then at the newspaper on the table.

'EXPAT MURDERED!' screamed the headline, and in only slightly smaller print below, 'MAID (NOW SECOND WIFE) ACCUSES EX-WIFE OF MURDER!'

They all looked at the headline, trying to digest the implications.

Annie said, 'But Sarah Thompson isn't even in the country.'

Stephen sighed heavily. 'I'm afraid she is,' he confessed. 'Sarah's been staying with us this last week. I didn't mention it to anyone before this because it might have embarrassed Mark. When I heard Mark was dead, my wife thought we should keep Sarah's presence in Singapore quiet if we could.'

'But we have to tell Inspector Singh!' exclaimed Annie.

'Not now, we don't,' said Stephen wryly, gesturing at the paper.

-six-

'Upon the solemnization of marriage, the husband and the wife shall be mutually bound to co-operate with each other in safeguarding the interests of the union and in caring and providing for the children.'
Section 46, Women's Charter, Chapter 353

Inspector Singh sat at a round table on the verandah of the old civil service club on Dempsey Road. The day was perfect in the way that is possible only on a Saturday afternoon in the tropics - balmy and breezy, blue skies with streaks of wispy white clouds. Inspector Singh, however, was indifferent to nature's attempt to woo him. He was scowling at the young policeman sitting opposite him. The young man was trying to wipe his fingers clean with a damp, scented towel. Its scent triggered a sneezing fit. Inspector Singh had just tucked into a South Indian banana leaf lunch. He had eaten with his fingers. Corporal Fong had tried to follow suit but had not mastered the art, dirtying both hands including his palms. He was now compounding his sins by ineffectually wiping his hands rather than washing them.

Two banana leaves, neatly folded in two, disguised the remnants of lunch. Inspector Singh did not see an unsolved murder as a reason to abandon long lunches. Long-grained fragrant rice, three varieties of vegetables; aubergine, ladies fingers, and spinach, a rich lentil gravy, fresh water 'tiger' prawns, deep-fried slices of fish, plain yogurt, a garlic pickle and crisp *poppadums* had been accompanied by a large bottle of cold beer to wash down the food. This would usually have left the older man with a feeling of languid contentment. But watching the young policeman picking at the food nervously, avoiding the spicy and therefore tasty bits and drinking iced lime juice had impaired his enjoyment. The Inspector realised that none of the sources of irritation justified his dispensing with the services of the constable. The young man had come highly recommended, straight out of the police academy where he had topped his class.

Singh belched and made his way to the long sinks along the wall of the restaurant. He washed his hands, rinsed his mouth and then walked back to the table. He sat down heavily and ordered a glass of *teh tarik*. He looked inquiringly at his companion who shook his head, turning down the hot tea, strained from tea dust and mixed with sweetened condensed milk.

Corporal Fong asked, 'What do you think about this case, sir?'

The Inspector gave no sign of having heard him, staring out into the middle distance.

When the Corporal was just about to risk repeating himself, his superior answered. 'What do I think about this case? I think it is going to be very difficult indeed.' He grinned maliciously at the other man, 'I think it is going to make or break careers…but more likely break them.'

•

The next few days passed in a blur for Annie. The office

remained closed. There was the awkward visit to the widow. They had gone together, the remaining partners. Even Reggie had decided to come along although Annie suspected that he was motivated more by curiosity than sympathy. Sophie had come, muttering something about doing the right thing by Mark. Conversation at the Thompson residence had been stilted. The widow was wearing unrelieved black, contrasting with the paleness of her skin.

Maria Thompson had received their condolences with a hint of disbelief, a shrug of the shoulder conveying her thoughts more accurately than her formal words of acceptance. She was willing that Stephen organise the funeral as long as it was held in Singapore but was adamant that 'the murderer' not be allowed to be present.

'She's not the murderer, she's the mother of his children, for God's sake,' said Stephen, his patience tried to breaking point.

'She will try to kill me too, I know it. I have asked the police to watch her,' was the uncompromising response.

'We can hardly have expected her to be grateful for our sympathy or advice. She knows how shocked everyone was at the marriage,' pointed out Rahul when they had escaped the house as soon as was decent and were standing outside in the sunshine.

'I'll bet she did it, anyway,' commented Reggie. 'That woman would stop at nothing.'

The funeral took place a few days later at a local crematorium. The Singapore expatriate community turned up in force, rallying around one of their own - or seeking more fodder for the gossip machine. A murder made a welcome change from the routine of luxury. The crematorium was bedecked with flowers. Stephen, now acting Senior Partner, had supplemented the offerings from third parties out of office funds. The coffin remained closed. The damage to Mark's head was beyond disguise. The funeral service was brief.

Stephen had stripped it of all religious content. Mark had been a militant atheist. This did not prevent Maria Thompson from wearing a crucifix encrusted with precious stones. She stood alone, a consciously romantic figure, appearing almost to relish her physical isolation.

Mark's children attended the funeral but not his ex-wife. Sarah Thompson had spared Stephen the necessity of telling her she was not invited by refusing point blank to attend. The children stood side by side, both teenagers, with the coltish awkwardness of youth. They acknowledged condolences in a dazed manner, unable to come to terms with the occasion. Both avoided the new wife. Annie could barely imagine how the children felt: losing their father, first in an estrangement over his second wife and then, a second time, on this occasion without the hope of reconciliation. Mark's son read Emily Dickinson, Mark's favourite poet. 'What fortitude the soul contains, That it can so endure, The accent of a coming foot, The opening of a door.' Stephen gave the eulogy, speaking of Mark's legal ability and wit, his love for his children, telling a few amusing anecdotes from his practice. 'Glossing over rather a lot,' said Reggie snidely later. Tears were shed for Mark by his daughter and by Sophie. Annie remained dry-eyed. She stood there like a stranger, trying to understand that it was Mark who lay enclosed in the polished wooden box. Mark, who was moving silently on mechanised wheels through a plain heavy curtain, returned to ashes and dust by the hissing gas flames.

Inspector Singh attended the funeral in an ill-fitting suit, buttoned across his large midriff. He stayed discreetly in the background. Directly after the funeral, he headed home, forsaking the opportunity to speak to the mourners. Once home, he released his belly from its restraints with relief and sat down in the armchair reserved for his use in the living room. It creaked silently and enfolded him in its familiar embrace, contours snug to his ample frame.

His wife darted into the room. A tiny, alert woman, she was more likely to castigate him for a forgotten errand than greet him warmly. Mrs. Singh's hair was drawn severely back from her face. It gave her face the tautness of a facelift. She was dressed in a brightly coloured *batik* caftan, signaling to her husband more clearly than words, that she was not intending a social visit nor expecting anyone to drop by. Otherwise, she would have been clad in a *salwar khameez*, the richness of the silk judged to a nicety for the social occasion. She would have worn thick bands of gold about her arms to complement the thick rope of gold around her neck.

She placed a mug of sweet, milky tea at Mr. Singh's elbow. He grunted an acknowledgement but paid her no heed beyond that. This ritual, performed every evening that he was home from work, with its air of domestic subservience, masked the iron will of the woman that the Inspector had married thirty-seven years before. He had seen her for the first time on their wedding day. As she was brought to him doe-eyed and downcast, his uppermost feeling had been one of relief that she was not burdened with a wooden leg or squint. After thirty-seven years, his gratitude was limited to the same things.

She said to him now, 'I was right.'
This continuation of a conversation that had been going on for several days was another feature of their marriage. She would begin to relate one of several overlapping tales, usually involving the scandalous doings of one of the relations, and continue it over a series of encounters with him - at breakfast, as he dressed for work and when he came home in the evenings. The Inspector would listen with half an ear, confuse all the separate strands and respond only if he felt the vitriol was too unpleasant to pass without some mild reproof.

She said again, more smugly this time, 'I was right,'

and then continued darkly, 'I told you what would happen.'

Another feature of these stories was the regular vindication of her views by unfolding events. Inspector Singh nodded agreement, not knowing nor caring what she was talking about.

'They let him go to America, to…to the mid-West,' she continued doubtfully, not sure whether her information as to location was accurate.

'None of our people are there. Now he has married an American girl.' And she continued, triumphant at the climax of her story, 'He did not even need a green card, he had already got it!'

The Inspector sipped his tea and was pleased to hear the doorbell ring.

Mrs. Singh peeped out from behind a curtain and said, 'Someone to see you.'

He asked, moved by curiosity, 'Who is it? How do you know he's here for me?'

She said disdainfully, 'Chinese,' and left the room.

The Inspector thought ruefully that she would have made a good detective. It was true that, despite living in multi-racial Singapore, for someone of his generation, a Chinese visitor would almost definitely have to be a work connection.

It was Corporal Fong, diligently following the Inspector home to report on his various assignments. Inspector Singh listened as he delivered a summary of his report in an admirably brief manner. There was nothing in it to surprise the Inspector but he had to go through the motions and cover the angles. Now he said, 'To sum up, nothing in the register at the front desk, no cards issued for that floor except as accounted for by the partners … so one of them killed him … or Mr. Thompson escorted his killer up.'

Corporal Fong said, 'I agree, sir.'

'That's a relief,' remarked Inspector Singh.

Fong continued to nod enthusiastically and his senior

was left to rue this inability to detect sarcasm and to wonder whether, despite his top marks in the academy, the policeman should be allowed out to question anyone.

He said curtly, 'Check the C.C.T.V tapes.'

'I have asked for them, sir. But the cameras were being serviced, so no tapes were running.'

Inspector Singh was impressed by this diligence.

His response gave no sign of it, 'The murderer is a lucky man ... we will have to change that.'

'Yessir!'

'You can go, unless there's anything else?'

Corporal Fong looked embarrassed and said, 'A partner from the firm has been trying to contact you, sir. But you had left the office and your mobile was off. He was so insistent that they put him through to me ...,' he trailed off.

Inspector Singh, his interest piqued, asked, 'Who was it? What did he want? Did he confess?'

'No sir, it was not one of the partners in Singapore. This partner has just flown out from London and wants you to call him.'

Inspector Singh grunted, 'Sounds like trouble to me.'

-seven-

'Whoever, knowing or having reason to believe that an offence has been committed, causes any evidence of the commission of that offence to disappear with the intention of screening the offender from legal punishment, or with that intention gives any information respecting the offence which he knows or believes to be false, shall, if the offence which he knows or believes to have been committed is punishable with death, be punished with imprisonment for a term which may extend to 7 years …'
Section 201, Penal Code, Chapter 224

Maria Thompson was on the phone. She was angry.

'What do you mean, I must wait? I need the money. It is my money!' She paused for breath. 'What does it matter to me if he is killed? I did not do it. It was that woman, his first wife. Why should I wait for what is mine? He said the insurance is for me!'

The response at the other end was not to her satisfaction. Her red nails gripped the phone like the talons of a bird of prey.

'I cannot wait!'

She slammed down the phone and glanced at her slim wristwatch. It was almost time to set out. Further argument with the insurance people would have to wait. She was not going to risk being late. Maria rifled through her clothes in the walk-in wardrobe. Bright-coloured designer labels predominated. She chose a hot pink pantsuit with wide lapels and a broad belt. She spent twenty minutes on her face erasing every sign of age and care with the help of her cosmetic set - a case so bristling with jars, potions and brushes that it looked liked a schoolboy's chemistry set. Finally, she slipped on a pair of high-heeled Jimmy Choo's and climbed into the backseat of a limousine service. She said, 'Take me to the airport.'

•

The office opened for business again the day after the funeral. Annie arrived at work early. She was the first to get in. She felt uneasy in the semi-darkness. Then she shrugged and flicked on as many light switches as she could, bathing the office in fluorescent light. Putting her briefcase in her room, she went slowly to the pantry to get a cup of coffee - and saw Mark's room at the end of the corridor. Memories washed over her. Mark, laughing, officious, dogmatic, drunk. Then, slumped in a chair, blood in his hair, down his face, on the carpet. Annie realised with a start that the bloodstains on the carpet would be a gruesome reminder to the staff of what had happened less than a week before. She doubted that the police cleaned up when they were done with their forensic analysis. They were more likely to leave their own distinctive signature of chalk outlines and fingerprints.

She made her way along the deserted corridor to Mark's room. One side was lined with filing cabinets, the other punctuated by office doors, with a desk by each door for the secretaries. It was as deserted as it had been the evening of the murder. Annie felt her steps slowing as she approached the door. There was a terrible feeling of déjà vu in her every action. Was it only the previous week that she had opened the door and found a dead man? The doorknob to Mark's room was cold and she could feel the hairs on her arm stand to attention. She had to do something. She could at least cover the stains or lock the door. Taking a deep breath, she slowly opened the door.

She looked around her in amazement. Mark's room had been cleaned out. The furniture was still there, but the books and files and other paraphernalia of practice had been cleared away. The contents that had made the office his own; the pictures of his children, the paintings on the wall, even the stationery on his desk was gone. The carpet bore no trace of blood. In fact, it looked like a new carpet. Only a hint of disinfectant in the air suggested that the changes to the room were recent. Her absorption in her surroundings kept her from hearing the firm, light tread along the corridor. Someone came up silently behind her and grabbed her arm. Annie gave a convulsive shudder and swung round.

The man asked sternly, 'Who are you? What are you doing in here?'

Not answering, she stared at the stranger, eyes wide and dark with sudden fright.

He spoke again, 'You shouldn't be in here. This room is off limits. Are you Mark's secretary?'

At this question, Annie recovered some of her equilibrium. She scowled at the man.

'I think, the proper question is, who the hell are you and what are you doing in this office? How did you get in? What do you want?' She shot out the questions like a machine gun firing on automatic.

His reply was measured, 'I'm sorry, I should have introduced myself, David Sheringham.' He stuck out his hand but she ignored it. He let his hand fall back to his side and said in a conciliatory tone, 'I've come out from London to manage the office for a few months. Stephen Thwaites will brief everyone.'

Although she gave no hint of it, Annie had recognised his name. David Sheringham was the firm's trouble-shooter. Based in London, he was a partner with a thriving banking practice. He was also always first on the scene if there was trouble in the offing within the firm. Angry clients, potential litigation, misbehaving partners, any hint of fraud or impropriety; if it affected the firm's interests, David was sent out to solve the problem. His resolution of any crisis was always in the best interests of the firm, but rumour had it, rarely in the best interests of the lawyers involved.

'I didn't know murder was within your remit,' Annie said pointedly.

An eyebrow went up as he realised that she knew who he was.

'Only where the suspects include the entire partnership of an office,' he replied easily.

'I'm Annie N--, associate partner and according to you, a murder suspect. I suppose you think I'm in here destroying the evidence?' she asked with blistering sarcasm.

'A bit late, I think, don't you?' he said, looking around the pristine office. 'What were you doing in here anyway?' David asked again.

Remembering her original plan to hide the bloodstains, she revealed a dimple in her left cheek, 'Destroying the evidence,' she said, and left, leaving a puzzled man staring at her receding back.

Later, at a gathering of all the staff, Annie studied David with interest as he launched into an explanation of his presence in Singapore to the staff. He was in his mid-thirties, just over six feet tall, loose-limbed and clean-shaven. Eyes were very dark, under unexpectedly delicate, winged brows. Hair was liberally sprinkled with premature grey, and cut aggressively close to a well-shaped head. A wide, thin-lipped mobile mouth and a straight nose with slightly flaring nostrils gave him an ascetic, cruel look. David's voice, however, was an even tenor, fluid and soothing. It was having its effect on the lawyers and staff who were beginning to nod in agreement as he explained his temporary role helping tide them through their immediate difficulties.

The meeting of partners later was less sanguine.

'So London is concerned that one of us will turn out to be a murderer and has sent you down to investigate,' said Rahul matter-of-factly. David shrugged.

'What right do you have to investigate us? What happens when you decide who it is?' asked Julian angrily.

Stephen was less antagonistic, more pragmatic.

'We might as well make the best of it,' he said. 'If David takes responsibility for liaising with the police and managing any bad press, we can carry on as normal. I am perfectly sure that Mark surprised some stranger who killed him and the sooner the police here work that out, the better.'

The others fell silent, recognising a *fait accompli* when they saw it.

'Is Sarah Thompson still in town?' Reggie enquired of Mark's ex-wife.

'Yes,' Stephen replied, 'The police have asked her not to leave.'

'Does that mean she's a suspect?' asked Reggie, brightening.

'Convenient as it may be for us, Reggie, I don't see how she can be. How would she have got into the office?' Rahul asked.

'Mark might have escorted her up?' suggested Reggie.

'They being such good friends and all,' Rahul replied witheringly.

'Let's all refrain from flinging accusations around,' said David. 'Assume that anything you say might leak out to the press.'

'Worried it will be held against the firm?' asked Ai Leen.

'It won't help the firm, and it won't help any of us either,' was David's response.

'Who cleared out Mark's room?' Annie heard herself asking.

'I arranged for it to be done,' said David.

'Where's his stuff?' asked Rahul. 'It's all been boxed and put in my …, in the room I'm using,' he answered. The only slip in the performance that day.

•

Maria Thompson had her face pressed up against the glass wall at the arrival hall of Changi Airport. She scanned the passengers with anxious eyes. She spotted them. Two slim children, a boy and a girl, holding hands and looking worried. An airline employee loaded their small suitcase onto a trolley and then escorted them towards the exit. Maria had not seen her children for five years. She moved forward slowly and then with a rush, enfolding them in a fierce embrace. Tears smeared her makeup but nature stepped in to erase some of the lines of care that had developed in the intervening years.

-eight-

' Any person domiciled and resident in Singapore who is of or above 60 years of age and who is unable to maintain himself adequately (referred to in this section as the parent) may apply to the Tribunal for an order that one or more of his children pay him a monthly allowance or any other periodical payment or a lump sum for his maintenance.'
Section 3, Maintenance of Parents Act, Chapter 167B

Corporal Fong waited patiently in the lift lobby of his apartment tower block. A couple of small children were playing marbles in a corner. He glanced up. Flowerpots had been known to fall off balcony ledges, killing unwary people below. The lift door opened and he stepped in. The lift stank of urine and there was a bag of rubbish in the corner. Someone had been too lazy to ride down to dump the garbage in the skip under the building and had left it neatly in the corner of the lift, hoping someone else would take it out. Fong usually did it. The stink and the rats, if he did not, were more than he could stand. Today he could not be bothered. He had already spent the whole day dancing to the Inspector's tune. He would be damned if he did anyone else's dirty work. He had known working with the large Sikh with the even larger reputation would be hard going but had hoped to impress. After all, he had finished top of his class at the police academy. This was his first assignment and it was a complex case full of political undertones as the privileged expatriate class found itself under investigation. There was plenty of room to shine. Unfortunately, the Inspector appeared to believe he was good to shine shoes and not much else. He had been sent to fetch documents, told to take notes, made to pack lunch for the Inspector and finally been sent to buy a newspaper and told to start a scrapbook of articles about the murder. He had not been near a witness or crime scene all day. Finally, he had been sent home while the Inspector went to interview that young, good-looking, part-Asian partner, Annie N--. He would not have minded going along for that. But the dirty old man had ignored his offers to go along.

Fong let himself into his home, a tiny, two-bedroom, subsidised Housing Development Board flat, shared with his parents. His mother was watching a Cantonese serial on T.V. She was guffawing loudly and barely acknowledged his entrance. His father lay on a bed in the living room. He was a paraplegic. He had been hurt in an industrial accident a couple of years before retirement, trying hard to do the work of a younger man to keep his job in the midst of a downturn in the construction industry. Corporal Fong saw that the old man had not been moved that day. He went over to him and, smiling reassuringly, turned his father on his side. If he was too long in one position, he developed bedsores. His mother hardly bothered these days. Any love she had borne for this man had long since been destroyed by the enforced intimacy of that living room. She would still spoon feed his father a thin soup twice a day but from the stains on the sides of his mouth and down his chin, even this was done impatiently. Fong sighed and wished again he had money to hire a nurse and move them all into a larger place. As it stood, his small constabulary salary was barely enough to cover the essentials.

Quietly, he sat down next to his father, wiped the old man's face with a wet towel and fluffed up his pillows.

•

In the easy chair on the veranda of her house, Annie sipped the last of a strong drink as she mulled over the events surrounding the murder. It was impossible to think about anything else, not even her father who had called to remind her to send the money she had promised. He had listened to her explanation for the delay with half an ear and remained oblivious to the fact that his only child might be suffering some distress from her proximity to a brutal murder. She had not hung up on her father this time. He was all the family she had and even his indifference had the ability to comfort. It proved that outside the immediate reach of the murder investigation, other lives were carrying on as normal. A pang of hunger drove Annie to the kitchen. To her relief there was a packet of instant noodles in the cabinet. The last thing she wanted to do was drag herself out to a food court to pack some dinner home. She put the noodles on to boil and wandered back to the front of the house, chewing on a fingernail.

A car drew up at the front gate and she looked at it curiously. She was not expecting visitors. The short, yet dignified, figure of Inspector Singh emerged. He was dressed, as always, in black trousers and a short sleeved white shirt that was starting to wilt after a long day. On his feet were his trademark white sneakers and he had, as before, a breast pocket full of pens, causing the pocket to sag and a blue stain to develop at its base where a pen had leaked. The Inspector walked slowly over, glancing about him at the convertible in the driveway, the single storey, black and white, old colonial bungalow and the glint of blue from the pool by the side of the house. Annie felt a stab of guilt at the luxury that her life as an expatriate in Singapore allowed her. But Inspector Singh showed no reaction to her home, either of envy or enthusiasm.

Annie did detect a mild pleasure when he accepted her offer of a beer. Apparently, he was willing to drink on duty. She got an icy Carlsberg from the fridge and a glass of water for herself. She gave him the drink and he took a healthy swig, draining a third of the glass immediately.

'I would like to ask you a few questions,' he said.

'Of course,' said Annie, 'Although I am not sure how I can help you.'

'All information helps. An investigation is a process of elimination,' he said ponderously.

'Well, if you can eliminate me as a suspect, I am happy to be of help.'

He did not respond and it was her turn to have a quick gulp of her drink.

He said, 'Tell me about the office.'

'What sort of thing do you want to know?' she asked.

'Anything, the organisational structure, the people.'

'Surely it would be better to get that sort of detail from Stephen Thwaites. He's the most senior person in Singapore after Mark.'

'I would like to hear it from you.'

Annie told him what she could, trying to stick to the facts and keep her opinions to herself. She told him that the partnership in Singapore consisted of seven people including Mark. There were approximately twenty-five associates and about thirty staff including all the secretaries and accountants and the tea lady. Only the partners had keycards that allowed access after hours. This level of security was considered necessary to protect client confidentiality. Others could get in but would leave a paper trail with the security guards downstairs.

'Did anyone sign the visitors' book that evening?' Annie asked.

'No.'

'But you can't think that one of the partners would kill Mark. I mean, why would any of us do that?'

'That is what we are trying to find out,' the Inspector said.

'Could anyone have borrowed the cardkey from one of the others?' she asked.

'No one has suggested that this happened.'

'What about Mark's key? Did he have it on him?'

'Yes.'

Annie's hope that it could still prove to be an outsider faded, and then flared again as the Inspector said, 'Or perhaps Mr. Thompson could have escorted his assailant to the office.'

'That would mean that he knew the person. He would not have let just anyone in, especially if he had just called a meeting of the partnership,' she pointed out, her thoughts immediately turning to the wife and ex-wife.

Annie remembered the last time she had seen Sarah Thompson. Sarah had found out that Mark had been sleeping with their Filipina maid. She had come storming into the office, crying and shouting - hysterical. The lawyers had come out of their rooms to investigate the commotion. Stephen and Sophie had gone to Sarah, tried to calm her down, and more importantly, to quieten her down. Annie had been in a meeting of clients. They had all tried to behave as though nothing out of the ordinary was happening. It had been an impossible task. Mark had finally appeared from his room. He had tried first to reason with Sarah and then to shout her down. Finally, he had physically dragged her into his office and shut the door. Snatches of conversation had still been audible. It had been horribly embarrassing. Annie had never liked Sarah, a large-boned, pale woman, with a braying laugh and a condescending attitude. But an alcoholic, philandering husband was a high price to pay for an expatriate entitlement complex. Could Sarah have done it? Perhaps that day, or when she had discovered later that Mark intended to marry the woman. But why now? Six months after the fact? In any event, Mark was unlikely to have escorted her up to the office.

Inspector Singh echoed her thoughts, 'It widens the pool of suspects slightly, perhaps to include the second wife, Mrs. Maria Thompson.'

'But not any mysterious strangers,' said Annie ruefully.

She turned her mind to the only stranger who had materialised that day - David Sheringham. It was a pity it was impossible to cast him in the role of murderer. He looked like one, hollow eyes and mobile mouth. But his military haircut suggested a trained, rather than untrained, capacity for violence. Bludgeoning someone to death with a paperweight was too disorganised. Annie wondered why she had taken such an immediate dislike to David Sheringham. Maybe it was the way he had manipulated them all into treating his presence as a benefit, rather than at most, a necessary evil.

'Admit it,' she said out loud, 'you're just annoyed because he mistook you for a secretary.'

'I beg your pardon?' asked the Inspector.

Annie blushed and hastily changed the subject.

'But what about Julian's key?' she asked.

'What about it?'

'He didn't have it that day. I had to let him in. I'm sure he's told you. He must have lost it. Anyone could have found it.'

'Mr. Holbrooke has not mentioned this loss to us. I will raise it with him.'

'Yes, do ask him,' said Annie. 'I'm sure that's the explanation.'

'It still would not explain why a stranger coming across a lost key would use it to murder your senior partner,' pointed out Inspector Singh.

Annie's optimism waned a little.

'In fact, unless Mr. Holbrooke lost it, if he has indeed lost it, in the building itself, there would be no way to be certain which office building in Singapore the cardkey was from.'

Her optimism now positively dampened, Annie nodded.

The Inspector drained his glass and made his way to his car. Annie watched him go, uncertain what the visit had been about. She felt rattled. Why had he come? He had asked her for information that he could more easily and better have obtained from any one of the more senior partners. She shook her head and ran a hand through her glossy black hair. She could not avoid the sensation that his visit had been some sort of test. Had she passed? Or failed?

-nine-

'Whoever commits murder shall be punished with death.'
Section 302, Penal Code, Chapter 224

Annie watched the police car reverse out of her gravel driveway, going over her conversation with the Inspector in her head. Then she fetched her mobile phone and rang Julian.

He picked up at once and said, 'Hello?' in a tentative voice.

'It's me, Annie,' she said, automatically trying to sound reassuring.

'Oh! I was expecting the good inspector,' he said, the relief audible. 'He just called me and the line got cut.'

It was Annie's turn to be surprised. 'He's just called you? But he's just been here.'

'Why? What did you tell him, what's going on?'

'Nothing important, you came up in the conversation only once,' she said, again trying to be reassuring. 'I just mentioned that you didn't have your cardkey that evening. I thought you might have lost it and whoever found it killed Mark.'

'Jesus Christ, Annie!' Julian exclaimed. 'I didn't tell him about the key. Now he's going to think I've been lying to him.'

'But why didn't you tell him?'

'Because he would have assumed that the only reason I would claim to have lost my key would be to widen the pool of suspects... create some doubt. There's no way that some stranger picked up the key and killed Mark. Why the hell would they?'

'Surely you're reading too much into this, Julian.'

'Don't be so damned naïve!' he snapped and hung up.

The next day, Annie, smartly if severely attired in midnight blue with a mandarin collar buttoned up to her throat, drove in to work with real reluctance. For once, she did not notice the daily irritations on her drive to work - the inept driving, terrible road manners and expensive cars lined up by the side of the road to wait for the electronic road pricing to be reduced by fifty cents. She did not notice the long queues of luxury cars at petrol stations offering slight discounts. Usually, Annie would arrive at work having had to overcome at least one incident of personal road rage. Today her conversation with Julian the previous evening occupied her thoughts to the exclusion of all else.

She mentally replayed events leading up to the murder. She had been cross with Julian, who had been supposed to go with her to Kuala Lumpur but cancelled at the last minute citing a conflicting deadline. It had been annoying but not that unusual. Things did crop up unexpectedly. Julian had been apologetic and appeared to regret missing the day trip. No surprise there. She sometimes wondered whether she should accept one of his offers of a date. They had a lot in common. They were good friends, both the same age, with the same ambitions and desires. But something had always held her back. A reluctance, perhaps, to begin something, that if it ended badly, would affect her professional life.

Her plan to bury herself at work and avoid Julian until he had had time to overcome his annoyance with her was thwarted when she checked her answer phone for messages. There was only one message, from David Sheringham, summoning the partners to a meeting that morning. Annie scowled. She thought of refusing to attend, then acknowledged that it would be a childish thing to do. Mark deserved her fullest co-operation. Whatever her resentment of David, she would have to be present. Fortifying herself with a touch of the light makeup she wore to work, she made her way down the corridor to the meeting room. At the door, she hesitated, thought about knocking and then decided against it. She was punctual so the meeting was unlikely to have started. To her surprise, the only occupant of the boardroom was David. He had not heard her come in. He was wearing an Italian suit. His shirt was a crisp white. Discreet cufflinks were visible at his wrists. The tie was heavily textured navy silk.

Annie cleared her throat.

He looked at her, 'I wondered if you would turn up.' This was closer to the bone than she liked.

Annie shrugged. 'I assume this has something to do with Mark. *He* deserves our best efforts,' she said with only the slightest emphasis on the 'he'. His was an ear trained to pick up nuances. She was happy to leave a trail of them for him.

'Look Annie, we seem to have got off on the wrong foot, I'm not sure why. But I'm glad you're early as there's something I need to discuss with you.'

She looked at him inquiringly but he did not have the opportunity to finish. The door opened and Julian and Rahul walked in. Rahul with his usual cheer issued a general greeting. Julian looked at Annie, then, rather sheepishly, came round the table, and gave her a quick hug. An apology for his rant about the key. She returned the hug with relief. Whatever was bothering Julian, they all needed to stick together.

Reggie and Ai Leen walked in, breaking off their low conversation as they stepped into the room. Ai Leen was dressed in her favourite pastel, today a delicate pink - almost too innocent a colour for her stern demeanour. Annie wondered again at this united front between Reggie and Ai Leen.

The only local Singaporean partner in the office, Ai Leen was an enigma. Annie had tried to be her friend on coming out to Singapore feeling that the two younger women in an office of men, both with Asian roots, should stick together. Ai Leen had responded politely but unenthusiastically. The women had slipped into a habit of friendly, but limited, intercourse. With her quick intellect and short temper, Annie had not been able to understand the quiet determination and steely ambition that characterised Ai Leen. She remembered that there had been a few snide remarks made about Ai Leen's success. She was considered 'a safe pair of hands', an expression used by the lawyers when faint praise was intended to be damning.

Reggie had been particularly scathing behind her back. He had made no secret of his belief that her partnership had been to lend 'colour to proceedings'. Despite that, in the end, he had been persuaded to support her candidature. By Mark, it was rumoured. Reggie's belated support had put the seal on her appointment. Annie remembered that Reggie and Ai Leen had arrived together on the evening of Mark's murder as well and wondered at it. They worked together and were civil to each other, but there was coldness at the heart of the relationship. This sudden fondness for each other's company was intriguing.

Sophie came in alone. Without a word to anyone, she pulled up a chair and sat down, staring at the painting on the opposite wall with unseeing eyes. The desultory conversation between the others petered out in the face of her concentrated misery. Sophie no longer looked unkempt. But there was something about her that suggested a tenuous control over her emotions. The veins in her neck were taut and prominent. She clasped and unclasped her hands in her lap as if considering an appeal for relief from some deity and then thinking better of it.

People started taking seats round the conference table. Rahul and Julian flanked Annie on one side. Sophie, Reggie and Ai Leen were on the other. Annie wondered if these were battle lines. David sat at the head of the table as if it was his position by right. The door opened again and Stephen Thwaites ushered in Inspector Singh. It was clear at once that no one with the exception of David had been expecting the police. There were a couple of stifled exclamations. Julian grew pale. Reggie muttered something to Ai Leen under his breath. It was inaudible to Annie and she hoped to the Inspector as well. It was bound to have been unpleasant. David invited the policeman to sit down. He did, nodding to Annie as he did so. Annie was not pleased to be singled out. Stephen sat down across the table from David and cleared his throat. Everyone turned to look at him expectantly.

'This meeting has been called to discuss the assistance we can provide to the police.' Stephen's deep voice managed to sound threatening.

Reggie interrupted him. 'We've done all we can. What else do they want?'

Stephen ignored him. 'Inspector Singh is here to briefly outline what he requires of us. Inspector?'

The Inspector pushed his chair back and rose to his feet. Annie saw Reggie run his finger round his collar as if it felt suddenly tight. It served him right. His attitude was appalling, varying as it did between hostility and servility.

'My team and I are currently investigating the murder of Mark Thompson,' began the Inspector. 'He was killed on these premises.'

Did he glance at Julian wondered Annie.

'Death was the result of several blows to the head last Friday between seven and nine p.m. The actual cause of death was either extensive skull fracture pushing fragments of bone into the brain or internal bleeding between the skull and the dura, that is the membrane covering the brain. It is not possible to determine the most proximate cause because of the severity of the attack.'

The Inspector paused to let the import of his words sink in.

'The pathologist has confirmed that the weapon used was a paperweight in the form of a pewter tiger - which the deceased kept on his desk.'

There was a stifled sob from Sophie.

'Suspects would usually be required to present themselves at the police station for questioning.'

Reggie's brow was gleaming with a thin sheen of sweat despite the cool of the air-conditioned room. Only David looked unconcerned.

Well, he's not a suspect, Annie thought irritably and glared at him.

'However, I have been instructed,' the Inspector paused, 'I have been asked to conduct this investigation,' again he paused, at a loss for the best form of words, 'in a more 'user-friendly' way. There are a number of reasons for this. This case has attracted a great deal of media interest, including the foreign press.'

'Meaning you can't control the content,' said Rahul, referring to the widely held perception that the authorities controlled the Singapore press.

The Inspector ignored him and continued, 'Mark Thompson was a leading member of the expat community in Singapore, there are a limited number of suspects, the Filipino community is up in arms …I want to keep the investigation out of the media spotlight…as far as possible anyway.'

He continued, 'I am going to hold the interviews with the partners and other members of staff here at these offices.

This will be more convenient for all of you and allow us to avoid the reporters camping outside my station.' This last was said with a small smile. 'Mr. Sheringham has volunteered to assist us with reviewing files. Finally, I have agreed that the firm may have an observer at the interviews, to provide independent testimony of proceedings, if this should be necessary.'

At this point the Inspector sat down heavily, shifted around in his chair until his posterior was properly wedged in and scratched his beard thoughtfully.

Stephen said, 'Thank you, Inspector Singh. It is in all our interests to co-operate fully with the police ... so we can get on with our lives and mourn Mark without a shadow hanging over us. I believe that Inspector Singh and his team will be commencing their interviews later this morning.'

The Inspector nodded his agreement, rose to his feet and left the room.

A babble of voices broke out the moment the door closed after the Inspector. Reggie was spluttering with anger at the thought of further questioning. Sophie suddenly came to life and turned on him, pointing out that Mark was dead and Reggie's ego was the least of anyone's concerns. Ai Leen wanted to know what the Inspector meant by 'limited suspects'. Surely they could not believe it was one of the partners? What did it mean that Sheringham would be reviewing the files? She thought London had sent him out to protect their interests. They were being protected, was Stephen's measured response. But a crime had been committed and they would all have to accept that there had to be an investigation involving them.

'But it's one of the bloody wives!' shouted Reggie.

'If you have any evidence, please share it with us,' said Rahul. 'Otherwise stop flinging accusations around, for God's sake.'

'Are we allowed to leave the country?' asked Julian.

Stephen shook his head.

'But I was going to London next week. I need to go

back. I tell you I need to go back!'

The sudden hysterical note in Julian's voice had the effect of silencing the room.

Annie turned to Stephen and asked, 'Who is this observer, anyway?'

'You are.'

The effect of this disclosure was electric.

'What do you mean, Annie is going to be observing? By what right?' This was Reggie.

'I want to do it. I want to see that justice is done for Mark,' said Sophie.

'Is she not a suspect? Why not?' asked Ai Leen.

'But I don't want to do this. It has nothing to do with me.' cried Annie.

David rose to his feet and waited. The cacophony of voices fell silent. Everyone turned to him in angry expectation.

Stephen said, 'David, perhaps you could take us through the reasoning of the partnership. The global partnership,' he added meaningfully. A timely reminder to those present that the partners round the table might call the shots in Singapore but that the firm was bigger than any of them.

'First of all, I must apologise to Annie for springing this on her.'

Looking at her, he continued, 'This is what I wanted to discuss with you this morning when we got interrupted.'

Annie did not respond.

'Mark's death is a tragedy for his family and his friends. However, there are other aspects to his death that cannot be ignored. Namely, that the Singapore partnership of Hutchinson & Rice looms large among a limited number of *practical* suspects.'

Julian caught Annie's eye. David had already heard of the missing cardkey.

David looked around the table reassuringly, 'I find

it impossible to believe that any of you had a hand in this crime and the sooner the police come to that conclusion the better. However, you are all …I repeat, all, suspects. This crime must be solved, both for the sake of justice for Mark …and so that you do not have to live with the suspicions of others for the rest of your lives. I think you will agree that a successful practice of law requires the trust of your clients … and of your colleagues - difficult if you are a suspect in an unsolved murder case.'

David stopped to allow his comments to sink in. From the slumped shoulders and sullen expressions, his audience was listening.

He continued, 'In the circumstances, I think it is in our interests to co-operate with the police. Inspector Singh has made it clear that he is under some pressure to bring this case to a speedy conclusion. Mark is …was, a high profile expat. The suspects are largely foreigners. The Singapore government does not want any bad publicity.'

Stephen added, 'The involvement of a Filipina suspect adds a political dimension. The last thing the authorities want is a second 'Flor'.'

Seeing some blank looks around the table, he explained, 'Flor was a maid accused of murder here. She was convicted and executed. The Philippine government and people viewed the whole thing as a miscarriage of justice and Flor as a martyr. The press in the Philippines is already painting the second Mrs. Thompson as being the victim in all this.'

'Victim? She's nothing but a whore!'

David interrupted Sophie's outburst, 'Hold on a second, I am not expressing a view.'

Sophie subsided but Annie said irritably, 'None of this explains why I have to eavesdrop on these interviews …'

'It is not eavesdropping, Annie,' said Stephen.

Annie looked at him in surprise. It was unheard of for her to be at the receiving end of a rebuke from Stephen.

'To cut to the chase,' said David, 'the police have

agreed,' he ticked them off on his fingers, 'to hold the interviews here, to accept my help to review files to highlight confidentiality issues and to allow Annie to sit in on the interviews. From their point of view, this is a safeguard against any *ex post facto* allegations of impropriety. To that end, they will not allow any non-participants, for want of a better word, to fulfill that role. They refuse to accept an independent observer. The authorities might lose face for having agreed to such a step if it leaks.'

Annie sat straighter in her chair, but David pre-empted her interruption, 'The reason Annie is being asked to play this role is because she is the only person acceptable to both the senior partnership and the police.'

'What if I refuse?' asked Annie in a small voice.

'If you refuse,' said Rahul ironically, 'I would guess that no other person will be allowed to sit in and we will all be dragged down to the police station at regular intervals for the judicious application of thumbscrews. At some point, one of us will be selected to hang from the neck until dead. In the circumstances, unusual though this procedure might be, Annie has my vote.'

There were a few nods around the table, a shrug from Reggie and no response at all from Ai Leen or Sophie.

Taking silence as assent, Stephen said in his booming voice, 'Thank you all for your time. If we stick together I am sure we will see this thing through.'

Annie looked round the table. His optimistic words fell on infertile ground. What had always been a friendly and effective team, now sat at the table in silence, not looking at each other, staring at their hands, or at the opposite wall, doodling on bits of paper. The personal foibles of individuals that had previously come across as amusing, even endearing, were now perceived as character flaws. Strange alliances were being born. Old friendships were being tested to breaking point. Already she had exchanged cross words with Julian and been ticked off by Stephen. What divisions would appear next?

As the partners got up to leave the room, David said, 'Annie, if I might have a quick word?'

She sat rooted to her chair as the others left, filing out of the room morosely. Only Rahul spared her a backward glance and a reassuring smile. David moved round the table to sit opposite her.

'Thanks for agreeing to do this,' he said.

'You didn't leave me with much choice.'

'Actually, you have your friend the Inspector to thank for that. He insisted that no one else was acceptable to the police.'

Annie's consternation showed. 'Really? But why would he do that?'

'I was hoping you could tell me.'

'But I have no idea.'

'I think it might be your being Asian. He might have just felt more comfortable with that.'

'I suppose it's possible,' she said wrinkling her nose doubtfully. 'But what about Ai Leen? She's not a half-breed like me and she's Singaporean.'

He raised an expressive eyebrow and grimaced, 'Would you choose her? Anyway, the fact that you are only part-Asian might have been a factor, a bridge between two worlds and all that.'

Annie snorted in derision at the suggestion and provoked the first genuine smile she had seen from David. It changed his face. The harsh lines on his face became lines of laughter, the indents on his cheeks, dimples. His eyes crinkled at the corners. He looked ten years younger.

His next words destroyed the image completely. 'I have to ask you this next question because it might have a bearing on your role and the general perception of it.'

'What is it?' asked Annie.

'Are you and Julian Holbrooke in any sort of relationship that might affect your impartiality?'

Annie could not imagine what he was talking about and then remembered the morning's apologetic hug. Her famously short temper immediately got the better of her.

'It's none of your damned business!' she said and slammed the door on her way out.

She walked back to her office, seething with anger. To her surprise, Ai Leen was sitting in the chair across from her desk.

'Hello, Ai Leen. What can I do for you?'

'Why did they choose you?' Her voice was brittle, tense.

Annie looked puzzled, 'I beg your pardon?'

'The police! Why did they ask you to sit in?'

'I honestly don't know,' Annie replied. 'God knows I don't want to do it!'

Ai Leen fell silent. The two women looked at each other, a study in contrasting styles. Ai Leen, slight, dressed in pastels, face carefully painted, heels, not a strand of hair out of place. Annie, on the other hand, conservatively dressed, hair loose and curling around her shoulders, no cosmetics except for a dash of lipstick and low-heeled court shoes.

'It's always so easy for you, isn't it?'

'Ai Leen, I have no idea what you are talking about.'

'Friendship, partnership - whatever you want, you get. And now this…we are all suspects in a murder, except you!'

Annie was caught off-guard by the hostility radiating from Ai Leen.

'I don't understand what you are trying to say, Ai Leen. Of course I'm still a suspect…and we're both partners!'

Ai Leen rose slowly to her feet. She looked at Annie carefully, as if searching for an answer to her questions. Her own expression was unreadable. The mask, that had slipped to reveal genuine anger at Annie, was back in place.

-ten-

'(1) A police officer making a police investigation … may examine orally any person supposed to be acquainted with the facts and circumstances of the case and shall reduce into writing any statement made by the person so examined.
(2) Such person shall be bound to state truly the facts … except only that he may decline to make with regard to any fact or circumstance a statement which would have a tendency to expose him to a criminal charge or to a penalty or forfeiture.'
Section 121, Criminal Procedure Code, Chapter 68

Annie made her way with some trepidation down the corridor to the room that had been assigned to the police for the interviews. She was still shaken from her encounter with Ai Leen. She knocked on the door, timidly at first, then more firmly. A voice that she recognised as the Inspector's invited her to enter. There were two other people in the room, David Sheringham and a young Chinese policeman in the dark blue uniform of the Singapore police force who was introduced as Jackie Fong and whose hand, when she shook it, was clammy. She wondered what was worrying him. Probably it was his first case of such magnitude. She suspected that the Inspector would be an exacting taskmaster.

She looked around the room. It was a moderately large room that had been cleared of all its usual contents; desk, files and the other paraphernalia of legal practice. A table about six feet by three had been placed across the centre. On it were a couple of files, a few pens and a blank note pad, all set neatly at right angles to each other. There were two leather chairs on one side of the table facing the door. The Inspector sat in one of them. As she watched him, he made a minute adjustment to the notepad on the table to ensure that the display was symmetrical. A man with an obsession for detail - for absolute accuracy? Or a man who would not see the wood for the trees? Their fate rested in his hands.

Across from him, there was a single chair. For the poor suspects, Annie guessed. Behind the table and to the left of the Inspector, there was a small desk with a laptop and portable tape recorder on it. On the side of the main table furthest from that single desk, a few feet away and facing the table at right angles, was another small desk completely bare. A chair was behind it with its back to the wall, immediately below the only window in the room. The blinds were raised and Annie could see the waterfront and a choppy angry sea, reflecting the gathering clouds overhead. A massive storm was brewing out across the South China Sea. The spindly trees planted randomly on grassy fields of reclaimed land along the waters' edge looked inadequate to their task of preventing the ground being washed back into the sea.

The walls of the room were bare except for some empty shelving and a picture hook from which no picture hung. Annie could not remember if that had always been the case or whether a painting had been removed. She did not know what a police interview room looked like but every effort had been made to make this particular office as soulless as possible. The atmosphere within was oppressive.

'I am surprised we haven't burnt cigarette holes in the carpet,' she said looking down at the cream pile on the floor.

'I beg your pardon?' asked the Inspector.

David grinned. Annie shook her head at the Inspector to indicate that her comment had not been important. Indeed, she felt guilty about being flippant in the face of their sombre task.

'What are the arrangements then?' she asked the Inspector, indicating her willingness to be co-operative.

He said, 'You sit over there,' nodding to the desk by the window, 'Take notes if you like but nothing can be taken out of the room without permission. Anything of importance will be placed in the safe overnight and distributed again in the morning.'

Annie saw that in her earlier appraisal of the room she had missed a squat gunmetal grey safe squatting on the floor in a corner.

'In any event, Corporal Fong,' he said nodding at the young policeman, 'will be recording the interviews as well as taking verbatim notes. Sheringham here will help explain the files being worked on by any of the lawyers - which might have a bearing on the case.'

Annie realised that David Sheringham had no plans of leaving her, a suspect, as the sole witness to the proceedings. Earlier, it had surprised her that the partnership had appeared willing to go along with it. Now she understood that it had probably never been their intention to do so at all. Knowing that any outright attempt to be present might have met with refusal or at least a reluctance that might have soured relations with the police, David had approached the matter obliquely and was now well placed to be present throughout. Strictly speaking, that made her presence redundant. She knew that she could not point this out. If the Inspector took steps to limit David's presence, she would be *persona non grata* amongst the senior partnership. Not a risk she could take if her life and career were ever to get back on track.

The Inspector said to her, 'Here is the list of interviews,' and handed her a piece of paper. Her own name headed the list. That made sense. She was still a suspect despite her new role as 'police liaison' or 'spy' or whatever you wanted to call it. She had to be interviewed first to prevent her tailoring her story to coincide with the testimony of the others. She took the chair opposite the Inspector. She expected David to sit down next to him in the other leather chair but he continued to stand - behind her so that she would have to turn in her chair even to see his profile. Fong walked to his desk. He caught his thigh on the corner of the table as he made his way around it but only Annie saw his grimace of pain. Poor bastard, she thought sympathetically. However, he sat down at his desk, snapped open his laptop, and checked the cassette in the tape recorder with a calm efficiency that contradicted his earlier nervous clumsiness.

Annie decided that it was like being in a dentist's waiting room: a reluctance to be there, an urgent desire to leave, a nervous expectation of something unpleasant and the certain knowledge that, unpleasant though the wait was, the reality would be worse. Annie looked at the Inspector's hands that were shuffling a couple of the files around; stubby callused fingers with little tufts of hair growing between the joints; tobacco stains on his index and middle fingers from years of smoking; grubby nails. Not quite a dentist's hands. He looked up from his files and solemnly intoned the time and date.
'You are Annie N--, associate partner of Hutchinson & Rice?' he asked. She nodded.
He said, 'Please speak your answers for the record.' The clicking sound of Corporal Fong commencing to type punctuated his remarks.
'I am,' said Annie clearly.

'We are investigating the murder of Mr. Mark Thompson. You were the person who discovered the body. Would you please recount the events leading up to your discovery?'

'But I've told you all that already,' said Annie.

'If you could tell us again… we might discover something that was missed previously.'

Annie shrugged. She had no issue with repeating herself if that was what the Inspector wanted. If he were hoping that she would be caught out in a contradiction, he would be disappointed. She had stuck to the exact truth the first time and events were as fresh in her mind as in the immediate aftermath of her discovery.

Annie explained again how she had been in Kuala Lumpur and had gone from the airport directly home that evening.

'What time was this?' he asked.

'About six in the evening,' she replied firmly.

'Your flight, SQ 118, landed at 5.15 that evening. That was a fairly quick trip home,' the Inspector remarked.

Annie was dismayed that he had been checking on her movements with such diligence but all she said was, 'I travelled first class and without any check-in luggage.'

'What did you do between the time you got home and took the call from Mr. Thompson?'

'I had a drink and fell asleep in the easy chair on the verandah.'

'Your phone records show that you received a call from the office at exactly seven in the evening. The last call Mr. Thompson appears to have made was to one of your colleagues approximately fifteen minutes later. Between that time and nine p.m. when you found the body, he was murdered. What did you do after you received his call?'

This is it, thought Annie, the moment to produce the alibi. Unfortunately, she didn't have one.

'I drove to the office,' she replied.

'That took an hour?'

'Well, I had a shower and watched the eight o'clock news before setting out,' Annie responded, a hint of sarcasm in her voice.

'It is best to be precise in a murder investigation,' said the Inspector heavily, ignoring her fit of pique.

'What happened once you got to the office?' he continued.

Annie explained that she had met Julian in the car park.

'By accident or design?'

'Accident!'

'When did he first mention that he had lost his swipe key?'

'He was rummaging in his wallet at the lift lobby... when he could not find his key I took mine out.'

'Did his actions seem contrived in any way?'

'No.'

'What happened next?'

'We went upstairs. Everything looked normal. No one else had arrived...although, of course, at that point I did not know Mark had invited *all* the other partners. Julian went to his office. He was going to check his email.'

The Inspector interrupted her, 'Did you not think this was odd?'

'What do you mean?'

'You have said that it was very unusual for a meeting to have been called by the victim in such a manner, late on a Friday evening, demanding the presence of the partners ...isn't it a bit unusual that Mr. Holbrooke, having rushed to the office as you did, should then take his time actually going in to see Mr. Thompson. You, after all, went straight to his office without delay.'

'What are you suggesting?' asked Annie.

Almost outside her line of vision, she saw David shift. She glanced at him but his face was in the shadows. It was impossible to read his expression.

'I'm asking you whether, then or now, you thought his behaviour in anyway out of the ordinary in the lead up to finding the body,' said the Inspector.

'Hindsight is a wonderful thing,' said Annie angrily, 'but nothing struck me as unusual at the time.'

The Inspector did not press her.

'When you found the body, I understand that you became overwrought?'

'I was shaken, certainly.'

'When did you realise he was dead?'

'I walked over to him when he did not respond to my speaking to him. I'm not sure what I thought, that he was sleeping...maybe that he had fainted, it all happened so quickly. Then I saw the blood in his hair...and down the side of his face. And his eyes were sort of wide and staring. I realised that he was dead.' Annie shuddered.

'Then what happened?'

'I ... er ...called for Julian.' The Inspector raised his eyebrows. 'He came in, checked for a pulse, and confirmed he was dead.'

'Very cool behaviour,' remarked the Inspector.

Again, Annie found herself on the defensive. 'Well, he did what he had to do. But he wasn't all that collected. He was pale and I noticed that his hands were shaking.'

'Mr. Rahul Gandhi joined you at this point?'

'Yes,' replied Annie. 'We had just come out of Mark's room and were trying to decide what to do when he turned up. He thought at first that Mark had had a heart attack or something when we told him he was dead. He looked in on the body as well. I don't think he could quite believe what we were telling him ... I can't say I blame him, it was all too farfetched to be true ...'

'Was there anything unusual in Mr. Gandhi's reaction?'

'No, not really,' Annie said. 'Rahul is pretty phlegmatic. He only ever seems to get worked up over cricket.'

Inspector Singh nodded, 'All these Indians are cricket mad, eh? I myself follow cricket. In fact, I used to open the batting for Singapore in my younger days.'

Annie looked suitably impressed. The Inspector was lost in a distant reverie, no doubt recollecting the glory days as he strode out on the pitch in his whites. Then he dragged himself back to the present and turned courteously to David Sheringham, 'I will now discuss any work-related issues that might have a bearing on the case - feel free to correct me if I misrepresent the legal position.'

David walked forward and sat down in the chair next to the Inspector. He leaned forward, elbows on the table and steepled his fingers. Annie had ample opportunity to notice that his hands were quite different from the Inspector's. His hands too were large but his fingers were those of a concert pianist, long and elegant. His nails were in better condition than Annie's own. She nibbled the nail on her index finger of her right hand when deep in thought and had one ragged edge to show for the habit. His nails were clean and cut right back, with no hallmarks of any nervous habit. Probably goes for manicures, thought Annie dismissively.

'I believe that you are currently working on two files, both of which have been ongoing for some time,' Inspector Singh said.

Annie nodded, and then remembering the strictures of the Inspector, said out loud, 'Yes, that's correct.' He had been doing his homework.

'A Malaysian takeover and an Indonesian banking deal,' she said.

'I noticed the deceased was the designated senior partner on the Malaysian deal?'

'Yes, he was,' said Annie. 'I had almost forgotten that. That is normally just a cosmetic exercise… to reassure clients that someone senior is involved. I sometimes find that particularly useful. Being young, a woman and Asian, it's almost like three strikes and you're out…I sometimes have to prove myself to sceptical clients.'

'And to some of your colleagues as well, I'm sure,' said the Inspector.

Annie did not respond. She was not going to admit to any weakness. Turning up for meetings and having the clients look past her for the 'real lawyers' to turn up. They never said so but it was implied that for four hundred dollars an hour, they expected a white face at least. She was not going to share with him the uphill battle her partnership had been. In fact, Mark had been one of her staunchest allies. Remembering this, Annie's eyes filled with tears at his loss. She dashed them away angrily.

'Did Mark Thompson play no role at all in the transaction?' the Inspector continued.

'He attended the kick-off meeting. All the senior people at the company were present as well as a few Government bigwigs. It seemed a good idea to have him along.'

'And was it?'

'What?'

'A good idea?'

'Yes, I think so. Mark was always very good with people.'

Except when he was drunk, she could have added but didn't. David probably knew more about his drunken binges than she did. The Inspector would have to find out from someone else.

'So it is possible that a client may have approached him directly?'

'What are you driving at?' she asked.

'Merely that the clients might have gone directly to him…if something came up.'

'I guess so,' she conceded grudgingly. Honesty compelled her to add, 'Especially if the issue related to me.'

'Were there any issues?'

'Like what?'

'You tell me. Money issues. Reputational issues. Any major disagreements. Poor decisions by any of the lawyers involved.'

She shook her head doubtfully, 'I don't think so.'

'Nothing at all?'

Annie hesitated, then she said, 'Well, I'm not sure how this could have a bearing on the case but the only issue, if you like, was that we suspected...suspect, one of the executive directors of the company of insider dealing. Unfortunately, the director we suspect is very well connected and would probably have pulled the rug from under the whole deal if we informed on him.'

'Who knew about this?' asked the Inspector.

'In the firm? All the partners.'

'Including Mark?' David asked the question this time, his curiosity getting the better of him.

'Yes.'

'What was his reaction?'

'He thought we should adopt a 'wait and see' attitude.' Annie's disgust with this policy was evident by the sudden curl of her lip.

'You disagreed?' asked the Inspector.

'Yes. I felt we should not condone any illegal activity.'

'What did Mark think of this view?'

'He said that I was being naïve,' she replied.

The comment still rankled.

'What did he mean by that?' again, David asked the question.

Annie had a quick look at the Inspector. He was impassive.

She shrugged and said, 'It was a bit of a money-spinner for us, the deal. Mark did not want to lose it.'

'What about the others?'

'Others?'

'Other lawyers?'

'The senior partnership, and Julian, the other lawyer on the deal, agreed with Mark. Anyway, I don't see what relevance any of this has to Mark's death. Unless you think I committed a murder because he would not let me prevent a theft?'

The Inspector responded, 'Ah my dear child, every

little bit helps us form a picture of the victim. I will decide what is important or not.'

Annie was speechless with irritation at being addressed as a child and treated like a little woman. She saw David's lips twitch and knew that he was trying not to let his amusement show.

She headed for the pantry. She was mentally bruised by the encounter. She had been distracted by her new role in the investigation. And had been unprepared for the cross-examination, the detailed examination of her movements and the hostility. She tried to remember what she had said, whether she had divulged anything controversial. They had been trying to persuade her to say damning things about everyone in the office. The police were looking at everyone's behaviour with the benefit of hindsight - reading sinister intent into the most innocuous of circumstances - Julian losing his cardkey or checking his email. Building mountains out of molehills about her deal in Kuala Lumpur. She belatedly understood the panic of Julian and Reggie in the face of the investigation. The process could make the most innocent among them feel guilty and soiled, secretive and defensive.

She pushed open the double swing doors of the pantry to find Reggie and Ai Leen with their heads together.

She caught the tail end of Reggie's angry whisper, 'For God's sake, you've got to do it,' and saw the vehement head shake by Ai Leen before they saw her.

Ai Leen gave her a defensive smile but Reggie said, 'Well, well, it's the double agent.'

Annie said crossly, 'Oh for goodness' sake, Reggie, do you think I want to be in this ridiculous position?'

'I didn't see you turn it down.'

'You know there was no way I could do that. Otherwise I would have.'

'What's been going on in there so far?' asked Ai Leen.

'I've just been given the third degree,' said Annie.

'Was it bad?' asked Reggie.

'Yup,' she said flatly.

'Well,' he said, his face turning red with anger and the veins showing in his forehead, 'I have said all along…'

Rahul, who walked in the door with Julian, interrupted him 'We know, Reggie. You've said all along it must have been the widows and they have no right to question you and blah, blah, blah. We've heard it all before. So just drop it will you!'

Reggie subsided into an angry silence.

'How's it been so far?' Julian asked Annie. 'Should we be running yet?'

'If you killed Mark,' said Annie, trying to lighten the atmosphere.

'What's that supposed to mean?' asked Julian angrily.

'Oh, please!' she said. 'It was meant to be a joke, in bad taste I grant you, but still a joke.'

They were all still glowering at each other when David Sheringham walked in. 'Annie, it's time to start again.' He nodded pleasantly at everyone and walked out the door again. Annie glared after his receding back, fetched a Coke from the fridge, counted to a hundred under her breath so that David would not think she had hurried on his account and went back.

-eleven-

'brothel' means any place occupied or used by any two or more women or girls whether at the same time or at different times for the purpose of prostitution..."
Section 2, Women's Charter, Chapter 353

On the door, someone, the industrious Corporal Fong probably, had taped an A4 sheet of paper with the words 'Interview Room - Strictly Private and Confidential'. Annie walked in the door. Only David was in the room. He shrugged to indicate he did not know where the policemen were.

'Who's next for the hot seat?' she asked.

'Starting at the top, I think, Stephen.' Annie nodded. That was consistent with the list she had been given.

David said, 'I presume I don't have to remind you that everything said in here is strictly confidential.'

Did he think she had been briefing everyone in the pantry?

All she said rather tiredly was, 'Don't be ridiculous.'

An uneasy quiet fell between them. Annie sat at the desk by the window and nibbled her index finger. David, stood easily, feet akimbo, arms crossed, apparently deep in thought. He stood with natural grace and did not fidget or shuffle his feet or look uncomfortable as most people do when standing and apparently doing nothing. Annie went back over the conversation in the pantry in her mind. She remembered Rahul shutting Reggie up and smiled. David looked up, saw the smile, and returned it. Once again, she was struck by the change a smile made. It was possible in that instant that the mutual antagonism might wane. Then Annie turned her face back to her notepad. David grimaced. The door opened and the Inspector waddled in. Corporal Fong followed him.

'Excellent, you are both here. We can start the next interview. Perhaps you would be so good as to fetch Mr. Thwaites.'

This last remark was addressed by the Inspector to his Corporal who correctly interpreted it as a command. The Inspector collapsed into his chair, patted his brow with the largest, whitest handkerchief Annie had ever seen and then bent over with some difficulty to retie the shoelace on his left white trainer, which had come undone.

He sat up again, drummed his stubby, grubby fingers on the table and said irritably, 'How long is that boy going to take?'

As Corporal Fong had only been out of the room for thirty seconds, this appeared to Annie to be the height of unreasonableness but she made no comment. There was something about the young policeman, a lack of physical presence or an aptitude for computers that would always annoy men like the Inspector. David as well, she suspected although he might hide it better. She made up her mind to try to be nice to the young man. Corporal Fong came in alone.

'Well, where is he?' snapped the Inspector.

'He said he would be here in a few minutes, sir. He was just finishing something.'

'What? Listen boy, when I tell you to fetch someone, you do it. We are conducting a murder investigation. No one, I repeat, no one keeps me waiting.'

This last shout was still resonating around the room when there was a firm knock on the door and Stephen Thwaites walked in. Although the Inspector must have been perfectly audible outside the door, Stephen gave no sign of having heard anything amiss. He nodded to Annie and David, ignored the Corporal and stuck his hand out to the Inspector. They shook hands briefly.

Stephen said, 'Sorry to keep you waiting,' in his rumbling tones.

The Inspector responded with an elaborate shake of the head and wave of the hand, 'No problem, no problem at all. We understand that you are a busy man. Please sit, sit.'

'Of course, of course. Everything going well so far?' asked Stephen as he took the seat across from the Inspector and leaned back in it comfortably, shuffling his large bulk in the seat like a man without a care in the world.

'Yes, Ms. N-- here has been very helpful and given us a number of leads.'

'Good!' said Stephen, nodding to Annie but unable to hide his slight puzzlement.

She sat there aghast. What the hell was the Inspector talking about? What in the world, would Stephen, her boss, imagine she had said?

'Fong!' barked the Inspector in a peremptory voice.

The Corporal leapt to his feet, almost overturning his table as he did so.

'Fetch Mr. Thwaites a drink. What will you have? Coffee, tea?' he asked.

'A glass of water would be good.'

'Very well, you heard him,' he said sharply to the Corporal who bolted from the room.

He turned back to Stephen. 'Our job is similar in many ways,' he said expansively. 'We both have to nurture and guide the young, teach them the job before we let them fend for themselves.'

'True, true,' said Stephen who was determined to match the Inspector's theatrical bonhomie. 'We can begin whenever you are ready,' he added.

'No particular hurry,' said the Inspector, 'no one is going to run away, eh. Not while I have your passports anyway.'

He gave a hearty guffaw that was met with a weak smile from Stephen Thwaites. Corporal Fong came back in with a glass of water that he placed carefully in front of Stephen. Annie saw that he had professionally wrapped the glass in a serviette so that the condensing moisture would not bother the drinker.

The Inspector waved the young man to his seat and turning to Stephen said, 'I understand that your wife and the first Mrs. Thompson are good friends?'

Taken aback by the line of questioning, Stephen could not help fidgeting in his chair. His authority dissipated and he became the errant schoolboy across the table from a headmaster.

'I am not sure how that is relevant,' he murmured.

'We'll let me be the judge of that, shall we,' said the Inspector, still all smiling politeness and white teeth, but now predatory.

'Yes, they are good friends.'

'I imagine both of you had a lot of sympathy for Sarah Thompson, the wronged wife. Hell hath no fury, eh?' and again he chuckled.

Annie sucked in her breath audibly, appalled by his insensitivity, and got a warning look from David. The Inspector's sense of humour might be in bad taste but this was no time to go charging into the breach. Stephen remained silent.

Inspector Singh proceeded, 'In fact, you were a good friend of Mark's were you not?'

Stephen did not answer, wondering whether he should deny a close relationship. He did not see any particular trap, or perhaps an innate loyalty and honesty made him say, 'Well, yes. We were after all the two senior people in the office and had a lot in common, plus our wives got along.'

'But you did not always have your wives along, eh, when you were together?' said the Inspector winking elaborately at Stephen who looked bemused.

'What's that supposed to mean?'

'I believe that,' he made a show of consulting his notes, 'you were picked up with Mr. Thompson two months ago on a dawn raid of a Balestier Road brothel?'

Annie gasped aloud. Balestier Road was notorious in Singapore for its hotels that charged by the hour and there was no reason she could think of for either Mark or Stephen to be at one, except the obvious, which she would have preferred not to believe of either man.

Stephen opted for blank denial. 'I cannot imagine where you got such information. It is not true,' he said firmly.

'Come, come, Mr. Thwaites. This is not helpful. We are both men of the world. There is no doubt at all that you and Mr. Thompson were arrested and subsequently released without charge. Your positions in the expat community and the fact that you were not caught, how shall I put it, *in flagrante delicto,* were the reasons for your release. But the Singapore police keep very good records,' he continued and leered meaningfully at Stephen.

The Inspector leaned back in his chair, completely relaxed, confident that he had the upper hand. 'I am sure you agree that your presence requires some explanation.'

Annie could not help nodding her head in agreement. Fortunately, she was outside Stephen's line of sight. She could hardly believe the Inspector's allegation. But Stephen was no longer denying it. Visiting businessmen of a certain type thought a stopover at an Orchard Towers bar or club followed by an assignation in Joo Chiat Road or Balestier Road a must in Singapore. After hours trips to seedy joints peddling sex was an integral part of business in South East Asia, whether it was the notorious bars in Pat Phong in Bangkok with its sex shows and brothels or the equally unpleasant but less well known strips in Kuala Lumpur or Jakarta. But she would have thought that Mark and Stephen would have had too much integrity to frequent such places. Was she so naïve? Two months ago, Mark would have been married to Maria for only a few months; surely his loyalty to his new wife had lasted longer than that?

Like an echo of her thoughts, Inspector Singh said, 'I believe Mr. Thompson had been married to the second Mrs. Thompson for a few months only. He seems to have strayed very soon. And what about you? How many years of marriage has it been?'

'Thirty five!'

'Were you having some domestic troubles then?'

'It's really none of your business, Inspector,' growled Stephen.

'Ah, that's where you are wrong, Mr. Thwaites. In a murder investigation, everything is my business until I say otherwise.'

'But how could this have a bearing on Mark's murder?' asked Stephen almost pleadingly.

'I do not know yet,' confessed the Inspector, 'but to give you a possibility, perhaps Mark was blackmailing you over this incident and you decided to kill him to end his hold over you?'

Annie could not believe her ears. Her whole world was being turned upside down. The Inspector thought Stephen had killed Mark?

'I'm telling you that did not happen!' cried Stephen.

Damp patches were showing through his blue shirt now, under his arms. A tip for the future, thought Annie grimly. Never wear a blue shirt to an interview with the police.

'I am telling you that is not what happened,' said Stephen.

'I am inclined to believe you,' said the Inspector unexpectedly. 'But you will have to tell me the truth about that night. Otherwise, I may have no choice but to question your wife about the state of your marital relations.'

Stephen looked at him almost in disbelief. 'You wouldn't do that, would you?'

'If you leave me no choice.'

Stephen sighed. He looked around the room as if trying to remember where he was. His gaze met Annie's. She looked away, breaking off the eye contact. She could not look at him in the same light. Annie's reaction made Stephen's mind up for him.

'You leave me with no choice,' said Stephen, addressing the Inspector directly. His voice steadied, he sat more upright in his chair and his hand went to his throat to straighten his tie. 'I had hoped to protect Mark. But your threats to spread these half-truths to my wife and the need to clear my name before my colleagues,' he nodded at Annie, 'have changed my mind.'

'On the night in question, Mark called me and invited me out for a drink. I could tell he had already been drinking heavily. If you do not know yet, Inspector, I am sure you will soon find out that Mark had a drink problem. I decided to join him and try to get him home at least. I did not want any scenes in public which would have embarrassed the firm.' He sighed again, 'Besides, he was my friend.'

He continued, 'I was frankly surprised to receive the call from him. My wife refused to acknowledge Maria, which curtailed our association with Mark as well.'

'When I met him that evening, he was already extremely drunk. He said Maria was moonlighting as a prostitute. He had received an anonymous letter saying so.'

Inspector Singh's ears pricked up at the mention of an anonymous letter. 'Did he show you the letter?'

'No, I am not even sure that it existed. It could just have been the excuse for his suspicions.'

'Why would he have suspected her of this?'

Stephen said, 'I am sure I don't have to tell you, Inspector, that it is not completely uncommon for some of the foreign workers in Singapore to get involved in that racket. They are mostly here for the money, after all, with large families back home to support.'

'But why would she continue after marriage to a wealthy man?'

'That was one of the arguments I put to Mark. He was not very clear but he seemed to think she might still need money, I don't know why.'

'Hmmm,' said the Inspector. 'It should be possible to find out.' He turned to Corporal Fong. 'Make a note of that,' he barked.

Stephen continued his narrative. Mark had dragged him to a bar in Orchard Towers, a place notorious for its seedy bars and discos. They had weaved their way between tables and onto the dance floor. The strobe lighting, bodies gyrating and smell of cheap perfume had almost overwhelmed him. He had tried to keep up with Mark who was swaying on his feet and getting dirty looks from the clientele as he grabbed slim young women by the arm and forced them to look at him, unable to be sure in his drunkenness whether any were his wife. Other Filipinas sashayed up to him to ask him to buy them a drink. A group of Bangladeshi men had become aggressive with Mark and he had dragged him away from what was developing into a dangerous confrontation. Hoping that was the end of it, he had urged Mark to give up and go home.

'But he took it into his head that he was going to Balestier Road to hunt for her in those cheap rent- by- the-hour motels along the road. I did my best to persuade him not to. I had these horrible mental pictures of him bursting in on half our clients and accusing them of using his wife as a prostitute!' Stephen shook his head, 'In the end I went with him again. I thought I might be able to stop him getting hurt.'

'What happened?' asked the Inspector.

'We got to one and went in. Mark could barely walk

in a straight line. I suggested to him that he wait while I had a look round. He refused. We were still in the middle of this argument when the police raided the place and arrested us. I think you know the rest.'

'So you never did find out if she was there?'

'Of course she wasn't there,' said Stephen. 'It was just a fit of drunken jealousy.'

'A pretty extreme case,' said the Inspector.

'This would be relevant only if the corpse was Maria's!'

'Does anyone else know of the events of that day?'

'I did not tell anyone, not even my wife. I'm sure Mark didn't either…assuming he could remember any of it.'

'Was his behaviour any different subsequently?'

'Not noticeably. He was still drinking a fair bit. As far as I am aware, he and Maria remained together.'

The Inspector slumped in his chair as if the revelations had placed too heavy a burden on his shoulders. He was nothing if not a ham actor, thought Annie. She herself could not decide whether she was more dismayed by her original suspicions or Stephen's explanation. The break-up of Mark's marriage had appalled everyone. Conventional wisdom was that Maria had married Mark for his money and that the second marriage would not see the year out. The reality was even more sordid. However unacceptable Mark's behaviour had been, having an affair, getting caught and then marrying Maria - it was this last point which had really electrified audiences. Annie felt sorry for the way things had turned out. Mark must have thought that he was embarking on a new beginning. Instead, six months later, he was dead.

'Let us turn to his murder, Mr. Thwaites,' said the Inspector. 'Perhaps you would be kind enough to tell us where you were the evening of Mr. Thompson's death.'

'I am afraid I do not have a very convincing alibi.'

The Inspector waited for him to continue, making no comment.

'I popped into the office briefly in the morning but then went over to Bintan,' Stephen mentioned a popular Indonesian island resort not far from Singapore, 'for a round of golf with a client. We played nine holes in the blazing sun and then were rained off. I had a couple of beers with him at the clubhouse and then took the ferry back. It must have been early evening when we got to Singapore. The crossing was choppy because of the storm and I am not a great sailor. I switched off my mobile phone when I got home, climbed into bed and slept soundly till the morning. When I switched on my phone the next morning, there was a message from Mark ordering me to the meeting. Of course I had missed it. A short while later, Rahul Gandhi called me with the news.'

'So you were asleep during the murder?' asked Inspector Singh, letting a disbelieving note creep into his voice.

'That's my story, I'm afraid. I realise it would have been better to have been the keynote speaker at a conference of hundreds.'

His attempt at humour fell on stony ground. The Inspector did not appear to have heard him.

'Did anyone see you come home? Can anyone vouch for you being home?' asked the Inspector impatiently.

'I'm afraid not.'

'Wife, children, maid? Surely someone must have seen you.'

'My wife was away that evening on one of those overnight casino cruise ships, with Sarah Thompson, if you must know. She was home the next morning. My children are away at university and the maid had the day off.'

'Pity you're not having an affair with the maid, eh?' Again the belly laugh from the Inspector.

Annie winced.

The Inspector was once more full of exaggerated

friendliness. 'Well, thank you very much for your time, Mr. Thwaites. I realise you are a busy man so I won't keep you any longer.'

He stood up, shook Stephen's hand vigorously and escorted him to the door, yanked it open, waved him through with a flourish and shut it firmly after him.

He turned back to the room. 'Well, well, well. That was very interesting, eh? We make progress,' he said, rubbing his pudgy hands together like a cartoon villain.

Annie had to remind herself that he was one of the good guys.

'Now I think that I will return to the station with Fong here and we will resume tomorrow.'

Seeing Annie's startled face, he explained, 'It will be best if I go back and follow up on some leads.'

'What sort of thing do you have in mind?' asked David, his curiosity overcoming his reticence.

Inspector Singh hesitated, as if wondering whether to share his thoughts with them and then said, 'That's for me to know and you to find out, eh.'

Gathering his papers, he nodded to the two of them and walked out the door with Corporal Fong trailing after.

'What do you think he's gone back to find out?' Annie asked David.

'Finding out why Mark thought his second wife would need money and whether there is any truth in this prostitution allegation, searching for the anonymous letter, if it really existed, confirming Sarah Robinson's alibi…and that's just for starters.'

'Can he do all that?' asked Annie.

'I suspect they will find a way,' was his response. He continued, 'Whatever one might think of the good Inspector's methods, the police are pretty organised. Knowing about Stephen's and Mark's escapade!'

'Yes, and knowing what time my plane landed,' said Annie.

'I suspect that once he decided that you would be the only acceptable witness, he checked up on your story first.'

'Well, he still thinks of me as a suspect …"

'A suspect but not a front runner!'

Annie grimaced and rubbed the back of her neck. The strain of the interviews had made her head and neck ache.

A clap of thunder reverberated through the room. Both turned to look at the only window. The dark clouds that had been gathering so ominously on the horizon had unleashed their full might over Raffles Tower. Rain lashed against the reinforced glass. It looked as if someone was chucking buckets of water at the window; individual drops were all but indistinguishable. From time to time, the sky was lit up with sheets of lightning. It was so dark outside, night might have fallen. Annie and David were both silent, admiring the ferocity of the storm.

'You forget, don't you? The sheer power of storms in this part of the world. You get used to icy pinpricks of rain all day in the U.K!'

Annie wanted to ask him if he had been in Asia much but stopped herself. This was still the spy from head office. Everyone in the office was 'kowtowing' to him already. She was not so easily convinced of his good intentions. Having made up her mind firmly on these points, Annie heard herself asking, 'Where are you staying? I can give you a lift on the way home if you like.'

'That would be wonderful,' he replied enthusiastically. 'I was not looking forward to trying for a taxi in this weather,' he said looking out the window again. His face was plunged into light and shadow as another fork of lightning cleaved the air. 'I'm at the Raffles. Is that on your way?'

Annie raised an eyebrow at him. There was no stinting on the expense account if he was staying at Singapore's luxurious Raffles Hotel.

He correctly interpreted the look and grinned, 'There must be some perks in a job that involves going round offices accusing your colleagues of murder.'

Annie shrugged. He was right. The firm could afford it anyway. 'It's on my way. Shall we go?'

-twelve-

'Every will shall be signed at the foot or end thereof by the testator… in the presence of two or more witnesses present at the same time …'
Section 6, Wills Act, Chapter 352

Corporal Fong waited patiently for the elevator. He had been sent to fetch the car. Inspector Singh did not deign to make the trip to the car park. It had been an interesting morning. He did not quite know what to make of Inspector Singh's methods. There had been nothing in the academy about his style of questioning. Still, he had had the lawyers off balance. Producing the brothel visit had been a masterpiece. He, Fong, had not even known about it. At this thought, he grimaced. Whatever his view of the boss might be, the boss had far too low an opinion of him to share vital information. He did not mind the errands so much. He had done his compulsory national service in the army. He knew the uniformed generation that viewed anyone of junior rank as a glorified servant. There was no room for a sense of self-importance. He would just have to knuckle down and produce results. Nothing else was going to make an impact on the fat bastard.

•

Annie walked down the corridor to her office. The secretaries, whose desks lined the walls, turned in unison to look at her and then hastily busied themselves. A lull in the wild speculation going on in the passageway. Annie could see that one of the women had not even turned her P.C on, although she was industriously typing away. Annie could not blame them for being curious. None of them had been in such a situation before. One of their bosses was dead. The rest were accused of his murder. There were plenty of insights into the expatriate lifestyle in the tabloids to keep their interest titillated. Annie was fairly sure that the 'sources close to the company' that had provided information to the newspapers on Mark ('he was sometimes very drunk in the office') came from the ranks of the secretaries. Who could blame them? The informants got their fifteen minutes of fame as well as cash. She had not noticed any particularly untruthful quote even if a few were exaggerated. Or were they even that? It was difficult to judge how others saw them, especially taking into account the huge cultural divide between the local staff and the mostly expatriate lawyers.

Annie noticed that Dora, Mark's ultra competent and extremely loyal secretary, was not at her desk and wondered where she was. She kicked herself for not having found a way of comforting her and making sure that she did not feel that her job was threatened. She hoped someone else had been more organised but was not optimistic. The lawyers were primarily concerned with their own well-being. In this crisis, with their own interests very much in jeopardy, it was unlikely they had spared a thought for Dora.

'Is there any news? Do they know who did it?' A strident whisper from a senior secretary, Yoke Lin. A fat buxom woman in heavy makeup and a tight-fitting floral dress, she was an intelligent and warm-hearted woman who was popular with the other staff and lawyers. Everyone within earshot stopped pretending to work to listen.

Annie shook her head. 'No, no developments yet.' She gave them a warm smile to show that she was not evading the question but telling the truth.

A head popped round a door. It was Julian.

'Annie! Come in here for a moment.'

She walked over to his office and he opened the door a crack to let her in, his behaviour, she thought, unnecessarily furtive. Rahul was in the room, leaning back in a chair, the buttons on his shirt straining as usual and a few food spots on his tie. A complete contrast to Julian's slightness, emphasised by his fitting light pink cotton shirt. She smiled at the two men.

'What's up?'

'You tell us. What's going on in there? We saw Stephen go in and now the Inspector has left.' This was Julian, excited and nervous.

'What have you two been doing all day, watching the door?' she asked, laughing, and then realised it was not far from the truth.

'Stop evading the question,' said Rahul, only half jokingly. Annie had not been, but this was a reminder that she was sworn to secrecy.

'Stephen's been interviewed. I guess the Inspector plans to go on tomorrow.'

'Why? What did Stephen tell him?'

'Come on, you two. You know I can't be telling you the details of what went on in there.'

'Jesus, Annie! You're supposed to be our friend,' Julian was quick to put her on the defensive.

'Of course we're friends,' she retorted angrily. 'But there is no way I can tell you anything. It's completely unreasonable of you to expect it of me. Surely you can see that?'

'Annie has to do what she thinks is right.' There was no acknowledgement from Rahul that he thought she *was* right. Annie scowled at them both.

Julian looked angry but apologised, 'Sorry! This thing has got me right on edge.'

She accepted the apology at face value. 'Me too. I'll see you two tomorrow.'

She turned and left the room to avoid more damage to their long-term friendship. Neither of the two men tried to stop her. She was no use to them except as a source of information. If she insisted on maintaining the proceedings as confidential, neither of them were able to move beyond the current situation to maintain the relationship. She would be lucky, she thought ominously, if they found the killer before she was stripped of the respect and friendship of all her colleagues.

Annie stopped again at Yoke Lin's desk. The plump woman looked up at her expectantly.

'Where is Dora?' she asked.

'The new guy, Mr. Sheringham, gave her the week off. He said that she should have some time away from the office to make things easier. When she returns she is going to work for him, Mr. Sheringham that is, until there is a replacement for Mr. Mark. Dora said that he was very kind.'

'Who?' asked Annie confused.

'Mr. Sheringham,' said Yoke Lin.

This was a rebuke that it had required the intervention of a stranger to take steps to reassure Dora. Annie nodded, accepting the criticism.

'Everyone is really stressed.' It was an explanation, not an excuse. 'I am glad that David was helpful.'

Annie walked to her room. She sat at her desk and looked around. Her room was clean and bare and functional. She did not clutter the place with mementos and other personal effects. Reggie's room was crowded with pictures of his three children and his wife, souvenirs from his childhood to the present and curios brought back from his business and holiday travels. The only personal stuff Annie had in her room was a large potted plant and a small photo of her mother, a petite, bubbly looking Caucasian woman, smiling broadly for the camera. Her mother had died when she was seventeen. A short, desperate, losing battle against cancer. As for her father, she had sent him the money he had asked for. He would have no more of her, and need no more - until his next financial crisis.

Looking at the time, she saw that she was late to meet David. He was already at the reception.

'Sorry,' she said breathlessly, having dashed down the corridor.

'No problem. What happened? Cross examination in the corridor?'

She guessed he had seen her get waylaid by the secretaries. There did not seem much that escaped his notice. 'Yes, and Rahul and Julian dragged me in for a briefing.'

Immediately, there was a sense of constraint between them. David was struggling not to repeat his admonition to keep proceedings confidential. Annie was annoyed with herself for giving him the impression that she might have been indiscreet.

'Don't worry,' she said, 'all the cats are still in the bag.'

He wrong footed her by asking, 'Look, are you sure you want to give me a ride home? I am sure I can hail a cab.'

This last was patently untrue as the storm was still raging outside.

She shook her head, 'Let's go! Before we get stuck in traffic as well as this storm.'

'There speaks someone who has forgotten how lucky they are to work in Singapore,' said David as they stepped into the lift lobby.

'What do you mean?' asked Annie.

'That there is hardly any traffic here, not even during rush hour.'

'Quite true, although rain and rush hour do occasionally cause a few hiccups.'

'You need to be dashing through freezing rain, to a crowded Underground station, to be packed like sardines into an overheated train which then crawls forward a few yards into a tunnel and stops because there is a leaf on the track …,' he said with a grin.

'No car?' she asked enquiringly.

'Oh! I have a car, just nowhere to park it in the city.'

'You're quite right that, after living here for a few years, one loses all sense of perspective. I get cross if it takes me more than fifteen minutes to get home.'

The lift arrived and the doors slipped open silently. Sophie King stepped out. There was a drabness about her. Sombre clothing, grey, worn face and dour expression. A woman labouring under a heavy load. She did not notice the two waiting for the lift and walked past them without a word or a glance. Annie's half smile was frozen on her face. David made as if to take a step after her and then stayed where he was. The doors starting to close reminded them of their original purpose. David put a hand out and the sensors stopped the doors. He ushered Annie in before him and she walked into the lift, ignoring the glares and scowls of the people inside. The occupants of Raffles Tower did not appreciate waiting.

They stood next to each other. Annie could see, looking at their reflection in the lift doors, that she barely reached up to his shoulder. She was pleased for an opportunity to study him discreetly. After all, she could not help but look at the reflections, directly in front of them. He was a distinguished looking man. She could see that a few of the women in the lift were stealing glances at him. Annie did not blame them. She would probably be doing the same if she did not already know and dislike him. She turned her attention to her own reflection, wondering what a stranger would see. This was unusually introspective for Annie. She was a tall woman, and slim, elegantly but practically dressed. Sober colours and sensible shoes. Far from beautiful, she acknowledged grudgingly. The firm chin and wide mouth were too distinct. And as for the big brown eyes, it was a wonder anyone took her seriously, she thought in disgust.

In the car park, David gave Annie's car an admiring gaze and ran his hand along the roof. 'This is nice!'

'I know,' Annie responded shamefaced. 'I swear it's my one extravagance.'

'No complaints from me. Pity the top has to stay up.'

He had to raise his voice as Annie drove out of the car park and the heavy rain drummed down on the roof. Both fell silent as Annie drove slowly through the storm. It was almost impossible to speak above the rain and the intermittent claps of thunder and Annie was concentrating hard to make out the other cars on the road, their rear lights barely discernable. Despite having to proceed slowly, they were soon approaching the Raffles Hotel. Through the rain, it was still possible to see the beautiful white building with long bay windows, surrounded by palms and flowering plants.

Annie turned into the gravel drive and David said, 'Why don't you come in for some tea?' He sensed her hesitation and said, 'You said you felt like a cuppa. Where else to have it but the Tiffin Room?'

'Sounds too good to refuse,' said Annie making up her mind.

She pulled up at the front entrance. A large Punjabi man, resplendent in a gold braided white uniform with shiny buttons and a turban which added six inches to his already impressive height, unfurled a massive golf umbrella and held it over Annie's door. She got out and handed the keys to him as he escorted her to the patio. David, not waiting for similar treatment, joined her, brushing the drops of rain off his jacket and running his fingers through his glistening wet hair. In the lobby, Annie stopped as she always did, to admire the polished old wood, thick carpets, gleaming chandeliers and heady scent of fresh lilies in a massive floral display in the centre of the room. A couple of backpackers behind her were stopped by an attendant and turned back because they were dressed in shorts and sandals. David, who was either inured to the splendour, or hungry, was already at the entrance to the Tiffin Room and as she came up to him she heard him ask for a table for two. They were shown to a quiet table by a window, a moderate distance from the sumptuous tea spread.

David looked at the food on display and said, 'Hmm ... I was planning a trip to the gym and instead I fear I am going to have the high tea.'

Annie nodded. 'Good! I won't feel so greedy if I have company.'

David ordered himself a pot of tea while Annie loitered around the buffet table, raising covers one by one. She walked back to the table, a heaped plate in one hand and a bowl in the other. She sat down and accepted a cup of tea from the waiter, adding a generous dollop of milk and sugar.

David looked at her plate and exclaimed, 'Good God! What is that stuff?'

Annie grinned at him, dimples showing.

'I am all Asian when it comes to food,' she said, 'and this is what we call tea.'

Her selection merited some remark. Her plate was heaped with brightly coloured deserts, pink and white stripes, green slices, a bright orange sliver, yellow bits - in all shapes and sizes, squares, rolls, triangles, balls.

'What are these things made of, anyway?' he asked.

'To be frank, I'm not sure,' she said. 'Coconut, pandan, durian, water chestnuts, corn and who knows what else.'

'Durian! A fruit that proves the non-existence of God.'

'You can't be serious, it's the King of Fruit!'

'Apple pie on a bog.'

'Rubbish! It's scrumptious,' laughed Annie. 'Are you aware that the theory of gravity was discovered by a Malay farmer long before Newton? Unfortunately, he was sitting under a durian tree ...'

Annie stopped and stared over his left shoulder. Curious, he turned to follow her gaze. A sleek, distinctive woman with long straight hair to her waist, heavily made up, wearing conspicuously expensive clothes and jewellery, was standing at the entrance holding two children by the hand.

'The second Mrs. Mark Thompson,' Annie whispered.

'Who are the children?' asked David.

'Must be hers,' Annie said. 'They're carbon copies of her. I had heard that she had a couple of children - from a previous marriage, but I thought they were in the Philippines.' And then under her breath, 'Damn, she's seen us.'

Maria Thompson looked over at them, her oval face expressionless. Debating whether to ignore them, acknowledge them from a distance or come over to their table. Still holding the children by the hand, she came over.

'Maria, how nice to see you. How are you holding up?' asked Annie.

'It is not an easy time for me,' she replied. 'First Mark is killed and that woman is sure to try and kill me also.'

Feeling quite unequal to responding to this, Annie said instead, 'Are these your children? They look so much like you.' Maria nodded and her expression as she looked down at them standing quietly by her revealed a fierce maternal pride.

'Erik and Gloria. Mark would not allow me to bring them to Singapore while he was alive. But now...,' she trailed off and shrugged.

David said, 'Mrs. Thompson, you do not know me but I have been sent by the London office to help out in Singapore and try and find out who did this terrible thing.

My name is David Sheringham.'

Maria sniffed, 'What is there to find out? I keep telling everyone, it was that bitch. I keep telling the police. But no one listens and soon I will be dead. Then who will look after my children?'

She finished near a shout and a few people at the other tables turned to look. A few whispered comments suggested that she had not gone unrecognised.

David signalled to a waiter and said to Maria, 'Won't you and your children join us?' and as Maria visibly hesitated, he continued persuasively, 'You can explain to us your suspicions and perhaps we can help you.'

This was an offer she could not refuse. Behind her, Annie glared at David. They all maintained a discreet silence as a couple of waiters dragged over a table to adjoin theirs and create sufficient room. Maria bent over her children and whispered a few instructions in Tagalog and they both headed off to the buffet.

David said, 'What about you, Mrs. Thompson? Won't you have something from the buffet?'

'No, no! I come for my children to enjoy. I will have a cup of tea. I need to keep trim, you understand,' she said, flashing him a look from under her long (and false I bet, thought Annie) lashes.

David recognised the role he was to play.

He leaned forward and said, 'Come now, Mrs. Thompson, I am sure you know there is no need at all for you to watch your figure, the rest of us will do that.'

Maria laughed and said, 'You can call me Maria.'

David poured out her tea, added milk and sugar at her nod, and gave it to her. Maria may have started out as a domestic worker in Singapore but she had gotten into the habit of being waited on.

'Now, Maria, tell me what the firm can do to help you. We will do anything in our power of course.'

Maria snorted her disbelief. 'You say you will help, but I know that Mark's office only wants to protect that killer.

Your Mr. Thwaites and his wife are protecting her.'

David said, 'It is true that Stephen and Joan have a personal friendship with Sarah Thompson, but the firm would still like to help you. You are Mark's widow.'

'Ha! At least you see this. I am the widow. She is nothing. An ex-wife. History! But you all act like she is the wife.'

Annie felt like pointing out that Sarah had been his wife for thirty years and was the mother of his two children, unlike Maria who had married him for his money six months previously. She knew that David would not thank her for it. The children returned to the table with laden plates and started tucking in enthusiastically. David looked at them and hesitated, reluctant to discuss the subject further in their presence.

Maria said, 'Do not worry about the children. They know. I have explained everything. And anyway their English is not so good.'

She continued, 'You want to know how she did it? I will tell you.'

David nodded encouragingly and even Annie leaned forward in her chair.

'She said she wanted to kill him…and me. When Mark wanted to marry me. She wrote bad letters.'

'Threatening letters?' asked Annie.

'Saying I was a slut, a prostitute…things like that.'

'When was this?' asked David.

'For months and months after we married.'

'Right up until the murder?' This time it was Annie with the question.

'The letters stopped two months ago. She is not so stupid. When she decided to come to Singapore and kill him, she stopped the letters so that no one would think it was her. But I know!' she said triumphantly, leaning back in her chair and looking at both of them.

David ignored the obvious difficulties with this line of deduction and asked, 'Did Mark see her on this trip?'

'Of course not,' Maria said scornfully. 'Why he want to see her? She is old and ugly. He did not want her anymore.'

'But perhaps to discuss the children, maybe their studies or money?'

He had touched a raw nerve because she said, 'He would not see her, but if he did, she would ask for money. She always wanted more money. She paid the lawyers to send many letters asking for money from Mark. She is a very greedy woman. But I said to Mark that he had given enough. We should have some to enjoy as well.'

'And his children?' asked Annie.

'They hate him too. He has not seen them for many months, since the divorce.'

'That must have been really hard for him,' said Annie. 'Perhaps your children helped to bridge the gap?'

'My children? This is the first time they come to Singapore. Mark did not want them. Even when I sent money for them, I keep it a secret from him. He would not give me any money for them at all. I had to send part of the house money.'

'That was very bad of Mark,' said David, leaning towards her sympathetically. 'Why did he feel this way?'

'I do not know,' she said wearily, the strain starting to show. 'Maybe jealous? I do not know…but it was very hard for me.'

Hard enough so that she had to kill him? That was the question in Annie's mind. At least the question of why Mark believed that Maria needed money sufficiently desperately to moonlight as a prostitute was revealed. If he knew that he was keeping her short of money for the children, he would assume that was her motive.

Maria looked at her two children, who returned her look expectantly. She smiled at them and then turned to the other two and looked at them defiantly, 'I know that many people think I killed him. That would make it easy for you. But I did not kill Mark, so you will have to find someone else to blame.'

David said, 'Maria, nobody will accuse you of anything you did not do. I give you my word that I will not let that happen.'

Maria looked sceptical. 'I am a Filipina in Singapore and I do not trust the police to be fair.'

She rose to her feet and picked up her purse.

David got to his feet too. He took Maria's hand in his and said, 'Don't worry too much. We will do what we can for you.'

She nodded her thanks to him and accompanied it with a small smile. Annie she ignored as she swept out of the room. A few men turned to watch her go.

'Well, that's Maria for you, every arrival is an entrance and every departure, an exit!' muttered Annie.

'You can see why,' remarked David. 'She really is an exceptionally sexy woman.'

'It was quite clear you thought so …all that fawning,' said Annie. She had intended to sound sarcastic but could not help but feel she sounded more aggrieved.

David thought so because he turned to her with one of his captivating smiles and said, 'Don't worry! She doesn't hold a candle to you.'

A remark calculated to aggravate.

Annie glared at him, ' I'm not worried. Your opinion is of no importance to me. I realise that she oozes sex appeal. Presumably that's why Mark married her and no doubt why she will have no difficulty finding comfort, from you or anyone else, in her so-called grief.'

David prudently changed the subject, 'Why do you think Mark would not have her children here?'

'Who knows? It seems out of character. And not letting her send money to them. No wonder Mark thought she might need to get extra cash by whatever means. I wonder what happens to Mark's money?'

'I know the answer to that,' said David.

He did not elaborate so Annie said, 'Well, aren't you

going to tell me?'

David beckoned to a waiter and gestured to his cold tea. The waiter came over and dexterously swapped cups and poured out a steaming cup of fresh tea for him. When he was out of earshot again, David turned his attention to Annie. She had no illusions about the little pantomime. He had been buying time, trying to decide whether to answer the question or not.

'She scoops the lot,' he said at last.

'What does 'scoop the lot' mean?'

'Maria is the sole beneficiary under the will. Not an awful lot though, about fifty thousand dollars all told. Sarah Thompson got herself a hefty divorce settlement and there is already a trust fund for the children.'

'Maria might think it a lot,' pointed out Annie.

'She might,' agreed David, 'although to be frank, I think she would have been expecting millions. There is also an insurance policy with her as the beneficiary, Maria that is, for another million dollars.'

'That should keep her in designer underwear for a while,' was Annie's shaken response.

'That's a motive and a half isn't it?' he said.

'But insurance won't pay if she killed Mark,' Annie said.

'No, they won't.'

Annie shook her head in disbelief, 'I suppose the comfort is that any motive I might have must pale in comparison.'

'Nah! You do yourself an injustice,' said David, 'If Mark was going to fire you for some misconduct, you would have lost more than that in the long run.'

'Very funny,' said Annie.

She drained the dregs from her teacup, stood up, pushed a tendril of hair firmly behind one ear and said, 'Well, I'm off. See you tomorrow.'

David contemplated her receding back. She had a determined stride and had disappeared out the doors in a few moments. He compared it to Maria's stately exit and smiled to himself. Annie did not play to the galleries.

Annie drove herself home, the top of her convertible down, as the rain had finally stopped. A few minutes earlier, Maria Thompson had summoned a hotel limousine with the Raffles 'R' emblazoned on its side and was handed into it by a liveried doorman. She had nodded her thanks but refrained from tipping him. She had worked hard to come by her money and was not going to hand it out to some uniformed car jockey who was doing no more than his job. Besides, she might well be short of ready cash waiting for the insurance to come through.

Once again, she congratulated herself on persuading Mark to take out the policy. It had not been easy. He had not wanted to think about his own death, to acknowledge the age gap between them. She had tread carefully so as not to confirm his fears that she had married him for his money. Married him for his money? Well, of course she had! Mark had been in relatively good shape for a man of his age with an alcohol habit. He had not been overweight, although his flesh had been fatty, covered in a pale, almost translucent, hairless skin with skein of blue veins showing - she shuddered to herself at the recollection. Would that have been her choice? Certainly not. She would have found herself a young, sinewy Filipino man, bronzed by the sun. He would have strong, work-roughened hands - not the desk job softness of Mark's that had felt like a woman's hands on her skin. Well, she could find herself a real man now, she thought with pleasurable anticipation. A new father for her children. One who would teach them to fly a kite and gut a fish. They deserved better than an old man who had refused to meet them. But his money would pave the way to a better future for them all. They owed him something for that.

-thirteen-

'When two or more persons agree to do, or cause to be done —

(a) an illegal act; or
(b) an act, which is not illegal, by illegal means,
such an agreement is designated a criminal conspiracy…'
Section 120A, Penal Code, Chapter 224

The main investigator in the case, Inspector Singh, was sitting at a table close to the entrance of a Chinese coffee shop. He had his elbows on the faux pine Formica surface pitted with cigarette burns and missing strips. His large rear end was balanced precariously, but expertly, on a red plastic stool. Above him, a ceiling fan turned slowly, ineffective to cool the steamy evening. In front of him, an ice-cold bottle of Guinness stood on the table next to an empty, clear glass mug with Carlsberg written on the side. Little rivulets of condensation ran down the side of the bottle and puddled around its base. Inspector Singh watched these little rivulets for a while and then reached out and grasped the bottle firmly in one hand and the mug in the other. He tipped both toward each other and commenced pouring carefully, from bottle to mug. As the mug filled, he straightened it ever so gradually until it was vertical again, filled to the brim with the drink and a layer of snowy white foam. He placed the bottle on the same spot on the table, marked for him by the circle of water. With the mug still in his left hand, he brought it to his mouth and had a full, long, slow swig. He put the glass down, only two thirds full now, and drew the back of his hand over his mouth, wiping away the layer of white foam that had adhered to his moustache and formed a peculiar contrast to his full black beard. He sighed pleasurably.

•

Corporal Fong was at his desk at the station. He was supposed to be writing up the notes from the day's activities. Instead he was looking at a glossy brochure for private health care. Comprehensive services were on offer. Round the clock care, resident doctors, private apartments. He knew he could not afford any of it. But the problem of what to do with his father was becoming more urgent. He could not bear the state he found the old man in when he got home. During his police academy days, his hours had been regular and he had been able to manage. Now, always at the beck and call of that black-hearted devil, he was in a fix. He threw the brochures into the bin. That was not the solution.

•

Annie tossed and turned all night, sleeping only in snatches. It had been a relief to hear the alarm and get out of bed. She set out on her morning bike ride, half an hour round the old abandoned cemetery ten minutes away from the house. It was a wonderful, old place, full of large semicircular tombstones - the most recent dating back to the 1930's - decorated with floral tiles and carvings, protected by grotesque gargoyles, parodies of frogs and lions and - Annie's favourite - guarded by two stone sentries with handlebar moustaches and curly beards, stone rifles by their side. Black and white photos of the dead were glazed onto the headstones; the faces of neat men and prim women. The pictures were of the young, but the dates made it clear that this was the last vanity of the dead. Occasionally husband and wife, or wives, were buried together and marked by the same gravestone. There were also pictures of men with a space reserved next to them for their wives. For whatever reason, the wives had not been buried there and the spaces had remained blank through the years. Undergrowth lapped the sides of the tombs and narrow road through it. Huge trees spread out overhead. In every fork in the branches, epiphytes sprouted voluminously. Orioles, the colour of the sun, and shiny blue kingfishers flitted from perch to perch. Swallows swooped through the air, diving for insects. High above, circling slowly, flew birds of prey. Annie loved the place, enjoying the solitude and the background chorus of cicadas, birds and frogs shrieking, whistling and groaning. Occasionally, there was even a monkey chattering to her earnestly. She enjoyed her dawn bike ride through the mystical old place three times a week before setting out for the office.

•

As usual, Annie's first stop of the morning at the office was the pantry. She put on the coffee percolator and watched it bubble and boil hypnotically.

'I'll have a bit of that.'

Annie started. Reggie had walked in. She had not heard the swing doors.

'Good morning, Reggie,' she said as she took the coffee jug from the percolator and poured a cupful into the proffered mug, 'You're an early bird today.'

Reggie was notorious for never being at work on time.

'Couldn't sleep,' he confessed.

'Me neither,' she said, feeling almost in charity with

Reggie, although he was someone she had always cordially disliked and now that emotion had sharpened on the back of his petty displays over the murder.

'What's on the agenda today?' he asked.

'More interviews, I suppose,' replied Annie.

'A bit of a strain?'

'That's an understatement,' she said. 'Being treated like a suspect, watching colleagues being treated as suspects ...,' she trailed off.

'I see what you mean, not much fun having a front row seat.'

'No,' she agreed.

'Any sign yet that that woman might have done it?'

Annie chose to be obtuse, 'Who do you mean?'

'The lovely widow of course,' Reggie responded tetchily.

'I have to say, I don't think she did it,' said Annie. She had not come to a firm view on the subject but felt obliged to contradict Reggie.

Her interruption was a very small stone in the stream as he carried on relentlessly, 'You can't be serious, Annie. It must have been her. It can't have been one of us. She is not exactly a moral woman, is she?'

'Reggie!' exclaimed Annie, protesting his logic. 'She may have broken up Mark's marriage, but that hardly demonstrates any criminal inclination, let alone a murderous one.'

'You may be right,' he said at last, 'but that means you're calling one of us a murderer.'

'I am not accusing anyone ... God knows I am in it as deep as anyone else, but Mark *is* dead and like it or not, we are all suspects.'

The doors to the pantry swung open, Western style, and Inspector Singh sauntered in.

'Good,' he said, 'you are both here. I checked in your rooms but there was no one to be found. But I guessed you would be here.' He beamed cheerily at them, pleased with his own deductive reasoning.

Reggie said, 'What do you want, Inspector?'

The Inspector appeared in no way put out by this rudeness. 'Interviews, interviews …,' he answered, 'the hunt for the truth must proceed.'

'My interview is scheduled for this afternoon,' said Reggie.

'Now then, Mr. Peters,' a parody of an English fictional policeman, 'I am sure you are the last person to want to delay our progress.'

Annie wondered if there was a touch of sarcasm in his tone. She would not blame the Inspector if there was. Reggie had not been a model of co-operation.

'This is unacceptable, Inspector!' Reggie blustered, 'I have meetings this morning, important work to do, I can't just cancel everything.'

'I'm sure that nothing you have to do is more important than finding Mr. Thompson's murderer,' replied the Inspector, a hint of steel in his voice. 'As a colleague and friend of his, no doubt you feel the same way.'

Reggie looked as if he was going to argue but the Inspector carried on, 'I do not want to inconvenience you unnecessarily, so you can have ten minutes to rearrange your morning.'

Unable to think of anything, not daring to refuse outright, Reggie turned away so hastily that hot coffee slopped over his hand from the mug he was still holding. He walked out of the pantry, dabbing his hand with a handkerchief and struggling to maintain some dignity. Annie raised a quizzical eyebrow at the Inspector. He had probably rearranged the meetings purely to unsettle Reggie. If that was the case, his plan had worked a treat.

'Do you think he will come?' she asked.

'Oh yes! He will be exactly five minutes late to demonstrate that he is not pandering to the natives, but he won't dare push it a minute beyond that.'

'And how do you feel about that?' asked Annie.

The Inspector gave one of his unexpected belly laughs, 'That's why I gave him ten, and not fifteen minutes.'

Annie followed the Inspector out of the room and down the corridor, feeling like a puppet on a string.

David was already in the interview room, seated in his chair, flipping through some papers. He looked up as they came in and smiled a friendly welcome.

'Good morning.'

Annie murmured a response and sat down in her chair. The morning sun was streaming in through the window behind her.

'What's the agenda today, then?' asked David, unconsciously echoing Reggie's words from earlier.

'We are having Reggie Peters in first,' said the Inspector.

David looked surprised. His eyes narrowed. Annie guessed that he had seen through the Inspector's tactics.

'Does Reggie know?'

'Yup,' said the Inspector.

There was a tentative and then a more forceful knock on the door, as if the person seeking ingress had regretted the timid nature of his first attempt and was trying belatedly to assert himself.

'Come,' growled the Inspector.

Annie was not surprised when Reggie walked in. She peeked at her wristwatch. The Inspector had been spot on in his prediction.

After the rather inflammatory beginning, the interview itself was rather low key. The Inspector was docile and Reggie was striving to appear co-operative. Reggie explained his movements the night of the murder. He did not have a particularly strong alibi. He had been at home. His children had gone to bed. His wife was out at a hen night. He had not actually spoken to Mark but found a message on his answer phone when he came out of the pool. He had wondered what to do. Then Ai Leen had called him explaining that she too had had a summons, wondering if he knew what this was about. He had offered her a lift as she was on his way. Annie itched to ask him about his newfound friendship with Ai Leen but knew that she did not have the *locus*. And besides she could not see how, curious though it was, it had a bearing on the murder.

Reggie claimed he had been a bit delayed getting to her place. Seeing as they were going to be late, Ai Leen had called the office to say that they were on the way and spoken to Rahul on the phone. When they arrived at the office, the police had interrogated the two of them. At this juncture, Reggie struggled to maintain his even tone. His 'treatment' at the hands of the Inspector still rankled.

When he had completed his uninterrupted narrative, the Inspector said, 'So who do you think did it then?'

Reggie looked surprised by the question but forbore from his customary accusations.

'I guess I don't know,' said Reggie. 'I just cannot understand who would want to do such a thing. I mean, it's ... it's outrageous!'

'Well, that's one way of putting it,' said Inspector Singh. 'So you have no idea what could have led to this?'

Reggie just shook his head.

The Inspector continued, going through his now familiar mantra, files worked on, Mark's involvement, issues, complaints, anything that might constitute a smoking gun. Reggie answered succinctly, reminding Annie that although he could and often did act the boor, he was a clever and successful man. Mark's involvement in his files was peripheral at best. As a senior partner, Reggie had had a free hand in both theory and practice.

The interview was over in no time at all and Reggie left the room in much better humour than when he had arrived. Expecting a hostile audience, he had been pleasantly surprised at the civilised tone of the interview. Annie looked at the Inspector curiously. She had expected far more fireworks. She supposed the Inspector had no evidence of wrongdoing on the part of Reggie. His alibi had been tenuous but so were most of their alibis. Even Reggie and Ai Leen were not alibis for each other. Either of them could have come into the office, killed Mark and then still been in time to meet the other before setting out once more. Again, she wondered about Ai Leen and Reggie. This time her thoughts were echoed out loud by David.

'Are Ai Leen and Reggie very chummy, then?' he asked the room at large.

It was the Inspector who answered, 'I can't speak for events prior to the murder but they have been as thick as thieves since.'

'What do you mean?' asked David.

'Well, they have been going to and fro work together most days and also spotted dining together a couple of times, usually fairly out of the way places with maximum privacy.'

Nobody asked the Inspector how he knew this. The two were being followed. Annie wondered whether she was being tailed as well. A disturbing thought. To what end?

The Inspector turned to Annie, 'Were they on good terms before?'

She shook her head, 'I have to say that I had no idea that they were close friends.'

'Friends?' snorted the Inspector. 'Any relationship that springs up around a murder investigation is very suspicious to me.'

'What next?' asked David.

'We ask Ms. Lim about her new-found fondness for Mr. Peters.'

He was as good as his word. When Ai Leen had been found, persuaded to attend the interview immediately and settled in her chair, the Inspector went on the attack immediately.

'You've been spending a lot of time with Mr. Peters of late?'

His remark was more a statement than a question.

Ai Leen was caught off guard.

'What do you mean?' she asked.

The Inspector made a show of fishing around his desk for a piece of paper, found it, looked at it carefully and then read out in a dry voice all the occasions in the past week when Ai Leen and Reggie had been spotted together. It was a long list and Ai Leen's dismay at the detail the police had of her assignations with Reggie was obvious. She tried to pull herself together but the fear in her eyes was a powerful thing.

'What does it matter? We are friends.'

'Quite a new friendship this, I understand.'

If looks could kill, Annie would have been prostrate across the floor. She tried to look apologetic and discreet at the same time. It would be difficult to win Ai Leen's forgiveness. And Ai Leen would tell Reggie and she would have both their hostility to contend with.

The Inspector continued, 'Well, Ms. Lim? I am waiting for an explanation.'

'Why do I have to explain anything to you? This is a personal subject, between Reggie and me. It has nothing to do with Mark.'

'I will be the judge of that, Ms. Lim,' the Inspector at his most cutting.

'We are friends, we support each other in difficult times.'

'How long have you been supporting each other?'

'A couple of months. We have known each other for a few years but we have become closer lately.'

'What triggered this?'

'We have a lot in common.'

'Give me an example,' said the Inspector disbelievingly.

Ai Leen glared at him, 'Our work! I am a banking lawyer too. We are both partners now.'

Ai Leen appeared to be dating her friendship with Reggie to her elevation to the partnership. It was not impossible Annie thought. Her improved status might have led Reggie to extend a hand of friendship. He had not done the same for her. But Reggie had not been much involved in the decision to make her a partner. Annie was not in his department and had not worked with him much. Ai Leen on the other hand had had to depend on Reggie's goodwill. Annie had heard on the grapevine that Reggie had started off being quite hostile to Ai Leen's partnership and been persuaded to change his mind. The other partners had thought she would make a good partner. Her being a local Singaporean was a boon. Maybe Reggie had felt it necessary to mend fences with Ai Leen.

The Inspector interrupted Annie's train of thought to ask, 'And is your husband aware of this new-found friendship?'

Ai Leen was a match for this. 'He is aware that Reggie is a colleague and friend with whom I occasionally have work-related dinners,' she said coldly.

'Quite romantic spots, you choose for these 'work-related dinners',' Inspector Singh pointed out.

'And why not?' she asked. 'We need privacy to ensure client confidentiality, and I personally am fond of good food, as I'm sure you are, Inspector,' she said allowing her gaze to drift across his large belly.

'You mean this?' the Inspector asked cheerfully, patting his ample stomach. 'This is not food. It's beer!'

Ai Leen managed to convey disgust with a slight flaring of her nostrils. She said to the Inspector, 'I really do not see what this has to do with the murder. I think you would be doing us all a favour if you tried to solve the crime rather than cast aspersions upon my character, or that of Reggie Peters.'

The Inspector changed tactics. In a much more conciliatory tone he said, 'Do you have any thoughts on who might have done this?'

'No, I do not. I only know it was not me. I am sure

that it was a stranger who robbed Mark and killed him. He must have snuck past the security guards somehow. In fact, maybe it was the security guards who did it.'

This was her final word on the subject because she rose to her feet, and at a nod from the Inspector, left the room.

David said, 'Reggie objected to her partnership at first, and changed his mind later. Maybe he was just mending fences and this friendship sprung up.'

These had been Annie's thoughts a moment earlier. However, when articulated, it was unconvincing. She shook her head. 'The Reggie I know would not be in the least bit concerned about having annoyed a partner.'

'What do you know about Ai Leen's partnership?' asked David.

'Not a lot. I was up for partnership at the same time. One hears rumours, of course …,' she continued.

'What sort of rumours?'

'Oh …the usual stuff. There was quite a lot of disagreement about her. Some partners were very keen to promote the local staff, others had doubts.'

'What sort of doubts?'

'Whether it was appropriate to support a candidate because she was Singaporean foremost, and not sticking to an objective test.'

'How did you feel about this?'

'Well, to be frank if I had been turned down, I would probably have been livid. But as we were both made partners…I can see why they wanted a local on the job. It looks better with local clients for starters. And she is a very good lawyer.'

'That's more or less what I heard as well,' said David. 'It was Mark who convinced Reggie to change his mind.'

'What's his wife like?' asked the Inspector.

'Reggie's wife?' Annie queried, 'Oh, a long-suffering blonde. I think she was his secretary but I could be wrong about that. He did have a habit of hitting on women in the office.'

'How do you know that?' asked the Inspector.

Annie looked embarrassed. The Inspector waited patiently for her response.

She said, 'Well, he's made the odd pass at me, you know, when drunk at Christmas parties and such like. For the sake of our tenuous working relationship, I have refrained from hitting him so far.'

'You should have said something. We do have policies about sexual harassment. You don't have to put up with nonsense like that!'

'Don't be so naïve, David. You know jolly well if I kicked up a stink, Reggie would get a slap on the wrist at most… and I, I would be branded a troublemaker. Anyway, I didn't 'put up with it'. I made it clear that he should keep his hands to himself.'

'And the next day?'

'And the next day we both pretend it never happened. At least, I pretend. He may genuinely forget.'

David still looked angry.

'It wasn't that bad,' Annie said bracingly. 'Anyway, I'm not really his type. He prefers the Oriental beauty …like the second Mrs. Thompson.'

'A nasty piece of work, this Mr. Peters,' said the Inspector, sounding almost pleased. 'I shall take some pleasure in hounding him.'

Neither Annie nor David responded to this. Reggie really was a nasty piece of work, whichever way you looked at it. Unfortunately, thought Annie, that did not make him a murderer. In fact, on the basis of the evidence against him to date - a tenuous alibi and an imponderable friendship - he was not even close.

'Whom shall we see next then?' asked the Inspector, rubbing his pudgy hands together gleefully. He seemed in a high good humour. Annie could not see the root of it. They had not achieved anything except to establish that Reggie was an unpleasant man. She at least had already known that.

'According to this,' said David, waving the interview schedule at the Inspector, 'it's Sophie King up next.'

'She's the one who walks around with the long face?' asked the Inspector.

Both Annie and David nodded. It was a fair description of Sophie post-murder. 'She looks like a woman who has lost her lover or her best friend…which is it?'

'Difficult to say,' said David. He turned to Annie. 'Do you know?'

'No, not really. I knew they were friends, been at the firm together a long time. I think they were trainees together - must be thirty years ago.'

David nodded his agreement and continued, 'She came out to Singapore about a year after he arrived here.'

'She was following him around?' asked the Inspector.

'It does seem so,' agreed David. 'In fact, rumour has it that they were more than friends once,' he shrugged, 'I have no idea if that is true or not.'

'The scorned woman, eh! My favourite suspect!' exclaimed the Inspector.

Annie looked scandalised.

'Well, let's have her in and ask her if she was sleeping with the boss, shall we?' the Inspector continued cheerfully.

Corporal Fong escorted Sophie in. She nodded to them and sat down on the edge of her seat, back straight, hands folded together on her lap, a grey lady - dressed in a grey suit, with greying hair and a grey drawn face.

The Inspector was as good as his word.

'Were you sleeping with Mark Thompson, Ms. King?'

He could not have been prepared for her response. It appeared that she was going to speak. She gave a small shake of the head - it could have signified denial or disbelief at the insensitivity of the question, but then she began to weep. She did not utter a sound but her body shook, racked with internal sobs. Silent tears coursed down her cheeks and dripped off her chin. Her hands twisted and pulled at a small white handkerchief but she made no effort to wipe her eyes or stem the tide. The suddenness of the collapse of control had caught them all by surprise. Corporal Fong sat at his desk, his hands poised over his keyboard, uncertain how to record her response. Annie felt like a voyeur, intruding on someone else's grief. A ringside seat to watching the disintegration of a fellow human being. A woman she had worked with, shared a drink with and considered a friend.

The Inspector showed no reaction to this outburst. He sat back in his chair, hands folded across his belly, like a large impassive Buddha, waiting for an answer to his question. Only David reacted. He came round the table to Sophie. He put an arm around her shoulders, gave her a comforting hug and produced a large white handkerchief from a pocket. He was speaking too, not saying much that was audible to Annie but in soothing reassuring tones. Slowly, he began to have an effect. The sobs became audible but intermittent. Sophie clutched the hanky in her hand and then began to dab her eyes with it, taking deep breaths to regain control.

She began to speak in an undertone, 'Sorry, I have no idea what came over me…just a shock, this whole thing has been a shock. The question, it was the final straw,' she looked at the Inspector fearfully.

Annie noticed a smugness about the fat man. She supposed the police had to be pleased if they provoked an outburst. Raw emotion was an honest response.

The Inspector said, all sympathy now, 'Take your time, Ms. King. I am sorry to have caused you so much distress.' And then, with no apparent irony, 'In a murder, the deceased is only one of the victims.'

This sentiment struck a chord with Sophie for she nodded her agreement and gave her face a final wipe. She nodded her thanks to David who rose to his feet, gave her a final sympathetic pat on the arm and then sat down in his chair again.

All eyes on her, Sophie squared her shoulders and then said, 'I will tell you everything.'

And she was as good as her word, in measured tones telling the story of her relationship with Mark. She was lucid and organised in her narrative, a far cry from her initial response. She and Mark had been good friends for almost thirty years. When they were trainees together, they had been lovers but had drifted apart. She had continued to love Mark but he had moved on. He had always been attractive to women and was not the sort of man to remain faithful to one woman when opportunity presented itself. Their relationship had become platonic but remained close. She, too, had other relationships but had never found anyone like Mark and had resigned herself to spinsterhood.

'I do not want you to think that I was unhappy,' she said with a small smile, 'I am very successful in my career. I have a lot of good friends and the occasional lover. I was not so naïve that I did not recognise that what was attractive about Mark was also what would make him a difficult person to live with.'

She had felt sympathy for Mark's wife when he married her and continued his philandering ways. She and Sarah had even contrived to be friends. She had watched with worry as Mark had started to drink heavily.

'Were you ever lovers again?' asked the Inspector.

Sophie shook her head.

'No, I would have lost the special position I had in his life and become just another one of his women. I would also, perhaps more importantly,' she said, 'have lost my self respect. Besides,' she continued, 'as Mark grew older, his tastes ran to younger women.' She smiled a little sadly. 'It is not an uncommon phenomenon, I believe.'

'How did you feel when he married Maria?' asked the

Inspector.

She paused, looking for the right word. 'Disappointed,' she said at last.

'Because you hoped to get him back?'

'Oh no! I still loved him but I was quite settled with my life. No, I was disappointed because I had put him on a pedestal, ignoring anything that reflected badly on him, his drinking or the philandering. But marrying Maria…well, that was a bit hard to ignore.'

Talking to them was having a cathartic effect on Sophie. She was finding solace in being honest, in telling them what had been bottled up inside her for so many long years. The initial passion of youth evolving into a deep affection for a flawed man and expressed in the depth of grief for the loss of both his life and an integral part of hers.

The Inspector asked, 'Do you have any idea who might have done this? Did he have any enemies?'

She shook her head, her confusion writ large on her face, 'Enemies? People did dislike him. He was successful, rich and arrogant. He had great personal charm, but he did not always use it on people he thought beneath him. But I cannot imagine anyone hating him enough to kill him, except Sarah maybe, and why would she wait all this time? It doesn't make sense.'

Annie was interested that her choice for murderer was the woman scorned, oblivious to the irony. But it appeared that Sophie did not categorise herself that way. She was more of the devoted retainer, who did not expect anything from the object of her affections and therefore was not disappointed to receive nothing. Was it possible to love someone for such a long time without feeling despair? Perhaps the first cut was the deepest, and nothing Mark had done since could affect her that strongly again. It was quite possible that her love had waned to a quiet affection that gave her an emotional outlet without the complications of a relationship. Annie could see the appeal. Plenty of time to devote to career without having to seek alternatives because the 'one man' was taken. Would she be able to adopt this posture of selfless devotion? She thought not. It was not in her nature. If she fought for but lost the man she wanted, she would try to retain her pride at least. She would walk away with her head held high, licking her wounds in private.

Sophie addressed a remark directly at her, 'Mark was very fond of you, you know. He thought you were a brilliant lawyer and was pleased with your progress.'

Annie smiled warmly at her. It was a generous gesture and she appreciated it.

Sophie looked enquiringly around the room. 'Is there anything else?' she asked. 'If there isn't, I should probably get back to trying to rebuild my life.'

Sophie rose to leave the room and both men instinctively stood. David took her elbow and guided her gently to the door and the Inspector opened it for her and shook her hand on the way out. Sophie had won their sympathy. The door closed behind her and the two men turned back into the room. As they stood side by side, Annie was not struck so much by the differences between the two men, but by the similarity. It was an effect created by their expressions, common purpose and personal self-confidence. An air about them, rather than the appearance of them, which hinted of sameness. Annie was intrigued by this insight. She had assumed the men to be poles apart in every way, a conclusion borne out by their contrasting personal appearances.

David looked at her quizzically and said, 'A penny for them?'

Annie was too embarrassed to reveal her thoughts and said instead, 'Worth a lot more than that I'm afraid.'

'Go on then, name your price. I am sure the Inspector will be happy to meet it on behalf of the police department …as I assume you have some clue as to who did it,' said David, giving the Inspector a jovial pat on the back.

David appeared to have developed a real fondness for

the quirky Inspector. She supposed that she had too.

The Inspector said, 'I do hope that you do not suspect poor Ms. King of any wrongdoing.'

'Do you think she is off the hook then?'

The Inspector sighed gustily. 'I do not see her in the role of the murderer of a man she loved so devotedly for so many years. However,' he continued, 'I have been bitterly disappointed in human nature in the past, and so I would not go as far as to cross her off the list.'

Annie said to the Inspector, 'You did not ask her about her alibi.'

Inspector Singh laughed out loud, 'You see,' he said to David, 'two days she spends in this room and now she wants my job.'

Annie smiled. It was a bit presumptuous of her to question the Inspector.

The Inspector said, 'She turned up at the office the evening of the murder, shortly after Reggie and Ai Leen. I asked her then. She lives alone and had been alone that evening until Mark called her for the meeting. So, plenty of opportunity.'

Annie noticed that he no longer hesitated to share information with her and David. Slowly, and unexpectedly, the three of them were starting to come together as a team. The rough edges of suspicion and doubt worn down by constant contact.

'But you didn't ask Sophie about her files,' said David.

The Inspector looked at both of them and laughed sheepishly. After a moment, the others joined in.

Outside, Julian was passing the door and heard the sounds of laughter within. He hesitated for a few long seconds and then walked on, his face creased with worry. Instead of going to the pantry as had been his plan, he took a lift to the main lobby, walked out to the taxi stand outside the building and climbed into the first taxi. A moment later, he was on his way.

-fourteen-

'...a person who...possesses information...that is not generally available but, if the information were generally available, a reasonable person would expect it to have a material effect on the price or value of securities... the insider must not... subscribe for, purchase or sell, or enter into an agreement to subscribe for, purchase or sell, any such securities...'
Section 218, Securities & Futures Act, Chapter 289

Across town, the police, equipped with the necessary warrants, were searching the Thompson home. Maria had flounced out of the house hours before, taking her children with her and complaining about harassment until she was out of earshot. The policemen were searching painstakingly, leaving nothing to chance. So far they had found nothing. The senior officer at the scene was beginning to suspect that he had been sent on a wild goose chase. He idly took a book from the shelf, a large volume on his own pet interest, the Pacific War. A sheaf of letters fell out as he opened the book at random. Curiously, he picked them up and leafed through the first few. He beckoned to a Corporal and gave him a few brief instructions. The Corporal, looking daunted, began taking books off the shelf and shaking them out one by one to see if anything was hidden in the pages. The officer reached for his phone.

•

Inspector Singh was furious at the absence of Julian. His interview was next on the schedule. There was no excuse for his disappearance. The Inspector's views were being forcefully expressed. Annie could not think of anything to say in Julian's defence. She had tried to explain that Julian would not have left when they were expecting him unless it was something really important. She had received a quelling glance from the Inspector and remained silent since. After all, Inspector Singh had a point. What could be more important than this murder investigation? Again she was forced to consider Julian's behaviour since the discovery of the body. Evasive, hostile, nervous. On the other hand, no one was acting in character. It was not just Julian. Stephen was worried and officious; Sophie had withdrawn into a shell. As for Reggie and Ai Leen, their response to the murder inquiry had been reasonably in character, she, inscrutable, he, aggressive and opinionated. But their united front? That was far from usual.

What about her own response? It was difficult to be objective. Annie was not adept at navel gazing. She was obsessed with the inquiry, spending all her free moments brooding over the murder. Everyone was desperately trying to point the finger of blame at someone else, happy to implicate each other. No one, except perhaps the Inspector, seemed interested in finding the truth. She had to acquit David of looking for a convenient solution as well. He was determined to identify a murderer, not a scapegoat. A phone rang. Corporal Fong answered the phone and handed the receiver to Inspector Singh. He listened to the caller for a few minutes. Finally, he issued a brusque, 'Good work, keep looking,' and hung up. The others looked at him inquiringly. He shook his head. 'Police business,' he said by way of explanation. Annie's pursed lips betrayed her annoyance.

David had remained quiet on the subject of Julian's disappearance, largely in order not to antagonise Annie further. He could hardly believe that Julian had made off when his interview was scheduled. What did he hope to achieve? He would antagonise the Inspector. There was no way he could flee the jurisdiction. Singapore was a small island. Controlling the borders was a relatively straightforward matter. Running would be a damned stupid thing to do. There was no evidence implicating Julian in the murder. Even if there was some motive for him to have murdered Mark, it would still be difficult to pin anything on him. Young fool, David thought contemptuously, forgetting that he himself was only a couple of years older than Julian.

The Inspector said, 'Well, no point wasting time. Let us see the Indian.'

Corporal Fong was sent to summon Rahul and in a few moments, he was in the room cheerfully greeting them in his distinct Indian accent, 'My turn for the third degree? That's alright...I haven't got anything to hide.'

There was no response from anyone to his jovial remarks.

Rahul smiled again and said, 'I guess this is no joking matter. Ignore me...I just get like this when I'm nervous!'

The Inspector said, 'There is nothing for you to be nervous about, Mr. Gandhi, unless you killed Mark Thompson.'

Here he stopped and looked at Rahul inquiringly as if to give him an opportunity to confess. When there was no response, he ran down the list of questions that Annie felt she knew by heart now, and received the stock answers. He had got a call from Mark. Arrived for the meeting. Been told that Mark was dead. Thought at first he must have had a heart attack. Was told it was murder. Had been suitably shocked.

He did not have an alibi for the couple of hours before the meeting. He had decided to stay in that evening, as he had not been feeling that well all day. Thought he might have been coming down with a cold. He had not been working with Mark on anything. His cardkey had been with him at all times. No, he could not even hazard a guess as to who had killed Mark.

The Inspector asked, 'Is there anything else you can tell us that might help?'

'What sort of thing?'

The Inspector shrugged. 'Unusual behaviour, before or after the murder…anything at all you might want to draw our attention to, however tenuous.'

Rahul made a show of thinking about it and then shook his head. 'Nothing out of the ordinary when you consider how extraordinary the situation is. Everyone is acting pretty jumpy. But then, who wouldn't?'

The Inspector nodded his agreement. 'Who did you have in mind anyway?' he asked casually.

It was Rahul's turn to shrug. 'I wish I hadn't mentioned it now,' he said, 'but since you insist, Reggie and Julian both seem especially nervous.'

Annie was surprised that he was willing to name two of his colleagues. If he had information of a factual nature, she would have understood. But to inform against Reggie and Julian when he had nothing concrete to go on? Fanning the flames of suspicion did not seem ethical or necessary. It cast him in a bad light. Annie was saddened to find another pair of clay feet, this time on the office bulwark. Once again, she regretted her role in the investigation. It revealed far more about her erstwhile friends than she would have wished ever to know. Rahul was dismissed from the room and spared her a fleeting smile on his way out. She reciprocated in full, grateful, despite her doubts about his conduct during the interview, for a hint of understanding from her co-workers.

Immediately on Rahul's departure, there was a knock

on the door.

'Come in!' called the Inspector.

It was Julian. His appearance at the door was met with silence.

Julian himself broke it saying, 'I say, may I come in? I'm terribly sorry but I forgot my earlier appointment, can you believe it? I popped out to run a few errands. Just got back and my secretary, efficient as ever, told me that one Corporal Fong was looking for me. That's when I remembered. I came at once, of course, but you were busy so I've been hanging around outside.'

He stopped at this point and looked at them inquiringly. The Inspector waved him in.

Once in the chair, Julian ran a hand through his hair and leaned forward earnestly, 'I still can't believe I actually forgot the appointment.'

'We can hardly believe it either," said the Inspector.

Julian continued disarmingly, 'You must forgive me, I hope I have not been too much of an inconvenience?'

The Inspector shook his head, seemingly at a loss in the face of this verbal diarrhoea.

'Thank goodness, I could not have forgiven myself otherwise. After all, we must get to the bottom of this, for Mark's sake and ours.'

Annie stared at him. The others might not be aware of it as they did not know Julian but he was behaving extremely strangely. First of all, it was impossible to believe that the man who had been waylaying her in the corridors for information and lying to the police should have forgotten his interview. Further, she did not understand this Wodehousian demeanour and address. He was playing a role, but why?

Julian was still talking. Unprompted by anyone, he was recounting finding the body and the events thereafter. He had been pub hopping when Mark had called. He had prepared a list of the places - he slid a piece of paper across the table to the Inspector - he had been to before coming to the office and meeting Annie in the car park.

'By accident or design?' the Inspector asked.

'I beg your pardon?'

'Did you meet Annie by accident or design?'

'Oh! By accident of course. I do try and meet her from time to time by design, but she's a hard lady to pin down!'

He said this last with a nod to Annie and a wink at the Inspector. Annie stole a glance at David and the Inspector to see their reaction to this attempt at humour. From the rigidity of his shoulders, she could tell that David was struggling to control his irritation.

'Is there anything else?' Julian asked.

The Inspector asked tartly, 'Has your cardkey turned up yet?'

Julian shook his head, 'I'm afraid not. I have absolutely no idea where the damned thing has got to!'

The Inspector continued, 'You are working with Annie…Ms. N--, on a matter in Kuala Lumpur?'

'Yes, the takeover…an interesting deal.'

'Why do you say that?'

'No particular reason, you know…good money spinner for the firm, interesting legal issues…,' he trailed off before David's sceptical gaze.

Only Annie could see that Julian's fingers were beating a nervous tattoo on the side of the chair.

'From what I understand, the only legal issues are criminal ones,' said David.

Julian nodded knowingly, 'You're talking about the insider dealing thing, aren't you? With all due respect, I think that's been a mountain made out of a molehill.'

'What do you mean?'

He was met with an indifferent shrug. 'Surely you can see. This is not London we are talking about. A bit of insider dealing in Malaysia…damn it, it's par for the course. I don't condone it of course,' he said hastily, 'I just think…you know, stuff happens.'

Annie had never heard Julian sound so much like

Reggie. In the glare of a police investigation, his shortcomings were thrown into stark relief.

David said, 'So, I understand from this that you do not think the motive for this murder lies in Kuala Lumpur?'

'Because of the insider dealing? No way,' stated Julian categorically.

The Inspector said heavily, 'Thank you very much, Mr. Holbrooke.'

Julian recognised his dismissal for he got to his feet, nodded to them all and walked out.

'Well, what do you make of that?' asked David.

'Mr. Holbrooke seems to have become more confident, I wonder why?' responded the Inspector.

Annie said nothing. She felt disloyal questioning the information provided by Julian who had been her closest friend in the office.

'Related to his disappearance?' suggested David tentatively.

The Inspector nodded.

'It's a possibility. Let's see shall we?'

He picked up his mobile phone and dialled a number from memory, 'Has the detail watching Julian Holbrooke reported in yet?' He was very quiet, listening intently to his subordinate. 'All right, all right! That's good. Tell them to keep at it.' He terminated the call and turned to the others. 'Interesting, really. He went to a branch office of a major bank.'

Annie said, 'I wonder why he went there?'

Inspector Singh replied, 'We don't know yet. There is no crime in going to a bank, not unless you rob it.'

There was a dutiful laugh all round at this attempt at humour.

The Inspector suggested that a break was in order and Annie gratefully got to her feet and led the way out of the door. Her knees were stiff from squeezing them under the too small desk, her low back ached, a recurrent pain, and her head felt as if someone had stuffed it with old socks, musty and crowded. Annie made her way to the pantry, debating between a cup of hot strong coffee or a long, cool iced Coke. The pantry was deserted. She felt a sense of relief at not being immediately subject to accusations and cross-examination by members of the office. Opting for the coffee, she poured a cup out and headed back to her office. As she walked along the corridor, impulse seized her and she knocked firmly on Julian's door. He was sitting at his desk.

He said, 'Report card time, is it?'

Annie looked puzzled. 'What do you mean?'

'I assume you are here to rate my performance in there,' he gesticulated with his head in the direction of the interview room.

'Was it a performance?' she asked.

'Why do you ask that?'

'You were so unnatural.'

'I suppose you shared your insights with your new best friends?' he asked bitterly.

'I said nothing to anyone.'

'Then why are you here?'

'I want to understand what's going on with you. I just don't get it,' she said almost pleading with him for some explanation.

'What do you really know about me?' he asked pointedly.

This so echoed Annie's thoughts from earlier that she was too vehement in her denial.

'Of course I know you. We've known each other for five years.'

He shrugged and said, 'I thought I knew you too.'

Annie said tiredly. 'Come on, Julian. Is there anything you want to tell me? Anything I can help you with?'

He looked at her. She thought that he was going to unburden himself. But he shook his head, a gesture of weariness and defeat.

Annie turned and walked out the door. And literally walked into David who was sauntering past. He grabbed her by both arms to steady her. It was the first time they had made physical contact. She was immediately aware of the strength in his long fingers as she regained her balance and looked at him. He held on to her, indeed his grip tightened. Then he saw the name on the door of the room she had just come from. He released her arms and walked down the corridor. He had not said a word. She watched him go, absently rubbing her arm where his grip had almost hurt her. A part of her wanted to run after him and say that she had not done anything or said anything to Julian, that she had stopped by his room to comfort an old friend - or perhaps to say goodbye to him - their relationship an early casualty of the murder investigation. But she did not. She had pride. David would have to trust her of his own volition.

•

'Any messages for me, Ching?' Annie asked her secretary, stopping at her desk.

'Not one,' said Ching.

Ching was always in the best of spirits and it grated on Annie's nerves to be met with such unrelenting good cheer. She nodded her thanks and had her hand on the door handle when Ching said, 'There is something.'

Annie looked at her inquiringly.

'He said it was not important. He just needed to check something. No need to tell you also.'

Annie asked herself for the hundredth time how she put up with her well meaning but insanity-provoking secretary.

'*Who* said *what* was not important?' she asked.

Ching looked sheepish and then said, 'Mr. Julian. He was here about half an hour ago. He wanted the Malaysian deal file. Said he had to check something. I looked for it but

I also could not find it.'

She looked at Annie reproachfully for having moved a file without informing her.

'I did not take it,' said Annie absently, 'Mr. Sheringham has it, I think.'

Ching continued, 'I said I would ask you where it was, but Mr. Julian said there was no need to tell you he wanted the file. It was not important.'

Annie sat at her desk and buried her face in her hands. The situation was getting away from her. At least the interviews were pretty much over. She was not sure how much more she could take. She gave herself a mental warning to avoid letting her self-pity overthrow her judgment altogether. She would one day put this episode behind her and move on towards a future. Such options had been taken away from Mark. Once again she felt a wave of anger against whoever the unknown perpetrator was. How had that person decided that his ends were best served by murder?

Ching called out, 'Phone, line two for you.'

She picked up the phone, a welcome distraction, 'Hello, Hutchinson & Rice, Annie speaking.'

'Annie! Good! I am glad to reach you. I was wondering why I have had no feedback from Mr. Mark. Maybe you can tell me?'

Annie said, 'I am terribly sorry but I'm afraid I do not know who this is.'

The man at the other end replied in his heavy Malay accent, 'Tan Sri. Tan Sri Ibrahim.'

Tan Sri was an honorary prefix like 'Sir', bestowed by a Sultan of Malaysia. It was a rare honour and indicated that the bearer was a senior figure in political or business circles. Annie recognised the name immediately. It was the Managing Director of the target company in her Malaysian takeover deal.

She said, 'Tan Sri! Of course. I do apologise for not recognising your voice at first.'

The response was cheerful, 'No problem. I call because I have not heard from Mark Thompson. I called him last Friday, to explain my concerns. He said he would look into it and get back to me. Of course, I explained that I was not making any accusations, but you know, certain quarters drew my attention to the problem so I had to raise it.'

Annie was completely at a loss for words. She had no idea what the Tan Sri was talking about. But he was suggesting that he had spoken to Mark on the day of his murder. Even more peculiarly, he did not seem to know that Mark was dead.

The Tan Sri, met by continued silence from Annie, continued, 'You see, I have been calling his mobile phone this morning. I just got back from Austria, my family and I were on a holiday. My son is a very keen skier. I, of course, do not ski. Too old for such young people's sports, lah!'

Annie said, 'Tan Sri, I am sorry to have to inform you that Mr. Thompson is no longer with us.'

'He has gone back to London? He did not mention this.'

'No, I mean that he is dead!'

'Dead! Ya' Allah! When did this happen?'

'Last Friday.'

'After I spoke to him?' He answered his own question, 'Must have been, lah.' He continued, 'I did not mean to give him stress, although of course it is a serious matter.'

Annie said, 'I am afraid that Mark did not have a chance to discuss the issues you raised with me, Tan Sri. Perhaps you could fill me in?'

The Tan Sri hesitated and then said, 'I called him because I thought it would be better to discuss it with a senior person at your firm. Is there anyone else - who has taken over?'

Annie said firmly and untruthfully, 'I am the most senior person on the file now, Tan Sri. I think it would be best if you explained the situation to me.'

The Tan Sri did not take much convincing. 'You see,

my analysts have told me that the share price of my company has been spiking from time to time in the last few months. They also say that it has coincided with some important disclosure about the takeover. So someone must be using his insider knowledge to trade the shares of the company. I am sure you know this is illegal in Malaysia.'

'And most places, Tan Sri,' said Annie automatically, her mind racing.

The company seemed to have got wind of the insider dealing that she had been so concerned over, but which the firm had decided to ignore. The Tan Sri had not finished with his revelations.

'Obviously, I was concerned by this,' he said. 'Insider dealing is not unheard of in Malaysia, but I will not have it in my company.'

Annie pictured the Tan Sri. A soft spoken, elderly man with white hair and a wrinkled brown face, one of 'nature's gentlemen'. Her first impression that he was an honest man had been correct.

'What did you do, Tan Sri?' asked Annie politely, still not sure where he was going with this lengthy explanation.

'Well, I had my senior staff investigated. There was no sign that they were involved. Finally, I discovered that the orders to buy and sell the shares came from Singapore.'

'What are you trying to say, Tan Sri?'

'I think, and I told your Mr. Mark Thompson, that one of your lawyers is insider dealing.'

-fifteen-

'Whoever voluntarily has carnal intercourse against the order of nature with any man, woman or animals, shall be punished with imprisonment for life, or with imprisonment for a term which may extend to 10 years, and shall also be liable to fine.'
Section 377, Penal Code, Chapter 224

The sun was setting over the Singapore Botanic Gardens. The sky was streaked with crimson. There was the merest whisper of wind. It swayed the treetops gently. The sounds of crickets chirping and clicking disturbed the stillness. The dusk air was heavy with the pungent scent of jasmine. Two figures stood under a massive flame of the forest tree - red and yellow flowers licked the sky like fire. The man and woman were engrossed in each other and had no eyes for the beauty around them. A jogger who caught sight of them from a distance thought that thus might Adam and Eve have stood in contemplation of each other. It was an uncharacteristic flight of fancy provoked by the general ambience. A more careful scrutiny would have changed his mind. But the jogger was soon far away and the image of innocence was the one he took with him.

A closer inspection would have shown him that, although the couple stood close together, their bodies were rigid with tension. Their conversation was in heated whispers, their faces contorted with anger. Suddenly, the man leaned forward and grabbed the woman by the throat pushing her face up with his thumbs until she was forced to look at him, gasping for air. For a fleeting second, it appeared possible that he might kill her. Use his superior male strength to throttle the life out of her body - squeeze until her last futile gasps were stilled. Instead, his body relaxed and he took a step back and then let go of her. Her hands went to her throat instinctively, protectively, but he made no further move against her.

He said in a menacing whisper, 'Listen very carefully to me, bitch! That was your last warning. If I suspect your nerve is going, I will snap your neck like a twig!'

She stood looking at him, fear and defiance fighting for mastery over her expression. She might have spoken but no words came from her hurt throat. The man turned and walked away. The woman watched him go and then spat violently on the ground where he had stood. It was a wasted gesture. Her trembling hands suggested that she knew it.

•

Later that night, across town, in a bar in Chinatown, a large man perched on a red leather barstool, polished smooth over the years. The bartender leaned over and tipped the last of a bottle of Chivas into his nearly empty whisky tumbler. He held it up to show the man that the bottle was empty and received a nod of acknowledgement from him. A quiet sort, thought the barman idly. But he had a big man's capacity for liquor. He had drunk steadily through a whole bottle of whisky. The only telltale signs were a redness around the eyes and a slight unsteadiness when he reached for his glass. The heavy front door of the bar was pushed open and the red lanterns that were strung across the streets were briefly visible. A young Chinese man came and stood at the entrance, blinking as his eyes adjusted to the dimness within. He was dressed all in black, in a body hugging short-sleeved shirt with large shiny ebony buttons all down the front, leather trousers and soft leather ankle boots with silver buckles. He had dressed in black to lend himself an air of sophistication but his youth shone through. He might have suspected as much as he nervously ran a hand through his thick spiky hair. After looking around the bar carefully, the corners of which were lost in darkness, he sat down on the stool next to the big man. The young man put his elbows on the bar. He had tanned, sinewy, hairless arms. His hands were clean and well manicured.

'What'll it be?' the barman asked him.

'Same as he's having,' he said, nodding at the glass of the man next to him. His request drew a bleary glance from the large man. The young Chinese man smiled at him in a friendly but tentative fashion. On receiving no response, he looked away in a hurt manner and sipped the whisky the barman put in front of him, idly playing with the beer mat in front of him. A large hand, with short black hairs on the back, took hold of his hand in a gentle but firm clasp. He looked up at the big man again and this time his smile was wide and confident.

•

Inspector Singh was in a deep dreamless sleep. He lay on his back, mouth open, a hint of spittle collected at the corners. His wife's stiff back was to him. The mobile by his bed rang. For a few semi-conscious seconds, his hand sought his alarm clock. Then he answered the phone blearily, making a silent promise that if the call was not important, he would have the badge of the policeman who had woken him. He hoped it was Corporal Fong. However, after listening on the phone for a few seconds, he grew alert and the sleep slipped from him like a blanket falling to the floor.

He nodded a few times and then shook his head vehemently, 'No! Not yet.' He was almost shouting. 'What's that? Oh, I see.' The Inspector thought for a moment. Then he said, 'He went willingly, didn't he?' There was an affirmative answer at the other end of the line. The Inspector said coldly, 'He's made his bed…my instructions are to wait.'

•

The following morning, Annie was up late. She had spent the night tossing and turning, snatching moments of sleep that too soon turned to nightmares and then to sweat-soaked awakenings. She lay in bed for a while, peering with heavy eyes through the cracks in the curtains at the sunny day outside. She was not sure whether she could bear to get out of bed and face the world. The day was fraught with potential incident. Annie, who usually greeted each new day with good cheer, now felt that to trust to fate in this manner was naïve. Her pillow felt hot under her neck and she shifted uncomfortably. Maybe she was unwell. That would serve as an excuse to avoid going into the office. She did not feel well, her head was heavy and her eyes scratchy. But she knew the only thing wrong with her was a sense of dread at what the new day might bring.

Her wakeful night and current malaise stemmed directly from her conversation with Tan Sri Ibrahim. If the insider dealing did indeed stem from Singapore, and Tan Sri Ibrahim had told Mark so, the insider would have had a cast-iron reason to have killed Mark. The consequences of being found out were enormous. Not only might the lawyer face jail time and lose his job, but he would never be permitted to practice law again - a huge blow for any of the lawyers in the firm with bright futures ahead of them. And this did not even take into account the public humiliation. With a sigh, she got out of bed and dressed for work, going through the motions by rote, unable to summon up any sort of will towards her routine tasks. Her mind played over the various possibilities for the thousandth time. Each time her thoughts led to the same inevitable conclusion. There were only two people on the file, aside from Mark, who had access to the information at the root of the insider dealing. She was one of them. The other was Julian.

Annie's phone rang and her answer phone clicked on. She heard her Father's gruff voice and buried her face in a pillow. She could hear him say that he had tried the office and her mobile but there was no reply. She knew she should pick up the phone; he was all the family she had. But she could not bear to do it. When there was no contact between them her busy life in Singapore meant that she did not think of him much. But when he needed something from her or she needed the comfort of family that had been lost the day her mother died, she was overwhelmed with worry and sadness for her father. His wasted life, his eternal optimism, the constant disappointment as each deal failed, as each idea petered out - it was like disappointment by a thousand cuts. And each year as he grew older, his diabetes and hypertension got worse and still he kept coming back with a new plan to recover his fortunes, to go out on a high. An unlucky gambler at the table of life. His only daughter was still picking up the pieces. Annie picked up the phone and rang her father back.

•

A diligent secretary patched a call through to the temporary office of David Sheringham. He picked up the phone and listened. Only his tightening grip on the receiver demonstrated his concern. His reaction was of white knuckled intensity.
He said, 'Are you quite sure?' He listened silently to the response. The instant the call was over, he leapt to his feet, grabbed his jacket and almost ran to Stephen's room.

Stephen was already in, sitting behind his polished mahogany desk, reading the Asian Wall Street Journal. He looked up in surprise as David burst in.

'What is it?' he asked. ' What's happened?'

David closed the door firmly behind him and said, 'It's not good, I'm afraid.'

•

Annie nosed her car into a tight parking spot, careful not to put a dent or scratch in her paintwork. She opened the door carefully to avoid hitting the car next to hers although he deserved a knock for his awful parking - taking up his own space and overlapping hers. As she eased herself out of the car, her mobile phone started to ring. She hurried out of the car and rummaged in her bag. Caller identification informed her that it was the office that had called. She considered returning the call and then decided that whoever it was could wait until she got in. She was only five minutes away. It was a minor act of rebellion but lifted her spirits. She made her way to the lobby, and then into the lift and to the reception area of the office. Exactly the route she had taken that fateful evening. But what a difference the daylight hours made. The car park had been full of shiny new cars. The lift was crammed with people going about their business. Each part of the building was brightly lit, not hidden in shadows. And at the office, the receptionist greeted her cheerfully.

Annie stopped by the ladies room. She flung the door open, stepped in and then stopped abruptly, the door swinging shut behind her, clattering into her heels. Ai Leen was standing before the large wall mirror above the sinks. At the sound of Annie's entrance, she whirled round, hurriedly trying to wind a pretty silk scarf around her neck. Not before Annie had got a glimpse of her throat. Annie started forward, looking at her in horror.

'Ai Leen! What happened? Are you alright?'

Ai Leen stared at her wide-eyed, her consternation at being found out apparent. It looked like she might confide in Annie, set aside their recent animosity, but then she had second thoughts. Pushing past Annie, she rushed out of the room, her face a mask again. Annie took a step in her direction, meaning to follow her and get to the bottom of the matter. But then she hesitated. Ai Leen had made it clear that she did not want to explain matters. Annie's natural reluctance to force the confidences of someone who was determined to maintain her secrets stayed her first impulse. She stood debating her next step, her uncertainty and hesitation completely out of character. Her phone rang again. Feeling guilty at her relief not to have to chase after Ai Leen, Annie reached for it.

David said, 'Jesus, where have you been? I've been trying to get hold of you for the last half an hour.'

Annie could hear the anxiety in his voice. 'What is it? What's the matter? Are you alright?'

'Me?' he asked almost irritably, 'Of course I'm alright.'

'Then what is it?'

'I can't tell you over the phone, you'll have to come down here as soon as you can.'

'Where?'

'The police station. Raffles branch.'

'But why? Why are you there? Has something happened?'

She was speaking to herself. David had hung up. She looked down at her phone, seeking answers from its backlit buttons. What in the world was going on? Why did she have to rush down to the station? Her blood ran cold. They might have arrested Julian. She had debated with her conscience whether to tell the Inspector about the Tan Sri's call. She knew she could not keep it a secret forever. But she had found it impossible to go straight to the Inspector with her information. There was only one possible way for the police to interpret what she had been told - that Julian had a motive for murder. In the cold light of day, Annie realised that her restraint might not be interpreted so unselfishly. The only other suspect was herself. Her silence might look like an admission of guilt.

It was one thing to try and protect Julian, to give him the benefit of the doubt that she feared no one else would. It was quite another to create the impression that she was covering up for herself. Tan Sri Ibrahim would eventually hear about Mark's murder and insist on speaking to someone else if she took no action. At most she had bought Julian a couple of days respite. She would have to confront Julian with what she knew. Give him an opportunity to tell his side of the story, to deny the allegations if he could. At least, forewarned would be forearmed. It was the best she could do for him. It was also the most she was prepared to do. It was what she owed him - for the years of their friendship. But it could all be a moot point if David's urgent summons was about Julian. David had sounded rattled, anxious, quite unlike his usual self. The animosity between David and Julian was obvious. And it was about her. She knew this in her heart and also that this was the reason that she was prepared to try and protect Julian against her own better judgment. She felt responsible for their mutual dislike. And she feared that David would be all too willing to accept Julian's guilt.

The Raffles Place police station. She knew that was the headquarters of Inspector Singh. No doubt he had a dingy office from which he ran the minutiae of the investigation. Those parts where she and David had no input. She stood at the door of the police station and felt an almost uncontrollable desire to turn away. Dismissing these hesitations as a weakness, she took a deep breath and walked into the station. It was a brightly lit foyer, cool compared to the outside, with an inquiry desk at one end and posters on the walls bearing messages from the Singapore police like 'Low crime doesn't mean no crime!' A message possible only in the highly organised, largely crime-free state of Singapore. The place where Mark had managed to get himself murdered. A fate that was so much more likely to have overtaken him in London or New York or any of the other cities in which he had worked than in Singapore, with its well ordered, highly policed society.

'Ms.N--?' Annie looked around in surprise and found the ubiquitous figure of Corporal Fong standing diffidently at her elbow. She looked at him inquiringly.

'Inspector Singh sent me down here to wait for you,' he explained, 'so that I can take you directly upstairs.'

Annie nodded her thanks and followed him to a broad flight of stairs.

As they hurried up, she asked him, 'What's this about?'

He said, 'Um...the Inspector will explain, I think. He did not tell me to say anything.'

It was on the tip of her tongue to say that he had not been instructed to breathe either. But she saved the energy for their ascent up another flight of stairs and arrived breathless outside a door with the words 'Inspector Jagjit Singh' in white plastic on black. Corporal Fong knocked on the door and entered with Annie hard on his heels, expecting to see Julian, convinced he was the reason for the call. There were only two men in the room. They were both standing, almost toe-to-toe, and it was apparent to Annie that she had interrupted an argument. The tension was palpable. The Inspector was in a rage, his brows drawn together in a frown and a scowl on his full lips. David was also angry, the lines on his face etched deeply and his lips pursed into a thin line. They both turned to the door as Annie walked in. The Inspector nodded to her curtly but the forbidding expression on David's face eased somewhat at the sight of her and he essayed a small smile.

'There you are,' he said.

Annie asked immediately, her worry shining through, 'What is it? What's happened? Is it Julian?'

The Inspector asked before David could say anything,

'Why do you think this is about Julian?'

Annie kicked herself mentally. She had been in the room thirty seconds and already she was on the verge of giving the game away.

She shook her head and said, 'No reason. I was just guessing, I suppose.'

Her voice did not ring true. She hoped the two men would not pick up on it. Vain hope. The Inspector gave her a searching look and she found herself unable to hold his glance.

He said heavily, 'Annie, I hope you know better than to withhold any information from the police?'

She decided, like Wellington, that attack was the best form of defence. 'What is that supposed to mean?' she asked angrily.

The Inspector duly retreated, 'Nothing, nothing! Just reminding you to be frank with the police, that's all.'

She nodded, as if mollified, secretly pleased to have brazened it out and deflected further questioning. She could sense David still looking at her curiously and did not dare look at him for fear that he would see that she was hiding something.

Instead she said, 'So tell me, what's going on?'

David looked at the Inspector who shrugged as if to indicate that he was resigned to David putting his version of events to Annie.

David said baldly, 'Rahul has been arrested!'

Annie did not know what she had expected to hear but she knew it was anything but this.

'Rahul? Rahul's been arrested? What for? You don't mean for the murder?' she asked looking at David in shock.

David said, 'No, not the murder.'

'Just tell me.'

It was the Inspector who answered, 'Buggery!'

She stared at him mystified.

David said, 'Rahul was picked up last night or the early hours of this morning, I should say. He was in bed with

with a young man.'

Annie stared at him, bemused, 'Rahul is gay? I never knew that.'

'No one did, it would seem,' answered David.

'But I don't understand. Why has he been arrested?' asked Annie.

'Homosexuality is still illegal in this country,' said David.

"You must be joking!" exclaimed Annie. She turned to the Inspector, who nodded his head in confirmation.

Annie said, 'But I know…,' and then stopped, aware that she was on the verge of naming other homosexuals of her acquaintance in Singapore who would not thank her for it.

David nodded at her, 'Exactly. That was the point I was making to the Inspector when you walked in. It may be the law but it is hardly enforced in Singapore so there is no reason at all to arrest Rahul.'

The Inspector said, 'What you say may be correct… but homosexual practices are still against the law here.' He dropped his bombshell, 'And might well be prosecuted where one party's youth is being exploited!'

Annie stared at him. What was he saying?

David said, 'I thought you said he picked up this chap at a well known gay bar?'

He was speaking through gritted teeth, betraying the struggle he was having to keep his temper in check. Annie admired him for it. He might have angered her in the past with the objective distance he was able to keep from the murder investigation, but when confronted with the reality of one of his junior partners languishing in jail, his humanity came through.

The Inspector said, 'That was indeed the case, but the young man was only seventeen. In these circumstances we have to make an example.'

'Rahul would not have known that he was so young,' said Annie angrily, hoping this was true.

Her whole world was being turned upside down.

Rahul was gay?

The Inspector shrugged. 'A crime has been committed. We are perfectly justified in arresting him.'

The lawyers were silent.

The Inspector said, 'Surely you see that we have been presented with a motive on a plate for the murder of Mr. Thompson?'

'What do you mean?' asked David.

Annie interrupted any answer the Inspector was going to make, 'You're not suggesting he'd kill Mark just to keep his being gay a secret, do you?'

The Inspector nodded. 'Of course I am. It's the best motive we've got.'

David said, almost shouting, 'But Rahul would not kill someone just because they found out he was gay!'

Annie nodded her head vehemently in agreement, 'Of course not. There is no stigma attached to being gay in our..., in Western society!'

If the Inspector noticed that Annie had ranged herself on the side of Western society on this point, he gave no sign of it.

Instead he said, words dripping with sarcasm, 'There was so little discrimination that he was comfortable telling all of you he was gay. Anyway, he may work for an international firm, but he is an Indian from Bombay. Not exactly the gay capital of the world.'

There was an uncomfortable silence.

Then David said, 'Look, there is no doubt there might be pockets of prejudice. But it would never amount to a motive for murder. Rahul may have kept his homosexuality a secret, but he would never kill anyone over it. That is just too absurd.'

Annie said to the Inspector, 'Anyway, you are making quite a few assumptions, aren't you? You are assuming Mark had somehow found out about Rahul...*and* that he was going to spread the news.'

David nodded his agreement with the point Annie

was making. He added, 'Mark was not one of those who would either be prejudiced against Rahul if he did indeed find out he was gay…nor would he have felt compelled to gossip about it. It was not in his character.'

In the face of this adamant response from both David and Annie, the Inspector's conviction wavered.

He said, 'I understand what you are telling me,' he said, 'but in this culture, his behaviour might be a motive for murder!'

David pressed home his advantage, 'But that is why we are here, to prevent cultural misunderstandings affecting the success of this investigation.'

The Inspector shook his head, 'I think Rahul and I are far closer in cultural terms than he is with the lot of you. I am prepared to release him from custody for now. We will decide later whether to charge him for this crime…or any other!'

On this parting shot, he walked out of the room.

Annie looked at David, her face full of concern. 'I've known him for five years and I never suspected he was gay. Why would he not tell us?'

David nodded. 'He has gone to great lengths to keep his secret.'

Annie asked tentatively, 'Do you think he might have done it?'

'Kill Mark? Over this? No, I don't think so. I really don't. But I must say I barely know what to believe.'

This was a real admission from David and Annie could see that he was shaken by the turn events had taken. She put a comforting hand on his arm. David, arrogant and confident, never failed to annoy her. But David admitting to doubt and confusion immediately won her sympathy. David took her hand in his and looked down at it. At the sound of the door opening, he gave her hand a quick squeeze and let go, turning to see who was coming in. It was the Inspector followed by Rahul.

'Rahul!' Annie exclaimed and rushed over to him,

giving him a tight hug, 'Are you alright?'

Rahul did not look alright. He was dishevelled and tired. He looked as if he had dressed in a hurry and not slept in a while. His eyes were bloodshot from exhaustion and worry and although he returned Annie's hug briefly, he would not meet her eye. Or David's when he too came over and clapped him on the back. Rahul just stood, a great shambling bulk of a man, and gazed unseeingly at the floor.

Inspector Singh said, 'Mr. Gandhi, I am releasing you for the present. We will decide whether to press charges at a later date. I already have your passport. You are free to go - for now.'

-sixteen-

'Whoever attempts to commit suicide, and does any act towards the commission of such offence, shall be punished with imprisonment for a term which may extend to one year, or with fine, or with both.'
Section 309, Penal Code, Chapter 224

Inspector Singh was watching videos. He sat in his ergonomic chair and stared at the screen with the concentration of a teenage boy with his first download of Internet porn. Every now and then he would gesture to Corporal Fong who was in charge of the remote controls. The Corporal had learnt over the last ten minutes which gesture indicated that he was to pause the tape, rewind or play a particular scene again, so the irritable outbursts that had punctuated the first part of the tape were now over. The film that Inspector Singh was watching was in black and white, of extremely grainy quality, the figures out of focus and distant. It did not seem to merit his absorption.

The C.C.T.V cameras in Raffles Tower were a comprehensive network that covered the lift lobbies as well as every public area. It would have been difficult to enter the building and avoid being caught on film. But the murderer had had a lucky break, and the cameras had been out of action. The Inspector believed there was always one lucky break for each side in a case and was still waiting for the dice to roll his way. And now, unexpectedly, Corporal Fong claimed to have found taped evidence. The hardworking young man had found something, not on the C.C.T.V tapes from Raffles Tower, but from the tape from a building half a block away. The Corporal had requisitioned all the tapes from a three-block radius without consulting the Inspector and watched every single one late into every night. On one of them, spotted by Fong's sharp young eyes but visible even to the rheumy old eyes of the Inspector, was Mark Thompson walking in the direction of Raffles Tower to attend his hurriedly summoned partners' meeting. Beside him, his young Filipina wife teetered along on high heels.

•

In the car, the quiet tones of Brian Ferry's 'Jealous Guy' were playing on the radio. In a sudden gesture of irritation, Annie leaned forward and switched it off. David did not say anything. Annie had wanted to go after Rahul when he had walked out of the police station but David had stopped her. He had felt that Rahul needed some time to himself before he would be able to face his colleagues. She had been less sure, deeply conscious of the change from the friendly, open personality that Rahul had been to the subdued creature who had shuffled out of the Inspector's room. In the end, Annie bowed to David's judgment. Perhaps he was right and Rahul needed some time to lick his wounds. Arrested, outed, humiliated and suspected of murder. It was a lot to contend with without the clumsy kindness of colleagues he had not trusted with a key part of his life.

She might protest that Rahul - big, calm Rahul -

would no more kill Mark than hurt a fly. But the police had a valid point in dismissing their assertions when it was obvious that they all knew so little about Rahul. It would be difficult to convince the police that the fear of being found out would not lead to murder. Singapore and Asia generally were still extremely conservative. Homosexuality was something that was hardly acknowledged. The general view was that it was an unhealthy practice limited to performers and hairdressers. She herself had Asian relatives who still thought that to be gay was to be merely happy. The Inspector might find it impossible to believe that homosexuality was no longer taboo, especially in light of the secrecy that had shrouded Rahul's sexual preferences.

She was so lost in her own thoughts that she did not hear David ask her a question. He repeated himself and this time, caught her attention, although she had no idea what he had said, just that he had spoken. He looked at her quizzically.

'Sorry, wool-gathering,' Annie said apologetically. 'I didn't catch what you said, I'm afraid.'

He said, 'I guessed that. Especially the third time I said it.'

'Was it about Rahul?' she asked.

He grimaced. 'Who else?' She waited for him to continue and he said, 'I told Stephen about Rahul's arrest.'

'I suppose it was impossible to tell him about the arrest without the reason?'

'Yes, especially as he would have assumed I was talking about an arrest for murder otherwise.'

Annie let her deep concern show on her face, 'Well, it might not be too long before that becomes a reality if the Inspector has his way.'

David nodded.

'I just can't believe that I didn't know… did not guess. Or for that matter that he didn't feel able to tell me. I thought we were friends,' she continued.

'I'm sure he was not hiding it from you. But it would've been a difficult façade to maintain if he had let anyone in on his secret.'

She knew that David was right. It would have been impossible for Rahul to be 'one of the lads', flirt with the secretaries, generally maintain a heterosexual persona if one of the observers knew the truth. He would have been hampered by a critical audience.

•

The Inspector took out a small sheaf of papers. These were the anonymous notes that had been found at the Thompson residence. There were four of the notes, almost identical to one another. The messages were on plain white, good quality paper. He guessed the notes had been done on someone's P.C, printed with a standard inkjet printer on A4 paper. Gone were the days, thought the Inspector longingly, of manual typewriters with their individual idiosyncrasies, bits of newsprint from identifiable newspapers and hidden watermarks leading straight to the desk of the writer. He supposed there were advantages to the anonymous notes in front of him. If they did find a suspect, he was sure someone like Corporal Fong would be able to prove that the notes had been written on a particular P.C. The young fellow had his uses. It had been a good piece of initiative to check the tapes from the neighbouring buildings. As for the messages, except that the writer was educated - the notes were grammatically correct and well punctuated, there was not much to be gleaned from them. As Mark had intimated to Stephen, the notes asserted that Maria was still earning an income from prostitution despite being married to Mark. 'Old habits die hard' as one of the notes pointed out.

He himself had not been able to find any evidence of Maria moonlighting either before or after her marriage. This was not surprising. If she had ever been caught, she would have been deported immediately. The Inspector had not confronted Maria Thompson with his suspicions. She would just deny the accusations outright. But now he had the tapes showing her presence in the city with Mark a short while before his murder. The time had come to have a word with the second Mrs. Thompson. David had told him that Maria had needed money for her children. It sounded as if Mark had preferred to avoid reminders of his blushing bride's past. The Inspector did not object to Maria marrying a meal ticket, but he drew the line at killing him. He knew that if Maria was indeed the murderer, it did not fit well with the meeting Mark had called of the partnership. But it was not impossible, despite his gut feeling that the two events were related, that the meeting had nothing to do with the murder.

•

Annie knocked tentatively at Ai Leen's door. There was no response so she knocked more firmly. She knew Ai Leen was in there because her secretary had told her so. Still, there was no sound from within. She tried the handle but the door was locked. Finally, she turned and went back to her room, walking slowly, head down, deep in thought. Inside the room, Ai Leen sat behind her desk, staring at the door. She guessed that Annie wanted to lend her support, be her friend, despite the recent past. It was too late for that. She was on her own. Sleeping on a bed of her own making. She had sacrificed so much, given up so much - had it been worthwhile? The luxury condominium, the big car, the club memberships, the partnership - her official badge of success. Had her self-respect been to high a price to pay for success? She knew it was too late for regrets.

•

Rahul Gandhi arrived home in a taxi. He lived in a modern apartment building, a steel and glass cube on the fourteenth floor. Inside, his furniture was minimalist, black leather couches and window blinds. On one wall, a plasma screen T.V hung, with speakers discreetly attached. A state-of-the-art sound system, Yakamichi, glowed blue, lit from within. The floor was carpeted in thick white pile that set off the starkness of the furnishings. Rahul went straight to the shower, and stood naked under a steaming jet of water, trying to wash away the past twenty-four hours, knowing that the life he had carefully carved out for himself was in ruins, destroyed by a moment of temptation in a Singapore bar. He was ashamed, as he had not felt since he had first discovered he was gay. The crude questioning at the police station dismayed him. He remembered the sympathy and confusion on Annie's face and felt tears mingle with the water coursing down his cheeks. How could he face her or anyone in the office again? They would never trust him in the future. He had no illusions about the murder investigation either. The Inspector had made it clear that he had moved to the head of the list of suspects. Rahul leaned his forehead against the cool tiles on the bathroom wall. He did not hear his phone ringing, and if he had, he would not have answered it.

•

In the office, Annie listened to the ringing tones and knew that Rahul would not pick up. She would have to see him face to face. But first, she would have to ask Julian about the Tan Sri's allegations. Whoever had done the insider dealing had generated a large profit. She had calculated last night that he might have made as much as half a million Singapore dollars in a fortnight's activity. A temptation for anyone. Perhaps Julian had had an urgent need for money that she did not know about. Something that had led him to take the risk. But he had misjudged the persistence of the company officers. And the trail had led directly to Singapore - to him. Sighing, she dragged herself to her feet and once again found herself reluctantly knocking on a door along the corridor.

This time the response was prompt, 'Come in!'

She entered tentatively, forcing a smile she did not feel.

'Annie!' said Julian in surprise, 'Good morning!'

Annie thought about the events the morning had brought forth already and felt unable to respond in kind. Instead, she flung herself into a chair opposite Julian, his heavily laden desk between them.

'What are you working on?' she asked casually.

Julian looked down at the papers spread across his desk and said, 'This and that. Nothing important…I'm struggling to concentrate, I'm afraid.'

Annie nodded, 'Tell me about it. I haven't had a fee earning moment in days.'

'Well, you've been busy, I suppose.'

This was said without rancour and Annie drew some heart from it.

She sat up straighter in her chair and said, 'I had the most peculiar phone call yesterday. From the Tan Sri.' Seeing Julian's blank look she added, 'You know the boss of that Malaysian company.'

His puzzled expression cleared and he said, 'Oh him! What about?'

She looked him full in the face and said, 'The insider dealing.'

He appeared unperturbed. 'What about it? He doesn't have a bee in his bonnet as well, does he?'

'He thinks someone in Singapore is responsible.'

'What do you mean?'

'What I just said, he thinks someone in Singapore has been insider dealing, something about the orders to the broker coming from Singapore.'

'And you think I did it, don't you? This precious Tan Sri tells you some cock and bull story and you come in here and accuse me of insider dealing.'

She said, 'He told Mark too.'

'What?'

'He called Mark and told him that he thought it was one of us…the night of the murder!'

Julian sat staring at his desk.

'Whom have you told?' he asked at last.

'No one.'

'Why not?'

'I don't know. I wanted to ask you first…I don't know.'

He looked at her, 'You really think I did it, don't you. Why would I? I don't need the money. Anyway, you're as good a suspect as I am.'

She nodded, 'I know it, but I also know I didn't do it.'

Julian said, almost in a whisper, 'Annie, you can't tell anyone about this.'

She looked at him, brown eyes full of worry.

He said again, 'They will think one of us killed Mark. Remember… you'd be a suspect too. Do you want to take that chance?'

'It will come out, you know. The Tan Sri is not going to let matters rest.'

Julian said desperately, 'But we can buy some time… they might have caught the murderer by then. Anything might happen!'

She could see the fear in his pale, blue eyes.

He got up and came round the desk to her, gripped her wrists in a vice, 'Annie, you have to believe me, I did not kill Mark!'

She was willing herself to believe him. A loud knocking on the door interrupted them.

Stephen came rushing in. 'Annie, come with me. Rahul's in hospital, he's tried to kill himself!'

-seventeen-

'A confession is an admission made at any time by a person accused of an offence, stating or suggesting the inference that he committed that offence.'
Section 17, Evidence Act, Chapter 97

Annie hurried after Stephen, breaking into a trot to keep up with his long strides. She tried to speak to him but he silenced her with a gesture.

'Not now, Annie.'

She saw his point. The staff were watching them, agog with curiosity at their hasty progress and grim faces. She concentrated on keeping pace with Stephen, her mind in a whirl. Why had Rahul tried to kill himself? Would he be alright?

Stephen maintained his silence until they reached the main lobby when he turned to say, 'My car is waiting.'

They stepped out into the glaring sunshine and the heat hit Annie like a breaking wave. Stephen's chauffeur beckoned to them. They hurried over and climbed into the cool interior of the dark blue Mercedes Benz.

Stephen barked, 'Mt. Victoria Hospital, now!' at the

driver and the car purred out of the foyer and nosed its way into traffic.

Annie asked timidly, 'What's happened?'

'I don't know the details. I just got a call from the hospital. Rahul is in critical condition. He took an overdose of sleeping pills apparently. His cleaner found him and called an ambulance.' Stephen spoke quietly so that his chauffeur would not overhear.

'Will he be alright?'

Stephen turned to look at her, his rumbling voice rendering his answer almost inaudible, 'I don't know.'

They sat in the car as it weaved its way through the traffic, each lost in his own thoughts.

'Where's David?' asked Annie.

'Don't know. I've been trying to call his mobile. There's no answer.'

Annie nibbled on her index finger. She said, 'Why do you think he did it - tried to kill himself?'

Stephen gave her a sideways glance.

She correctly interpreted it and said, 'But surely that's not a good enough reason. I mean, being gay is hardly a crime.'

Stephen said, 'On the contrary.'

'I know it's a crime here. But I don't think the Inspector will press charges. He's just using it as leverage because he thinks Rahul might have killed Mark.'

'All I know,' said Stephen heavily, 'is that Rahul behaves like a man with an unbearable burden of guilt!'

•

Rahul lay on a hospital bed in a private room. He was tucked in up to his armpits, both his arms lying still and limp on the covers. He was either unconscious or asleep. His Brooke Shields eyebrows and long sooty eyelashes were the only colour left on his face. The solitary sound in the room was the constant beep from the heart rate monitor - its glowing green line forming a hill, then a trough, at regular intervals. As a concession to the exorbitant rates of the private hospital, the curtains were a faded floral print. A picture, a print that looked as if it had been cut from a calendar and framed, lent a dismally decorative touch. Annie fought back tears.

Their brief vigil at his bedside was interrupted by the unforgiving routine of the hospital that slowed for nothing except death. Two nurses, in starched white, bustled in, one so thin as to be almost skeletal, with bony elbows and a forbidding expression. The other was younger and sweeter in appearance but went about her business with the same brutal efficiency. They flipped through charts, swapped drips, lifted Rahul's eyelids and peered into his eyes and checked machines. Then, acting in concert with the supreme co-ordination of synchronised swimmers, they changed the sheets; raising Rahul by the shoulders, fluffing up his pillows, replacing his sheets and somehow making his bed with a minimum of fuss despite the presence in it of a comatose man weighing not less than a hundred kilograms. Annie and Stephen shuffled their feet and tried not to get in the way. It seemed, despite Rahul's oblivion, to be an invasion of his privacy.

Finally, when it appeared that the nurses were on the verge of leaving the room without having uttered a sound between them, Stephen asked gruffly, 'How is he?'

The skinny nurse said, 'No change yet. The doctor will be back to see him in a few hours.'

'But, I mean, how is he now? Will he be ok?'

The nurse shook her head, her normal voice a stark contrast to Stephen's hushed tone, 'Too early to tell. They pumped his stomach. But a lot of the sleeping tablets had already been absorbed into his blood. He's in a coma now. The doctors are not sure if he will come out of it.'

Stephen nodded.

The nurse took pity on him and said, 'If you need more information, you can ask the doctor later.'

On another occasion, Annie might have noticed and been amused by Stephen's nervousness in hospitals, the nervousness of a person with good health who preferred to ignore reminders of the body's essential frailty. But she was too shocked by the nurse's chilling words. Rahul was in a coma. He might not come out of it. He might not survive. It was too much to take in. Big, friendly laughing Rahul, lying there. He already looked as if death held him by the hand and was leading him slowly away from those who held him dear. And the police would leap to the conclusion that this suicide attempt was as good as a confession.

Inspector Singh walked into the room through the door left open by the nurses on their exit. Corporal Fong sidled in behind him.

'Well, well! What do we have here then?' he asked in a booming voice that might well have been heard all the way down the corridor.

Annie had never disliked him more than at that moment for his deliberate insensitivity.

She said coldly, 'He's in a coma. He may not recover.'

If she thought to shock the Inspector out of his callousness by such a harsh description, she was disappointed.

He merely looked interested and said, 'Coma, eh! Save the cost of a trial if they have to pull the plug.'

Stephen exclaimed, 'What trial?'

Inspector Singh said nonchalantly, 'For murdering your boss, of course!'

'But why do you think he did it?' asked Annie.

'His lying there looks a bit like a confession to me.' And predicting Annie's outburst, he continued, 'And so does this,' and took a sheet of paper wrapped in cellophane out of the file he was carrying.

Stephen almost snatched it from his hand and he and Annie stared together at the single sheet of paper torn from a notebook. In black ink, in Rahul's unmistakable scrawl, were written the words, 'I'm sorry. I cannot face what I have become.' It was unsigned and undated.

Annie almost shouted, 'This doesn't prove anything!'

Stephen asked, 'Where'd you get this?'

'His bedside table, next to the empty bottle of pills.' The Inspector looked at Annie and continued, 'It's good enough for me.'

'But this could just mean his being gay. He can't live with that,' said Annie.

'I thought being gay wasn't enough of a reason to kill anyone.'

'Anyone else maybe, but not himself.'

The Inspector shrugged, 'It may be as you say. We'll keep looking into matters and wait to see if he recovers…'

Annie guessed that he was just throwing her a bone. His mind was made up. As Stephen had said, Rahul had behaved like a guilty man. The Inspector shared his view. They all stood and gazed at the comatose man unconscious of the heated words being bandied around the room. Rahul's debate was being conducted in silence. And the subject was not the crime of taking another's life but the sin of taking one's own. Of one accord, the two men and one woman filed out of the room. Corporal Fong, who had spent the time lurking quietly in the doorway, moved aside to let them pass and then followed, shutting the door gently behind him. The Inspector stopped a nurse and told her that a policeman, he nodded in the general direction of his Corporal, would stand guard outside Rahul's door for the time being.

Back at the office, they found David waiting in Stephen's room. He looked worried, brow furrowed and mouth grim.

As they came in, he looked up expectantly, and then seeing Annie's expression asked, 'What is it? What's happened?'

Annie did not answer but instead turned away from him and walked to the window. She stared unseeingly at the view, trying to compose herself.

Stephen flung himself into his chair, which groaned under his weight and said heavily, 'Rahul's tried to kill himself. Sleeping pills. He's in a coma…they're not sure if he will pull through.'

'My God! Why?'

'We don't know why, although the Inspector thinks he can guess.'

'What do you mean?'

'Rahul left a note, a confession.'

Annie said, 'It was not a confession!'

David asked, 'What did it say?'

She repeated verbatim, the words etched in her memory, 'I'm sorry. I cannot live with what I've become.'

David ran a tired hand over his face. 'I see. And the Inspector thinks he can't live with having become a murderer.'

Stephen said slowly and distinctly, 'It is not an impossible explanation…and if he doesn't make it…,' he trailed off meaningfully.

Annie rounded on him. 'There is nothing in that note to suggest Rahul killed Mark.'

David put out a restraining hand. 'Calm down, Annie. I agree it's not conclusive, but it is suggestive. We would be irresponsible to ignore the possibility that he had something to do with it.'

Annie looked aggrieved but did not respond.

David continued, 'The note is a bit strange if you think about it…I assume you think that it is the discovery of his being gay that he can't live with?'

Annie nodded curtly.

'Don't you think it's worded a bit strangely?'

There was no response from the other two.

David explained, 'He says he can't live with what he's 'become'…'

Stephen interjected excitedly, 'I see what you are driving at…he hasn't just 'become' gay, he's just been found out!'

David finished his thought for him, 'The only thing we know of that he might have just 'become' …is a murderer!'

'For God's sake! It's a suicide note, not a carefully drafted legal agreement. He scrawled it just before taking a bottle full of pills. You can't interpret every word of it… looking for hidden meanings,' said Annie.

Stephen shook his big head slowly, 'I'm not sure you're right, Annie. Rahul was…is, a lawyer. He would say what he meant.'

Annie looked at them with accusing eyes, 'All I see is that Rahul in a coma makes him a great scapegoat for the rest of us!'

David changed the subject, 'What do we tell the lawyers? We have to tell them that Rahul is in hospital. Do we need to mention suicide?'

'It's too late to keep that cat in the bag…I blurted it out in front of Julian when I was looking for Annie,' said Stephen.

'Ok, we'll have to call a partners' meeting,' said David.

Annie asked, her voice husky with anxiety, 'But will you tell them he was gay? That was Rahul's secret.'

'I don't know, Annie. I just don't know.'

The partners were gathered around the conference table once more, their number reduced again. The intervening week had wrought changes. Sophie had pulled herself together. She no longer looked as bereft as she had done in the immediate aftermath of Mark's death. This time it was Ai Leen who looked careworn and fragile, face pale under her makeup, bluish shadows under her eyes, a scarf wound unfashionably tightly around her neck, as if she was trying to ward off a chill. Her united front with Reggie appeared to have faltered. She shrank from him and sought the chair furthest away, avoiding catching his eye. Reggie, on the other hand, had gained in confidence. He was munching on a ham and cheese sandwich now, leaning back in his chair as if he did not have a care in the world. Annie felt her stomach turn as she saw him devouring his lunch. David, smooth, confident, Teflon-coated David, was looking worried - and involved. He, the outsider, had been sucked into their world where death stalked amongst them, murder and suicide his weapons.

Stephen said, 'Thanks for coming, all.' He looked around the room as if gauging to see if they had the strength to absorb further bad news and then said, 'You've probably all heard that Rahul is in hospital.' There were a few nods around the table. 'He is in a coma. The doctors are not sure if he will recover.'

Sophie asked, 'But what happened? Julian said he tried to kill himself. Is that true?'

Stephen said, 'I'm afraid so.'

No one said anything. To hear the rumour confirmed was a shock.

Julian finally broke the silence. 'But why? I don't understand.'

Annie saw David and Stephen exchange glances; this was the moment of truth if they were to reveal Rahul's carefully maintained secret.

Stephen hesitated and then said, 'We don't know, I'm afraid, why he tried to do this.'

Reggie, true to form, was the first to articulate the possibilities.

He asked abruptly 'Does it have something to do with the murder?'

'There is no reason to think so!' snapped David, despite his earlier position.

Reggie pounced on this immediately, 'How can you possibly say that? Why else would he have done it?'

'What are you trying to say, Reggie?' asked Sophie.

A cold voice answered, 'It's quite obvious, isn't it. He's

accusing Rahul of murder.' It took Annie a moment to realise that the thin, disgusted voice had been her own.

To his credit, Annie saw that Julian was quick to defend his friend, 'It can't be Rahul, I don't get it. Why would he kill Mark?' She rewarded him with a small smile for his loyalty.

Reggie asked shrewdly, 'What do the police think?'

Stephen said, 'They consider it a possibility.'

Again, there was quiet in the room as everyone took in his words.

A broad smile broke over Reggie's face, 'Well, that is good news.'

•

Mrs. Singh was aghast. Her husband had told her that the young Indian lawyer from Bombay was most likely the murderer. At first, she had refused to believe it. There was no doubt in her mind that murder was the product of poor upbringing and falling into bad company. If you could not trust a wealthy Bombay family to protect their son from the sort of influences that might cause him to be capable of murder, she did not know what the world was coming to. She firmly told the Inspector that he had the wrong man. It was one thing to maintain an ignorance of what he did at the office, quite another to let him arrest some Indian boy from a good family. Finally, irritated by her persistence, the Inspector told her that Rahul had been found in bed with a young Chinese man. It was difficult to discern whether she was more horrified by the homosexuality or the multiracial nature of his assignation. But she had no difficulty, after becoming privy to this information, in believing Rahul capable of any atrocity, including murder. Inspector Singh had known how she would react. He thought about Annie's insistence that being gay was not a secret worth killing for, or dying for. She should meet his wife.

•

That evening, Annie stopped at the hospital on her way home. The young uniformed policeman who had replaced Corporal Fong slipped out of the room and stood like a statue by the door. She sat by Rahul's bed, watching the gentle rise and fall of his chest as he breathed. After a while, she fished out the book she had brought, a convoluted legal thriller of the sort Rahul had been addicted to and read aloud from it to him. The other lawyers had visited Rahul during the day, en masse, seeking comfort in company. Annie had not gone with them. She felt too tired, too disillusioned by their scarcely concealed relief that a frontrunner among suspects had emerged.

To her surprise, the door opened and Reggie walked in. She stopped reading immediately. He was discomfited to find Annie in possession of the room.

'Any change?' he asked.

She shook her head mutely. Reggie walked to the bedside and stood staring down at Rahul's still form.

He asked, 'Why do you think the coppers are hanging around?'

Annie shrugged to indicate she did not know and did not care. She wished Reggie would leave. She could not imagine what his purpose was in coming to visit Rahul again. He had definitely been part of the earlier contingent. Julian had told her so.

Reggie beckoned to the policeman at the door and asked him, 'So, what are you doing here then?'

The young man hesitated for a second, wondering whether he should answer. He decided that there was no harm in it and said, 'In case he wakes up and says anything, sir.'

Reggie nodded thoughtfully, 'I suppose that makes sense.'

He took a quick turn about the room, stood fidgeting by the bed and then walked out.

Annie let out a gentle sigh of relief and picked up her book again. She continued where she had left off, 'The young man prised open the door with a credit card...' The policeman looked sceptical as Annie read on.

•

The next few days passed in a blur for Annie. She went into the office and worked in a desultory manner. She spent a couple of hours every evening reading to Rahul whose condition remained unchanged. She saw very little of David and nothing at all of the Inspector. At one point, she collared David in his room and demanded to know if the police had downed tools. He had been evasive. Finally, she had marched out of his room on the crest of a wave of anger and ignored him since. There was a discernable sense of relief in the office. Although there were pockets of genuine concern for Rahul's condition and a lot of lip service, the general feeling was one of relief. Rahul's homosexuality remained a secret. There was speculation as to what had led Rahul to such a terrible step. But on the whole, the lawyers avoided the subject. Least said, soonest mended. These were strange days - Annie felt like a piece of flotsam adrift on an ocean, no control over her own direction. There was a sense that they were all in limbo, expecting further developments. It was with dismay that Annie realised that the office was waiting for news of Rahul's death. As time stood still for Rahul, deep in his coma, so time stood still for all of them. Rahul awaited death, the rest awaited closure.

She had exchanged casual words with Ai Leen but respected her privacy on the subject of the awful bruising on her neck. She had met Ai Leen's husband only a couple of times and had thought him a gentle, good-natured man. He evidently had another side to his personality. However, if Ai Leen, an educated, successful woman was willing to give him another chance, she was not sure she should interfere. But was it the right decision? Annie worried about her own inaction. She had spoken to Julian as well, exchanging news of Rahul, avoiding the subject of the insider dealing. Annie knew that she would eventually be called to account by the Tan Sri but could not bring herself to confront Julian again or take her suspicions to Stephen. She postponed the inevitable.

•

On Friday afternoon, returning from a solitary lunch, she found a package on her desk. It contained her passport. She looked at the small, thick, scuffed book that had recorded her travel for the last five years. Annie buried her face in her hands. The police had definitely decided that they had found their man.

-eighteen-

'(1) Nothing in this Act shall authorise an act that causes or accelerates death as distinct from an act that permits the dying process to take its natural course.
(2) For the avoidance of doubt, it is hereby declared that nothing in this Act shall condone, authorise or approve abetment of suicide, mercy killing or euthanasia.'
Section 17, Advance Medical Directive Act, Chapter 4A

Corporal Fong was watching his father sleep. His breath came in asthmatic wheezes. The bedclothes were grimy. He would have to change them but it was a shame to wake the old man who had the terrible insomnia of age. His father was rarely able to fall into a deep sleep. His mother had gone to bed. The fact that the T.V was switched off was proof enough. Fong had snuck out of the office to check on his father. There were mountains of work to get through but he had a responsibility to the old man. If he were honest, he knew that there was no hardship to stay away, to bury himself in work. But his father depended on him. He could not afford any additional care, not on a rookie's wage. A cough rattled his father's chest. He lifted him up gently and turned the pillows. He went to his bedroom and got another - higher elevation might help his breathing.

He held the soft pillow in his hands and looked at the man on the bed. Only a flicker of life left. So easily snuffed out. Was that not the best option for all of them? His father easing into merciful death, his mother indifferent to his passing, and he himself - free at last. Free to work hard, save his money, move out, find a girlfriend - live his life. All the might of the police force was concentrating on finding the murderer of Mark Thompson. Yet, here in his flat, he could take a life with minimum fanfare. He bent down and kissed his father's forehead and went back to work.

•

On the weekend, Annie paced up and down the veranda, strolled about the garden and prowled around the house seeking distractions from her worry that were not to be found. This hiatus at home was not having its desired effect. There was no ebb in the tension washing over her. She called no one and spoke to no one. Except Rahul. But her monologues with Rahul did not amount to conversation. His passivity was so comprehensive as to be indistinguishable from death. The machines which kept him alive had more life than the inert figure on the bed. She did her best, injecting her voice with enthusiasm as she spoke to him or read to him, trying to penetrate the blackness that enveloped him. But at no point did she feel that she even flickered at the edge of his consciousness.

On Sunday morning, she rose bright and early, awoken by the din of mynah birds quarrelling over a snack. The small, brown birds sounded like a pack of children arguing over a sweet - high, shrill, argumentative, persistent. Annie decided to spring clean and then wash and polish the car. If she had not exhausted her sum of nervous energy by then, she would consider pushing her lawn mower around the overgrown garden, pre-empting the gardeners who were due the following week. She dressed in an old pair of gym shorts and a grey flannel vest that bore testimony to an aborted painting exercise she had undertaken months back, and set to work. By mid-morning, she was regretting her decision but still determined to see it through. She was dusty and dishevelled but could at least congratulate herself on not having spent the morning brooding over recent events. She got herself an icy bottle of golden beer, plucked a small lime from a lime tree in the garden, bit it in half - wincing at the sharp sourness - and popped one half into the bottle, flicking the other into the garden where it was eyed askance by the cat. She took a long cold swig and rubbed the back of her neck, sore from her efforts to take down the curtains earlier. With a crusader's single mindedness, she retrieved a bucket and some rags, the car shampoo that was more expensive than her own, tied her own hair back again and set to work hosing down the BMW.

She was on her hands and knees in the gravel, scrubbing the wheel hubs with a rag, up to her elbows in suds, damp with perspiration, hair escaping in tendrils and adhering to her forehead when a voice said behind her, 'Very busy, I see!'

She turned around in surprise, knocking over her bottle of beer.

She scowled at her visitor, wiped the sweat out of her eyes and said, 'What do you want?'

David chose to ignore the unfriendly tone and answered cheerfully, 'Came to check up on you. You've been wandering round the office like a bear with a sore head.'

Annie looked at him disdainfully.

He said, 'I'll help you finish up here.'

She looked at his immaculate white linen shirt, open at the throat and well pressed khaki trousers and said, 'That would probably be a mistake.'

He ignored her, grabbed a sodden piece of cloth out of the bucket and set to work with vigour. For a while, they scrubbed in silence.

Then David said, 'I would have called first but I was pretty sure you wouldn't invite me over.'

'And that didn't dissuade you?'

He grinned at her, the perspiration already starting to run down his face despite the patches of shade cast by overhanging trees.

He said, looking at her drink, 'A cold beer would go down well.'

Annie signalled her agreement by chucking her rag back in the bucket and standing up. He stood up too and she laughed, 'No way! You keep at this car and I'll fetch the beer.' Reluctantly, he retrieved the rag and got back to work.

Annie went into the house, blissfully cool and dark compared to the outdoors, fetched a six-pack and went back out. David had taken advantage of her absence to expedite the carwash and was already hosing down the car.

She yelled, 'That'll do, come over here!'

He gratefully abandoned his task, turned off the hose and joined her. She was sitting on the front step, long brown limbs stretched out before her.

It was a wonderful afternoon. Annie was to look back on it with longing in the days ahead, this interlude of laughter and conversation. David was humourous, interesting, controversial and comfortable in turn and at once. Occasionally, they would fall silent and listen to the birds. These silences were almost as pleasant as the conversation that preceded them. Of murder and its consequences, they said nothing. She drew his attention to the different species of birds in the garden and he told her of those he had seen trekking up Mt. Kinabalu, the tallest mountain in South East Asia. They were armchair sports fans and captivated by politics. Both were amused to discover that the other had been in Japan for the World Cup.

'We might have been sitting next to each other!' exclaimed Annie.

'I doubt I would have forgotten you!'

His admiration must have shown in his eyes for a second because a constraint fell between them for the first time that afternoon. Annie became aware of her grubby t-shirt and the patches of perspiration under her armpits. She did not meet his eyes but instead leapt to her feet and disappeared into the house. She regained her composure slowly, scowled at her appearance in a mirror, retrieved a bottle of Chardonnay from the fridge as her excuse for bolting and sat down on the step beside him. She realised that she had returned without bottle opener or glasses and made to get up. David caught her arm and she sat down again and looked at him. His face was too close, his grey eyes were smiling, and she felt her breath catch in her throat. He held her gaze and then leaned forward and brushed her mouth gently with his. And then, as she did not move away, he took her in his arms and kissed her.

Afterwards, they sat without speaking. Close but not touching.

Annie said, 'I have to go to the hospital…to visit Rahul.'

The ugly shadow of the recent past darkened the afternoon for the first time that day.

He nodded. 'Do you want me to come with you?'

She shook her head mutely. She would love him to come, but needed the space to regain her equilibrium. He understood, for he got to his feet, held out a hand to her and pulled her to her feet as well.

'I'll be off then,' he said.

She looked at him, unable to find words to make this parting a normal everyday affair. Trying not to think about the events of the day and doing nothing else, she showered and dressed in a pair of jeans and a snowy cotton t-shirt, slipped into her car and headed to the hospital.

-nineteen-

'The Registrar shall keep a register of ... persons convicted of any crime within Singapore...'
Section 4, Registration of Criminals Act, Chapter 268

Rahul was still in a coma. That much Annie could see the moment she walked into the room. The stillness of a coma went beyond that of sleep. In sleep, there was the occasional stretching and shifting, murmuring and muttering. For Rahul, the only movement was the barely discernible rise and fall of the chest, the only sound, the slight whistling of exhalation between parted lips, largely drowned out by the machine-generated sounds from the paraphernalia of life support. There was no policeman on duty and Annie wondered at it. She opened the bedside drawer and took out the book she had been reading to Rahul. She was heartily sick of it and hoped that boredom was not prolonging Rahul's inert state. She gave herself a mental scolding for being facetious in such a desolate place and read on, trying to inject some life and cheer into the words. After a while, she put down the book. She was not concentrating, missing words and sometimes whole sentences.

She looked at him, his hair neatly combed, the light veins showing on his almost translucent eyelids and said, 'I'm sorry, Rahul. I'm making a real hash of this book. It's pretty bloody awful anyway, isn't it? Rather like the last fortnight. The murder, the police, losing friends, suspecting colleagues, your ending up here in hospital - it's been a nightmare. And then today, David Sheringham came to visit me. I had been cleaning, first the house, then the car, trying to get this stuff out of my head, at least for a while. I was a real mess. And you should have seen what I was wearing. An old pair of shorts and a t-shirt with paint stains - from when I tried to paint the bedroom. You probably don't remember but I came to work smelling of turpentine for a couple of days. Anyway, I was not a sight to gladden the eye. We talked and drank a lot of beer. To cut a long story short, we were sitting there, chatting. Not about the murder. And he kissed me.'

Annie paused for a second to see if her revelation had provoked any sort of response from the man lying on the bed, but there was no sign of it. She shrugged and carried on, 'Where was I? Oh yes! He kissed me.' She smiled at the memory, less a smile than a general lightening of her features and a sudden brightness in her eyes. 'Did I tell you, the first time we met, he confused me for a secretary? Yes, the bastard thought I was Mark's secretary!'

'But I have to tell you Rahul, although you wouldn't appreciate it...I suppose you might appreciate it! That smile of his, it's a wonderful thing.' Her own lips turned up at the corners in a reflex response to the memory. 'His eyes go all crinkly round the edges, and he looks so young...and his eyes light up, I tell you what,' she said suddenly irritable, 'it's not a wonder I kissed him, I suspect most women would have!'

Again she looked at Rahul to see if he had anything to say but he remained shut away in a world of his own. Her voice trailed off as she became aware how desperately she wanted her interlude with David to be a beginning, not a passing moment. Annie fell silent. She forgot her purpose in visiting Rahul and sat lost in her own thoughts, like a teenager in love.

She did not realise she had company until a sudden movement caught her eye. She looked up in surprise at the youth who stood nervously by the door. If she was surprised, he was completely taken aback to find someone in with Rahul. She supposed she had been so quiet he had not noticed that there was someone in the room until actually in the door. He looked like a rabbit in headlights, trying to find the will to bolt.

Annie smiled at him in a friendly fashion and said welcomingly, if a bit doubtfully, 'Hello! Are you here to see Rahul?'

The youth managed a quick nod in response.

She smiled at him reassuringly, wondering why he was so nervous and said, 'Come in, I'm Annie, I work with Rahul. He's not very well, I'm afraid.'

The youth came in slowly and took her proffered hand. In a gentle voice, barely above a whisper, he said, 'I'm Ahmad. I am a …friend of Rahul.'

Annie gestured, inviting Ahmad to get closer to the bed and see Rahul for himself. Ahmad sidled up to the bed and gazed down at Rahul. Annie was surprised and touched to see a glint of tears in his eyes.

The youth stood by the bed for a while and then turned to Annie and asked, 'Will he get better?'

Annie said gently, 'I don't know. The doctors are not sure yet. He has not gotten any worse.'

The boy nodded and they both gazed at Rahul lying still in the bed, indifferent to his guests.

Annie asked, 'Have you known Rahul long?'

Ahmad looked up at her. 'Not so long, no. We have met a few times only.'

He was a soft-spoken fellow, speaking in the gentle undulating cadences of the Malay. Annie had to strain to hear him. Growing in confidence, the boy said, 'I read about him in the newspapers, so I came.'

Annie nodded. Rahul's attempted suicide had leaked to the press and there had been much speculation as to why he might have done it - the newspapers walking a fine line between titillating their readers and risking a potential libel suit if Rahul recovered and was not after all found to be a murderer. The unfolding story surrounding Mark's death was still very much grist to the tabloid mill.

Inspector Singh's bulk filled the doorway in complete contrast to the thin slip of a boy minutes earlier. He nodded cheerfully to Annie, glanced indifferently at Rahul and then subjected Ahmad, who looked like he would have fled if the Inspector had not been blocking his exit route, to a close scrutiny.

He said, 'Who are you then?'

Annie, shocked at the Inspector's rudeness, leapt to the youth's defence, 'This is Ahmad. A friend of Rahul.'

'A friend, eh? I'll bet he is.'

Annie was fuming now. 'What's that supposed to mean?' she asked.

'Just that, unlike you, I know a rent boy when I see one.'

Annie stared at him.

'Even so! Anyway, you don't have any proof.'

Ahmad stood quivering between the two powerful personalities squaring off.

'Proof! My twenty five years as a policeman is all the proof I need, young lady.'

Annie was trembling with rage now.

'Twenty-five years as a policeman! And you jump to conclusions like a...a Corporal. Rahul tries to kill himself and you think he's a murderer. You'll be driving this kid to the edge next!'

The Inspector burst out laughing, his belly rippling with humour.

'My dear girl, I should throw you in the lock-up, not him,' he said, gesturing at Ahmad.

Annie looked sheepish, knowing she was lucky to have provoked laughter, not rage.

The Inspector continued, 'And don't worry, I'm not going to arrest this young man. Not now. Only if I find him soliciting.'

This last was said sternly to Ahmad who nodded, aware that he had received a reprieve.

In a more gentle tone that sat uneasily with his earlier harshness, the Inspector asked, 'What are you doing here anyway?'

The boy looked at him and decided that prudence dictated honesty, 'We have met a few times. I thought we were friends.'

The Inspector nodded knowingly, 'You were a bit of a favourite, were you?'

Ahmad nodded and emboldened, said, 'Why does she say Rahul is a murderer?'

It was Annie who answered him.

She said scathingly, 'The police think that Rahul killed Mark Thompson, that expat who was murdered last week. *I* don't think he did it.'

'The *ang moh* who was his boss?' he asked.

She nodded.

'Rahul told me about it. He found the body.'

Annie shrugged, 'More or less.'

The Inspector's interest, however, had been piqued.

'When did he tell you about it?' he asked brusquely.

'When he came back that evening. He was with me but then he had to go to the office. I waited for him at his flat. When he came back, he told me that his boss had been killed.'

Annie started to speak but the Inspector put up a

broad hand to stop her.

He looked at Ahmad closely and said, 'Listen to me, young man. I am going to ask you a few questions and I want you to tell me the truth. If you do, you will not get into trouble. If I find that you have lied to me, you will never see the sun again, do you understand me?'

Ahmad nodded, terrified.

Satisfied, the Inspector asked carefully and slowly, 'Were you with Rahul the evening of the murder?'

Ahmad nodded fearfully.

'Both before and after Rahul went into the office?'

Again the nod.

'Do you know what time this was?'

Ahmad said, his voice barely audible. 'I meet him after work to go for a drink, then we go back to his flat and order pizza. He got this call. He say it is the boss. It was about eight at night.'

Inspector Singh interrupted him, 'How do you know what time it was?'

'The pizza arrive when Rahul was on the phone. I check the time because if they come late, they give you a discount. Then we ate some of the food. After half an hour, Rahul went out. He said he would be about one hour but he did not come back till midnight.'

The Inspector said, 'You were with Rahul until about eight thirty in the evening?'

Ahmad nodded, puzzled by his emphasis.

'And in that time, you did not go to his place of work?'

Ahmad looked shocked. 'Of course not. Rahul would not want to be seen with me!'

This rang poignantly true to Annie. The Inspector looked at Annie.

'Well, I guess that lets Rahul off the hook,' she said.

The Inspector took out his big white handkerchief and patted his brow.

He said, 'You don't happen to have your passport on you, do you?'

Annie's initial delight at Rahul's innocence was quickly tempered with reality. The Inspector had left with Ahmad, a firm grip on the young man's upper arm. She had remained to keep Rahul company a while. She understood Rahul's silence on having an alibi. He was so determined to keep his homosexuality a secret that he must have planned to brazen it out. When he was arrested and became chief suspect for the murder, he had probably not wanted to compound his immediate crime in the eyes of the police by producing another rent boy. It did not explain why he had tried to kill himself - unless he could not live with his homosexuality out in the open. And Rahul's innocence meant that there was still a murderer at large. This was a zero sum game. The exoneration of one person meant only that the killer was another of their colleagues - or the widow. And, unbidden, the thought came to her mind. Julian was the most likely candidate. He was the only other person she knew with a motive.

•

Inspector Singh sat in the backseat of a police car being driven back to the station. Next to him, Ahmad made himself as small and innocuous as he could. He need not have bothered. The Inspector's mind was on other things. He sat brooding about the day's developments. If he were honest with himself, he knew that there had always been a seed of doubt about Rahul's guilt. As that young woman had insisted, it had never been entirely probable that Rahul had killed Mark to keep his homosexuality a secret. And now it appeared that Rahul could not have been the murderer. The Inspector had been leaning back, the rear seatbelt dividing his mass into two wobbly protuberances. Now he sat upright, electrified by an idea. He reached for his mobile phone, cast a sideways glance at the boy next to him and slumped back in the seat again. It would have to wait until he got to the office.

•

David Sheringham lay on his back on the firm mattress of his hotel bed, with his hands under his head, staring at the ceiling. As if his thoughts had the power to compel action, his mobile phone rang. It was Annie calling him. He recognised the number as it flashed up on his display and he could not help a grin spreading across his face. He looked at his watch. Two hours since he had left her. She had not waited too long to call.

He picked up the phone and said 'Hello!' cautiously.

'David, is that you?'

'Annie? Yes, it's me. What's the matter?'

'David, it's Rahul.'

Immediately his voice became crisp and firm, 'What is it? Is he alright?'

'He's the same. No change in his condition.'

An impatient note crept into David's voice, 'What about him, then?'

'He has an alibi!'

'An alibi? What do you mean?'

'For the night of the murder. He was with someone. He left for the office just in time for the meeting. He could not have killed Mark.'

'Who was it? Who was he with?'

'Some friend of his, a young Malay boy. He came to the hospital while I was there. The Inspector turned up and it transpired that this lad, Ahmad, had been with him that night.' She continued less surely, 'The Inspector accused him of being a rent boy.'

'I see,' said David, and he did indeed see.

He saw now, why, despite having a watertight alibi, Rahul had preferred to pretend to have been alone that night and hope for the best. Annie had nothing more to say and did not know how to end the call without awkwardness. To act as if nothing had happened between them would be a challenge. To acknowledge the episode in any way was a concession she was not ready to make. She must at least come out of any relationship with her dignity intact.

She had been silent for too long because he said, 'Annie, are you there? Are you alright?'

She said hastily, 'Yes, I'm fine. Sorry. I'll see you tomorrow at the office.'

David said, 'Just so you know, I had a great time this afternoon!'

The line went dead.

Annie's phone rang and she grabbed it.

'It's Annie,' she said breathlessly.

'Annie, good. I'm glad I caught you.' It was the Inspector, not David calling back. Her heart slowed down again.

'Listen, don't tell anyone about Rahul Gandhi's alibi.'

'Why?' asked Annie.

'If people think that he's still the suspect, they might betray themselves.'

'Oh! I see what you mean.' She paused and then said, 'Inspector?'

'Yes?'

'I'm afraid I've already told David Sheringham.'

'Bloody hell! That was quick.'

'Sorry, I thought he would like to know.'

'Well, never mind. I'll call him and sort it out.'

-twenty-

'For all purposes, a person has died when there has occurred either ... irreversible cessation of circulation of blood and respiration in the body of the person ... or total and irreversible cessation of all functions of the brain of the person.'
Section 2A, Interpretation Act, Chapter 1

Every Monday morning the partners of Hutchinson & Rice held a meeting to discuss the week ahead - work, clients, marketing. It was a useful half an hour get-together, combined with coffee and croissants, that set the agenda for the week ahead. These meetings were normally good-natured events, an exchange of stories about the week that was and an upbeat assessment of the week to come. The partners were, after all, by and large, a collection of wealthy, successful, ambitious individuals with similar concerns and goals.

This Monday morning, Annie sat at the table with her fellow partners. No one was saying much. The coffee was being drunk but the croissants were largely untouched. Two partners were absent. One was dead, the other was lying as if dead in hospital. David was present, making up the numbers somewhat, sitting at one end of the table flicking through the papers he had brought with him. He had barely glanced at her as he came in and Annie was furious at his indifference. Now, looking around the table, Annie was amazed that she had ever liked, or even respected, these people. Her present attitude to each of them ranged from dislike to disgust, with little spikes of something that approached hatred when her gaze lit on Reggie. The meeting had not begun because they were all waiting for Stephen. He was late.

Annie wondered idly what was holding him up but then discovered she did not care. She was obsessed with a few subjects but had reached a pitch of indifference towards any others. Her balance was gone. She was filled with an overwhelming concern for Rahul and a deep worry over Julian. She had no interest in the firm and the manner in which it was weathering the crisis in its ranks. A meeting about client matters was so devoid of any possible importance, she wondered whether she would be able to sit through it without screaming. Her index finger was in her mouth. She tasted the warm iron flavour of blood. She had bitten her nail so deep that a droplet of blood was welling up in the corner between nail and flesh.

The door opened. The expectant looks around the table were rewarded with the sight of Stephen standing at the threshold. Slowly, he came forward, walking with the gait of an old man. He looked up and gazed at their faces. There was a stifled exclamation. Stephen's face was white and drawn, his jowls sagging - it was a cameo of what he would look like in twenty years. He cleared his throat once, and then again, and Annie had a sudden dreadful premonition of what he was going to say.

She whispered, 'No!' and he must have caught the breath of sound because he turned to look at her and seemed to direct his next remark exclusively at her.

'I'm afraid I have bad news. Rahul passed away a

couple of hours ago. He never recovered from his coma.'

A pin dropping would have sounded like a gunshot.

Julian asked, 'What happened?'

Stephen ran a hand through his thinning hair, 'Not sure of the details, the hospital just called and then Inspector Singh confirmed that he died in the early hours of the morning.'

Ai Leen was the next to find her voice, saying hesitantly, 'What does that mean for us?'

'It's not possible to try a dead man for a crime,' said Stephen.

The implications of this took a while to sink in.

Sophie stuttered, 'But that means we…we will always be suspects.'

'It's probably not as bad as that. Although there can't be a formal trial, word will get out that Rahul was suspected of the murder and tried to commit suicide. People will draw their own conclusions,' said Stephen.

Annie looked at David who shook his head. There would be time enough to reveal Rahul's alibi when the Inspector gave them leave. Let the people around the table believe that they were off the hook. The Inspector's reasoning that it might lead to carelessness on the part of the murderer was still sound. Rahul's death did not change anything except to make the murderer feel more secure that Rahul had taken the secret of his innocence to the grave. As for Rahul, he was dead. The suspicions of his fellows could no longer hurt him.

Reggie said, 'It's a terrible thing about Rahul, of course, but it's probably for the best. It would have been very difficult for Rahul to have faced a trial and would have reflected very badly on the firm. This is a bit of a let off, I think we can all agree!'

Annie discovered that the expression trembling with rage was not a figure of speech. She got to her feet and stormed out of the room.

In her office, she sat in half-darkness. She was dry-eyed. There would be time enough to weep for Rahul when his name had been cleared of murder. As she sat there, she knew that when this was over, when the murderer was found, and she had to believe that would happen, she would leave the firm. She could not work with these people. The well was polluted and she would not drink from it again. But there was no possibility of leaving now. She was a suspect in a murder investigation. Besides, she would not leave if she could. The murderer, having come amongst them had not just killed Mark, but destroyed Rahul. She would have to see it through to the end. There was a firm knock on the door. She did not respond. There was no one outside that door she wanted to see. After a brief pause, she saw the handle turn. It was Julian who came in. She looked at him with hostility, hating him for his part in the whole sorry mess.

He said, 'I can't believe it about Rahul.'

She saw that he had come to seek comfort. The three of them, the young partners in the firm had always stuck together, often spending time together at work and after. Now one of their number was dead, by his own hand. How had it come to this?

'I know, it's all unbelievable,' said Annie.

'And the murder? I just don't understand why he would have done it.'

She looked at him sharply. He was, after all, a prime suspect. He seemed genuinely puzzled and once again, she was assailed by doubt. Perhaps she was mistaken in Julian. He might have made some money illegally but she could not see him in the role of murderer. Feeling guilty at suspecting him as he stood there in need of a friend, she went round the desk and held open her arms.

He hugged her, saying again into her hair, 'I still can't believe it was Rahul. I really can't!'

Annie kept silent, not wanting to lie to him but conscious that Rahul's innocence was something that she could not share with him. Neither of them heard the quiet knock on the door. Annie raised her head as she heard the door open and found herself looking straight at David. He stood there at the doorway, one hand on the handle, absolutely still. If she had looked, she would have seen that his knuckles were white. Slowly and with great care, David shut the door. Julian had not even noticed he was there. Annie stood in Julian's arms and buried her face in his shoulder. He hugged her more tightly. David walked back to his room and shut the door behind him. He clenched his fist and slammed it against a cupboard door. He felt the sharp pain in his hand. David felt clear-headed and clear-eyed. The surge of pain-induced adrenaline had refreshed him - distanced him from the anger that had welled up at seeing Annie with Julian. This was not the moment to get angry. There was work to be done first.

•

Inspector Singh sat across from Maria in her living room. Their positions were almost identical to those they had assumed the night he had gone to break the news of Mark's murder. He sat in the straight-backed chair; she sat across from him on the red velvet sofa. There were changes to the room, subtle, but ripe with meaning. The pictures of her and Mark were gone. In the same frames were recent shots of herself and her children, by the sea, in a garden and in that very room. On the Afghan rug between them, a child had commenced building a train set complete with stations, miniature people and animals. Life now animated the room.

The Inspector was frustrated. Maria did not hide her lack of sorrow over Mark's death. She had looked at the anonymous letters with indifference, insisting that there was no truth in the allegations of prostitution and furthermore, that Mark would never have believed them. When he pointed out that Mark had gone hunting for her in room-by-the-hour motels on Balestier Road, not the behaviour of a man who had dismissed the claims, she had shrugged and looked disbelieving. When he had suggested to her that this provided her with a motive for murder, she had remained unimpressed, merely saying that he was picking on her because she was Filipina and she would complain to the embassy if she was harassed by the police.

He had one more card to play. He watched her, trying to gauge whether the time had come to show his hand. So far, she had exuded confidence - but was it the confidence born of innocence? The Inspector was convinced she was a woman with plenty to hide but whether that included murder, he was hard-pressed to say. He opened the manila folder he was carrying and slipped a black and white photo across the coffee table towards her.

She looked at it with mild interest and said to him, 'What is this?'

He said, 'A photo taken from a C.C.T.V camera two blocks from Raffles Tower.'

'Why do you show this to me?'

He said evenly, 'It was filmed on the night of the murder.'

She repeated the question, this time her voice was more high pitched, her Filipina accent coming through more strongly, 'What are you saying to me?'

He did not answer at first and her façade started to crack.

The Inspector stood up and folded his arms, a round figure with an air of menace.

'I am saying that you were near Raffles Tower on the night of the murder. I am saying that you lied to me when you said you were at home.'

She shrank back in her chair and crossed herself furtively, the profound Catholicism of the average Filipina putting in an appearance. Then she pulled herself together. It was a conscious, visible effort. Her back straightened and her hands fell to her sides. She lifted her chin and met his gaze without fear.

'So what?' she asked.

'I discover that you lied to me…that you were at the scene of your husband's murder, a murder for which you have an excellent motive, and that is all you have to say to me?'

She did not flinch. She was a woman hardened by experience. She had battled all the adversity that life had dealt her with such a generous hand, using her only weapons - her face and her will. She was not going to snatch defeat from the jaws of victory.

She stood up, a slight creature compared to him and said, 'You cannot prove that I killed my husband!'

'You were in the area that night. I know it and you know it. Did you see anything that would help me find out who did kill him?'

He could see that she was sorely tempted to say something, make something up perhaps. But her innate caution stopped her.

She said, 'If I go to the office, I might have seen something…but I did not.'

His gambit had failed. The Inspector knew that he was no further along than he had been when he rang her doorbell half an hour earlier.

He said, 'If you reconsider the lies you have told me, you can contact me at this number,' and gave her his card.

She took it reluctantly, her hand brushing against his fingers. She looked at him through half closed eyes, as if measuring him up for a suit and then came slowly round the table until she was standing toe to toe with him. She put one slender hand on his chest and felt his heart beating beneath her hand. She looked up into his eyes and a shadow of a smile played across her face, like a breath of wind through leaves.

'Can I help you in any other way?' she asked in a low tone, never taking her eyes off his face.

His large hand, with its stubby, grimy fingers, closed over hers and he stood looking at her, breathing in the delicate scent of her. She could feel that his heart was racing.

Then he said, distinctly, enunciating each word, 'There is nothing you can do for me.'

She could not disguise the flash of anger in her eyes at his rejection but she did not say anything. Instead, she took a step back, continuing to look at him. His personal space once again his own, the Inspector nodded curtly at her and left the room, hoping that she could not see the regret welling up within him, threatening to burst through the banks of his self control like flood waters after a storm.

•

Stephen went home after the meeting in the conference room. The Singapore office of Hutchinson & Rice was in disarray and Stephen was the man in charge. He knew that his life, that he had worn like a comfortable suit of old clothes, would never be the same again. Sitting in the office, replaying the memory of shock, and worse, of relief, that had played over the faces of his colleagues when he had told them of Rahul's death, he had longed to get away. He had grabbed his briefcase, and then stopped to put it down again - walking out of the room empty-handed. His secretary had tried to stop him, murmuring something about meetings and calls, but he had ignored her.

Now he sat, in semi-darkness, slumped in the leather armchair in his study, wondering how he had let his wife and the interior decorator turn his private room into this pastiche of commercial masculinity - dark wood, red leather, heavy curtains and, unbelievably, hunting prints and a ship in a bottle. Joan, his wife came into the room and he looked at her. He had thought that she had gone out for the day, with Sarah Thompson, that friendship still blooming despite the pressures of recent events. She had not seen him, sitting in a corner, lost in his own thoughts. He was going to draw her attention to his presence and then changed his mind. He wanted solitude, even from his wife. He watched her as she sat down at his desktop and switched it on, remembering the girl he had fallen in love with and comparing her to this middle-aged woman for whom he had a tepid affection based on a shared history and a commonality of mundane purpose.

He noticed with mild surprise that she was printing something - he would not have thought that she knew how to switch on the computer, let alone print documents. Stephen felt awkward. His desire to be undisturbed had left him in a position where he felt that he was spying on his wife. He saw with relief that she had finished what she was doing, gathering up the sheaf of papers and making for the door hurriedly. His phone rang. It was in his shirt pocket and its clarion call cut through the silence. Joan started with fright and dropped the papers, staring at him as if she had seen a ghost.

Stephen fumbled for his phone, saying to her, 'Sorry, love. Came home early.'

She continued to stare at him. Then galvanised into action, she started picking up the papers hurriedly. Stephen came over to her, intending to help. He stooped and picked up a sheet but she snatched it from his fingers. She turned to face him defiantly, still trying to shield the papers from his view. He had seen enough.

He said hoarsely, 'My God!'

•

David hurried through the fluorescent-lit hospital corridors, trying to ignore the antiseptic smell that assailed his nostrils. He overtook an old woman being wheeled gently through the corridors by three generations of family. Her husband keeping pace next to her, a daughter-in-law doing the actual pushing, and her grandchildren skipping ahead, indifferent to the pall of mortality that hung over the place. He stood impatiently at the lift trying to ignore the whispered conversation of two nurses on the shortcomings of their matron. The lift arrived and they all squeezed in next to a trolley bed containing a young Chinese man being wheeled back to his ward after surgery, muttering and groaning as the first hint of pain penetrated the blackness. The two orderlies pushing him, dressed in baggy green, discussed the latest football results with enthusiasm, inured to the pain and suffering around them. The doors opened and disgorged the contents of the lift. David held the door open for all and stepped out last, breathing a small, guilty sigh of relief to be distanced by space, and he hoped time as well, from these afflictions.

    He set off again in the direction of Rahul's ward, less hurried now that he was so close. He continued to guess at the reason for his summons. He reached the nurses station and found the Inspector standing there, waiting for him. He looked at him enquiringly but the policeman remained silent. Instead, he beckoned him into the room that had been Rahul's until so recently. Of Rahul, there was no trace. The bed was empty, stripped of its bedding. The life support machines had been cleared away. The flowers that had been wilting in two vases on his bedside table were no longer there. The only sign that Rahul had been in the room was the thriller that Annie had been reading him, which lay on the bedside table. David picked it up and felt a wave of compassion for the loss of the confused, unhappy young man whom he had hardly known.
    'Such a waste,' he said to the Inspector, not expecting a reply but feeling that he owed it to Rahul to acknowledge his passing before being taken up in the details of death rather than the life that had gone before.
    Still the Inspector remained silent. David sensed that this was not his usual impassivity. There was a turbulence within the policeman that was discernable in the dark hollows of his eyes.
    David asked, 'What is it?'
    The Inspector gave a small sigh, a delicate emission from the usually gross man. 'It might have been murder.'

'What do you mean? What might have been murder?' And then with dawning horror, 'Rahul?'

The Inspector nodded.

-twenty one-

'A person is said to use force to another if he causes motion, change of motion, or cessation of motion to that other, or if he causes to any substance such motion, or change of motion, or cessation of motion as brings that substance into contact with any part of that other's body, or with anything which that other is wearing or carrying, or with anything so situated that such contact affects that other's sense of feeling.'
Section 349, Penal Code, Chapter 224

Ai Leen sat at her computer, staring at the screen. The flashing cursor marked each second that she sat there, looking at the letter she had just drafted. Her hand stole to her neck, still wrapped in a gossamer scarf. She no longer felt any pain from the bruising but the gesture had become a nervous habit. She made up her mind and clicked on the print command, getting up hurriedly to go to the printer room to retrieve the letter before anyone else set eyes on it in that public place. She wrested the door to her room open and found Reggie standing there.

She took an inadvertent step back and he seized the

advantage to put a foot in the door. She considered pushing past him, but the interested glance of her secretary, her attention drawn by the frozen, silent tableaux, stopped her. Reggie propelled her back into the room by stepping forward and forcing her retreat. He shut the door behind them. Her eyes were drawn to the computer where the letter was still on screen. He looked her over slowly, insultingly, and put out a hand to touch her cheek with one finger. It might have been a caress but for her reaction.

She slapped his hand away, and shrunk from him, hissing, 'Don't touch me!'

He enjoyed her fear; there was a hint of a smile on his face.

He said, 'That's a change of heart!'

Ai Leen slipped behind her desk, creating a barrier between them. She said, unable to hide the tremor in her voice, 'I mean it, don't touch me.'

Reggie came round the desk and perched on the corner. He put up his hands in a conciliatory gesture and said, 'Look, I came in here to see whether we could make a deal.'

She did not reply and refused to meet his eyes.

He said sardonically, 'After all, we made a bargain before and I kept up my end of it.'

Ai Leen closed her eyes against the greed and ambition that had led her to this place.

Reggie waited a moment and said, 'Rahul killed Mark. Rahul is dead. End of story.'

She looked up at him at this, and then her gaze fell.

He said, 'Surely you see it? We have nothing to worry about now. The police are content. The firm is content. You and I can put this behind us. But I need your guarantee that you will keep your mouth shut.'

It was only through a singular effort of will that Ai Leen refrained from looking at the screen. Instead, she nodded, just once.

Reggie said, 'I want to hear you say it.'

She looked at him, hatred in her eyes.

He took a step in her direction and she whispered, 'I won't say anything.' Again, her hand went to her throat.

He did not miss the gesture. The tension went out of his body.

'Good,' he said cheerfully and turned away from her. At the door, he stopped and glanced over his shoulder.

'It's been fun!' he said and walked out.

Ai Leen watched him go, her palms damp with perspiration. She remembered her letter and hurried to the printer room. To her almost light-headed relief, the room was deserted and the letter was still there, obscured in a pile of other printed material. She glanced over it and was satisfied with what she saw. Then she walked over to the shredder, a fixture in any legal office, and fed the letter through, watching the remnants of it rain like confetti into the waiting bin.

•

Stephen sat across from his wife in their front sitting room. It was a comfortable place. The sofas were of good quality but well worn. The coffee table books were not the usual untouched hardcovers on architecture and spa resorts, but were well-thumbed travel guides and family albums. Pictures of family covered one wall, grandparents, graduations and holidays. It was a room that suggested that the domestic situation of the family living there was a fundamentally happy one. Stephen remembered that he had felt nothing but a mild affection for his wife of thirty plus years when he had seen her in the study. He realised now that she was of utmost importance to him - he had merely lost the habit of acknowledging it to himself, let alone telling her so.

He said, 'Joan, what in God's name were you thinking of?'

She sat across from him, knees drawn primly together, hands folded in her lap, hair shot with grey, tied back from an expressionless face.

She shrugged helplessly. 'It wasn't my idea, it was Sarah's …I thought it might help her, get the anger out. You know, a sort of therapy.'

Stephen exploded, 'Therapy?"

His gaze fell on the papers on the coffee table and he subsided, rubbing a tired hand across his eyes.

Joan said, 'I'm so sorry.'

He nodded wearily.

'Maybe you should tell me exactly what you did.'

Joan drew a deep breath. Her voice grew stronger. The act of telling was drawing the poison from the wound.

'When Mark left her for that woman, Sarah was beside herself. It was not just that she still loved him but the shame too, it was unbearable for her. She would come and talk to me and cry…she just could not understand how it happened.'

Stephen remembered that Sarah had spent a lot of time closeted with Joan after the break-up of her marriage. He had maintained a prudent distance, with all the reluctance of the male of the species for getting involved in a domestic fracas.

He nodded his understanding to her and she continued, 'She was convinced that Maria was no better than a prostitute, that she had basically lured Mark into bed…was after his money. She tried telling him so but he was besotted with Maria and would not listen. She wanted me to tell him. Of course, I refused. Then she hit on this idea of sending him anonymous letters. She thought the seeds of doubt might be planted if Mark kept getting reminded that Maria was in it for his money.'

Stephen remembered that fateful evening on Balestier Road and knew the plan had worked to perfection. He asked, picking up one of the letters gingerly, 'But what about all this stuff about moonlighting as a prostitute? Was it true?'

Joan shook her head, 'I don't know. I don't think Sarah did either. She just put in the worst things she could imagine.'

Stephen asked tiredly, 'But I still don't see how you got involved?'

'Sarah told me her plan. She knew she'd be the prime suspect if it came out. So she asked me if I would send the letters with a local postmark, while she went back to England.'

He raised one of his bushy brows, 'And you agreed?'

'She kept begging me to do it. I was very worried about her. In the end, I agreed. It seemed a small thing to do. The marriage was never going to last. Maria *was* a tramp...so she emailed me the letters from time to time and I printed them out and posted them to Mark.'

Stephen was puzzled, 'But what were you doing today?'

'Sarah stopped the letters when she came back to Singapore. But she was worried that there might be something incriminating in them. She asked me to print them out and take them to her so she could have a look,' she trailed off.

They stared at the letters lying between them.

Joan asked timidly, 'What are we going to do?'

He said, 'I don't know.'

•

David and the Inspector were in the hospital canteen drinking coffee. They had spoken to the doctor in charge of Rahul, heard his concerns and agreed that an expedited *post mortem* was the best way forward. The preliminary results were due early the following afternoon but neither the Inspector nor David had any doubt as to the outcome. The doctor had been young and diffident, expressing himself with frequent throat clearings and qualifications, but his underlying competence had carried a weight of conviction. Despite being in a coma, all Rahul's vital organs had been functioning normally; it was his brain that had, for want of a better word, short-circuited. His death however bore the hallmarks of suffocation and further examination had led to the finding of a few strands of white fluff about Rahul's nostrils. To put it succinctly, as the Inspector had done, when he had heard the evidence, someone had killed Rahul by the simple expedient of holding a hospital pillow over his face. In a coma, Rahul would not have known, understood or struggled against what was happening. He had crossed the border between dreamless sleep and easeful death. Perhaps he had made the journey without pain or fear or doubt. But as the Inspector said to David, the man or woman who had assisted him on his way was not going to have it so easy.

Inspector Singh was a very angry man. David had struggled to understand the policeman's ire - so much greater than over Mark's death. Then he realised the Inspector blamed himself for this second murder. He had removed the policeman who had stood guard over Rahul. The guard had been to ensure that any post-recovery confession was recorded. When it became apparent that Rahul had a watertight alibi for Mark's murder, he had seen no need to continue the guard. He had been wrong. And the murder of a defenceless man on his watch had hit him hard.

The Inspector said, 'I still don't understand it, unless perhaps the two murders are unrelated?'

David looked at him sceptically.

The Inspector sighed, knowing that he was clutching at straws. He said again, 'Then why?'

David could see how deeply the Inspector blamed himself for Rahul's death from this willingness to listen to ideas alone.

He said, 'It really wasn't your fault, you know!'

'Only to the extent that I did not hold the pillow over his face.'

Both men sat quietly, lost in their own thoughts.

At last, David said, 'How about this for a hypothesis, whoever killed Mark thinks that we all suspect Rahul because you insisted we keep his alibi a secret. The murderer knows that there is only one real danger - that Rahul wakes up and insists on his innocence. There would be no reason for anyone to think that Rahul would hide a perfectly good alibi unless they knew he was gay.'

The Inspector nodded, slowly beginning to see where the lawyer was going, 'So he kills Rahul. Now Rahul can't wake up and plead not guilty.'

David said, 'Only the murderer would think that the measure of doubt left by Rahul's death was better than the certainty of being found out.'

They both nodded in unison. It was guesswork on their part but fit neatly with the facts at their disposal.

The Inspector said, 'Unfortunately we are no closer to knowing who killed Mark, and now Rahul.'

-twenty two-

'Words spoken and published which impute unchastity or adultery to any woman or girl shall not require special damage to render them actionable.'
Section 4, Defamation Act, Chapter 75

Annie had stayed in her room after Julian had left her. She was still coming to terms with Rahul's death. She had known it was a possibility of course. He had been in a coma after all. And surely it was better to die than to have persisted in a vegetative state? She knew in her head that this was true. But her heart was heavy with loss. Annie could not fathom choosing suicide as an option. Blessed with a practical outlook and a general optimism, she usually felt able to see beyond the immediate - to believe that things would look up around the next corner. The current crisis was testing her sorely. But she believed that it would end. The murderer would be found. A knock on the door interrupted her fruitless musings. She hoped it would be David so that by word or action she could show him that, whatever he imagined was going on between her and Julian, he was mistaken. But it was not David who walked in but her secretary.

Annie looked at Ching in surprise. It was not the habit of this woman to knock. She usually drifted in as of right, bearing messages or documents, tidying shelves or putting away files. Ching came further into the room and then stopped, equidistant between Annie and the exit, as if she wanted to consider her options again before passing the point of no return. Annie felt a surge of impatience. She needed her privacy to grieve for Rahul without this theatrical interruption.

'What do you want?' It came out more harshly than Annie had intended. She asked, in a more conciliatory tone, 'Is anything the matter?'

The woman made up her mind and took another step forward. This generated unexpected momentum, and she rushed forward saying breathlessly, 'I did not realise it was personal or I would not have read it!'

'What are you talking about?'

'I thought it might be important.'

Annie said through gritted teeth, 'Ching, just tell me what you are talking about.'

She said, 'I was in the print room, looking for something I had printed for you...I was looking through this stack of papers and I found it. I read it before I saw it was personal.'

Annie said, 'Alright, you accidentally read something private but important in the printer room. What has this to do with me?'

Ching looked uncomfortable. 'You are helping the police ...,' she trailed off uncertainly.

Annie gave up any hope of getting to the root of the matter without invading the privacy of the author of this mysterious note.

She said firmly, 'What did it say?'

Her secretary took a piece of paper from the file she was carrying.

'You took it?' exclaimed Annie.

'Photocopy!'

Annie held out her hand and her secretary handed her the single sheet of paper and then stepped back from the desk hurriedly.

'I will leave it with you,' she said and almost ran from the room.

Annie looked down at the letter and began to read. She grew pale. Her hand went to her mouth. Annie read and then re-read the missive. She understood why her secretary had been so anxious to divest herself of the letter.

•

The Inspector's phone beeped twice. He read the text message, and then looked across at David, 'Stephen says he has something important to tell me, I am to meet him at my office.'

David asked, 'Any guesses what it's about?'

'Maybe he's coming to confess!'

The two men laughed as a phone rang again. It was David's.

He reached in his pocket and flipped it open, 'David Sheringham.'

'David, this is Annie, I need to see you.'

'Of course, what is it?'

'I can't tell you over the phone.'

David bit off the urge to persuade her otherwise, 'Shall I come back to the office?'

She thought a moment, 'No, meet me at home.'

'I'm at the hospital. I'll meet you there in half an hour.

Annie grabbed her briefcase and went to her secretary's desk, 'Ching, I want you to listen very carefully to what I have to say.'

The woman nodded nervously.

'I want you to forget the letter you gave me, I do not want you to mention it to a living soul, do you understand?'

Again, Ching nodded.

Annie carried on, 'I am going out now. I won't be back today.'

Ching screwed up the courage to ask, 'Are you going to do anything about it? You know, the letter.'

'Yes, I am going to see David now, to discuss the matter.'

Julian, coming round the corner, heard the last sentence. It was as if the blood in his veins ceased to flow for a second.

He said, 'Annie!'

'Not now, Julian. I'm in a rush. We'll talk about things tomorrow.'

He grabbed her arm as she rushed past him, 'But where are you going?'

She wrenched her arm free and set off again, calling over her shoulder, 'Home!'

Julian stared after her and then said to Annie's secretary, 'I thought she was going to see David Sheringham?'

'I guess she's seeing him at her house…'

Julian set off back to his office, grabbed his car keys and headed for the exit.

•

Stephen drove with a steady concentration that belied the turmoil in his mind. He had set up a meeting with the Inspector but he still did not know what he was going to say to him. He knew that he had to reveal Sarah Thompson as the author of the anonymous notes sent to Mark, accusing his second wife of being a prostitute, amongst other things. The police believed that Rahul had committed the murder. Perhaps they would not be too hard on Sarah for her ill-considered actions. He also hoped to be able to minimise the role of his own wife in the debacle, although he was not certain how he was going to do it. But he knew that, despite his misgivings, he had to come clean on the provenance of the letters. Stephen had never considered himself a particularly principled man. Life for him had not been sufficiently challenging to test his integrity. Although he had always been a man of his word and conducted his practice with honesty, the reality was that there had been nothing to tempt him from the straight and narrow. He drew some small comfort from the knowledge that, despite the inevitable backlash, he had not considered withholding information from the police.

•

David stood on a pavement along Orchard Road. His hairline and upper lip were beaded with sweat. He had loosened his tie but it had not made him feel any cooler. There was not a breath of wind. Shimmering waves of heat reflected off the tarmac. The stench of petrol fumes from the phalanx of vehicles inching forward on the road in front of him assailed his nostrils. He could feel his damp shirt clinging to his back. He saw another blue Comfort taxi and flagged it down authoritatively. The driver ignored him from the comfort of his air-conditioned interior. As he went past, David saw that he had a passenger sitting comfortably in the back. He scowled at the be-suited man. David tried to get a grip on his temper. He had not been aware when he had spoken to Annie that it was rush hour. The Inspector had left for the station in his car fifteen minutes before. David's mobile phone had run out of juice while he was on hold for a taxi. Now he was trying to flag one down by the road. He regretted not forcing Annie to tell him what was bothering her. She had sounded worried. His mind was playing tricks on him, imbuing her few quick words with hidden meaning. Was she in trouble? He tried to flag down another passenger-filled taxi.

•

Annie arrived home and sat in her car in the driveway.

Everything appeared so normal. The house gleamed white in the evening sun, the windows picked out in black. The cat was asleep on the veranda table, so relaxed he looked like a furry black and white rug. She looked at the briefcase next to her and the dangerous secret it contained. Was it enough to kill for? She glanced at her watch. She would mix herself a very stiff drink and wait for David. She heard a car pull up on the main road outside. David was early. Well, she would mix a drink for both of them.

•

Stephen stood looking at the various awards and certificates that adorned the Inspector's office walls, everything from sharp shooting to 'Completing the annual police fitness programme', and then at the books that lined a single shelf. They were an eclectic collection - criminal psychology, hostage rescue, gun manuals, theories of crime and punishment. The Inspector waited patiently. Stephen had asked to see him and now, having declined a seat, appeared to have arranged the appointment purely for the privilege of browsing through the policeman's bookshelf. Inspector Singh had been in this position may times before and recognised the sideshow for what it was. He knew that any attempt to hurry the bearer of information would only risk a change of heart. And anything that could cause a man of Stephen's experience and confidence to take down a book entitled, 'M16 v. AK47 - The Final Showdown' and flick through the pages with feigned interest, was worth hearing.

Stephen looked up from the book and said, 'I have a confession to make, I'm afraid.'

•

David was now queuing for a taxi in front of the Takashimaya department store. There was a long line of tired shoppers, weighed down with their purchases, ahead of him. Mothers looked harassed, teenagers indifferent and businessmen impatient with the long wait ahead of them. David made up his mind. He jogged up to the head of the queue, ran round to the back door of the waiting taxi and yanked it open. The young couple about to clamber into the taxi, looked at him in disbelief.

David said, 'I need this taxi. It's an emergency!'

The young man started to protest but David cut him off, 'I'm really sorry, you know. I hope you get another taxi.'

He jumped into the taxi and eyeballed the white shirted, sweating driver.

'Move!' he barked and the man, with much nervous grinding of gears, did so.

David looked out the rear window and saw the woman haranguing the man for not putting up a better defence of their taxi. He leaned back against the faux leather seat and let a cold blast of air-conditioning calm him down.

-twenty three-

'Whoever does any act with such intention or knowledge and under such circumstances that if he by that act caused death he would be guilty of murder, shall be punished with imprisonment for a term which may extend to 10 years, and shall also be liable to fine; and if hurt is caused to any person by such act, the offender shall be liable either to imprisonment for life, or to such punishment as is hereinbefore mentioned and shall also be liable to caning.'
Section 307, Penal Code, Chapter 224

    Annie unlocked her front door, mixed two stiff gins and tonic and walked back out, carrying the drinks carefully. She expected to see David and was astonished to see Julian standing on the veranda. She exclaimed and spilt some of the drink over her hand.

    She glared at him, setting down the drinks and licking her fingers, 'Jesus, Julian. What are you doing here?'

    He would not meet her eye but instead settled on a careful perusal of the middle distance.

    'Julian, now is not a good time.'

    He said in a pleading tone, 'I must talk to you!'

Annie's hot temper was getting the better of her. Irritation that he had followed her home was replaced by anger.

'Look. I said we would talk tomorrow. Now is not a good time. I'm expecting someone.'

'I know you are,' Julian said evenly.

'Well, if you do, I have no idea what you're doing here.'

Julian seemed to have a change of heart, or at least a change of tactics.

'Annie, I just need fifteen minutes ... please!'

She looked at him and at her watch, 'OK, you can have ten minutes.'

And not wanting David to find her with Julian again, she said, 'Let's go for a walk.'

They set out together, drinks left untouched. Annie, from habit, set a purposeful pace and headed in the direction of the cemetery.

As they entered the massive wrought iron gates, Annie, trying to keep the impatience out of her voice, said, 'OK, what did you want to say?'

Julian picked his way through the overgrown paths and sat down on a large squat gargoyle, covered in lichen and moss, guarding an ornate, tiled semi-circular grave. It glowed orange and green in the half-light. Annie remained standing, looking down at him, her arms folded. A statue of a young goddess looked up at her curiously.

He said, 'About the insider dealing ...,' and stopped.

'What about it?'

He looked miserable and Annie could not help but feel sorry for him.

She asked more gently, 'Did you do it?'

He nodded.

'But Julian, why?'

He grew sullen, kicking at a tuft of grass.

She said again, 'You have to tell me why.'

'It was so easy; there was so much money to be made.

It was madness, I guess. One day I picked up the phone and told my broker to buy some shares, not many. I sold them the next day and cleared ten thousand dollars. After that... after that, I was hooked. The amounts were larger. I grew careless.'

'It was just greed?'

He smiled at her wryly, 'Were you hoping to hear that I needed the money urgently for some life-saving operation for my mother - some reason you could rationalise? Sorry, I just wanted the money.'

'But it was illegal, criminal!'

The silence was punctuated by the low repetitive call of the nightjar. Bats, quick black shadows, flitted back and forth chasing unseen insects. Something brushed against Annie's cheek, a rush of velvet. She started, and then saw that it was an early owl.

She asked in a quiet voice, 'Why are you telling me this?'

'To ask you, no...to beg you not to say anything.'

It was Annie's turn not to be able to meet his eyes. She looked up into the trees and saw a pair of pale yellow eyes glaring at her - an owl, perhaps the one that had brushed past her a moment before.

Julian said, his voice cracking, 'You have to listen to me...it was different with the murder. This would have made me a prime suspect. But it was Rahul who killed Mark. I know this is bad...but I didn't kill anyone!'

Julian took her silence as evidence that she was wavering because he said, 'I'll do anything...give the money to charity. Or maybe,' he suggested diffidently, 'give you half...?'

Annie said in a voice vibrating with anger, 'How dare you try to bribe me? I thought you were appealing to our friendship. I have kept silent for these past few days...and now you try to pay me off. My God, Julian! Who are you?'

He shrank away from her anger, muttering, 'I'm sorry. We can't all inhabit the moral high ground. I thought you might need some spare cash, with your Dad and all. Look, I can't return the money. It doesn't belong to anyone. But I will give it away. It's not even in Singapore anymore.'

'What do you mean? Where is it?'

'I sent it to England that day I was late for the interview.'

'For God's sake, Julian. How suspicious is that?'

'Just please don't tell anyone.'

He stood up and grabbed her by both shoulders, looking into her eyes.

'Give me another chance!' he said pleadingly.

'Rahul did not kill Mark.'

Julian looked at her uncomprehendingly.

She repeated, 'Rahul had an alibi. He didn't kill Mark!'

Julian let his hands fall to his sides. He looked at her searchingly, 'My God, you think I did it!'

'I don't know what to think.'

'Annie, you can't believe I would kill a man?'

She said in an unconscious echo of his words, 'I can't believe that you did the insider dealing, but you did.' And when he did not say anything, she continued, 'I don't know what to think. It's a damn good motive.'

He sighed and walked over to the inscriptions on the gravestone. They were brief and to the point. Gold flaking paint giving the names and dates of birth of the patriarch and his two wives. He had been an old man when he died and both of his wives had pre-deceased him, one of them by a good fifty years. The intervening fifty years could not lessen the serene beauty of the woman who had died young. The black and white photograph of her embossed into the tiles testified to her eternal youth. Her husband had slicked back hair and a serious expression. He must have been no more than twenty-five when the photo was taken; he had died seventy years later. Annie watched him as Julian squatted down to look more closely at the images in the failing light.

She said, 'I don't know what to do.'

He got to his feet slowly and came over to her. He took both her hands in his and held them, bringing them up to the level of his chest. He looked into her eyes, the brown pools turned almost black as her pupils widened to catch the last light of the day.

He said almost conversationally, 'You have beautiful eyes.'

She tried to free her hands and turn away but his grip tightened.

'Let me go, you're hurting me.'

He continued to look at her, his pale eyes glistening in the encroaching darkness. She could feel his hands grow clammy, sweating from the contact of skin on skin in the humidity.

He said, 'I did not do it. I didn't kill him!'

Again, she tried to wrest her hands free. Julian grew angry, his body rigid.

'You think me capable of murder? What's to prevent me stopping you from ever telling?'

There was no mistaking his threat now.

Annie refused to be cowed. She met his gaze squarely and said scornfully, 'Don't be ridiculous, you're not going to hurt me.'

He ran a thumb over her hand and she felt the soft hair on her arms spring to attention like soldiers on a parade ground. For the first time, she felt a genuine flicker of fear. She tried to ignore it but when his grip tightened further, she could not prevent a small gasp of fright. She saw that it had emboldened him, empowered him to believe that he could hurt her - to protect himself, to protect his secret.

And then Julian whispered, 'I'm sorry Annie,' and let her go. As she made to turn away, the relief washing over her, he grabbed her again. One hand went over her mouth while the other arm went round her neck, yanking her head painfully back. Her back was to him, her body pressed up against him. Already, she could feel her lungs starting to tighten. She stamped on his foot with all her might, and as his grip loosened in shock, she bit the hand over her mouth as hard as she could. He released her mouth, exclaiming in pain and shock, but the arm round her neck tightened. She could scream now though and she did. She tried to control the rising tide of panic, knowing that the cemetery was deserted. Julian desperately tried to get his hand back over her mouth as she fought him furiously. Each struggle, each effort to pull free was further asphyxiating her against the arm around her throat. The blackness encroaching was not the onset of night but her vision starting to fade as she battled for air.

And then unexpectedly, blessedly - she was free. She fell to her knees, choking and retching, dragging painful gasps of air into her lungs. She turned to see where Julian was, poised to run despite the sharp ache in her chest. She saw that he was fighting her rescuer; a creature composed more of shadow than of substance. For a highly-strung moment, she wondered whether it was a figment of her imagination. Then she saw that it was a man. A man was fighting Julian. It did not take her long to realise that neither flight nor intervention was necessary. Julian was desperately lunging out, swinging wildly with both fists. But he was finding it impossible to make anything except chance contact, while his opponent's blows were landing with precision. There was a lull for a second. Julian stood swaying on his feet. Her rescuer hit him hard, fist to jaw, and Julian crumpled in a heap. It was David.

He came stumbling towards her saying, 'Annie! Are you alright?'

Annie scrambled to her feet, tears of relief wetting her face and walked into his arms. The figure lying on the ground behind them rolled over onto his back and groaned. David turned to look at Julian, shielding Annie with his body. She shook herself free. Julian tried to raise himself on an elbow but fell back to the ground.

•

Stephen had finally blurted out the sorry tale of the anonymous letters to the Inspector who had listened impassively through the whole narrative, betraying neither surprise nor indignation. Eventually, unnerved by the silent recipient of his confidences, Stephen had stopped talking. He looked at the Inspector expectantly.

The Inspector responded to the mute appeal by saying, 'Thank you for coming in to tell me this, Mr. Thwaites. We will look into it, of course.'

'Will there be any question of pressing charges? Against any of those involved?'

The Inspector smiled beatifically, 'It's too early to decide on that, Mr. Thwaites.'

And politely but purposefully ushered him out of the room.

•

In the end, all three of them returned to the house. All the fight had gone out of Julian. He limped back with Annie and David, visibly in pain from his bruises and a twisted ankle where he had fallen heavily. There was not much sympathy to be had and he did not expect any. He had started to apologise but Annie had shaken her head and he had fallen silent. There was tacit agreement between David and Annie that any explanations could wait until they were safely home. They trudged back and each heavy step beat out a question. Was Julian the murderer? How had David known where they were? Would she tell them about the insider dealing now? The questions spun round in her head like an out-of-control merry-go-round.

Her home came into view, a sight more welcome than ever before - windows glowing with a warm, yellow light. She saw that she had visitors. Even from a distance, she recognised the distinct outline of Inspector Singh. She supposed the slim shadow lurking behind him was Corporal Fong but could not see who the third person was. As she got closer, she saw that it was Stephen Thwaites.

She asked David in a hoarse voice, 'What are they all doing here? Did they come with you?'

She sensed rather than saw him shake his head.

He said, 'I came alone.'

As they stepped out of the darkness, Stephen leapt to his feet, 'What happened?'

His shock was understandable. Both Julian and David were muddy and dishevelled. Julian was by far the worst for wear - one of his eyes was almost shut, his bottom lip was split, there were cuts and bruises on his face and arms and he stood heavily on one leg, unable to put weight on the other. His defeated expression, eyes half shut, lips turned down, shoulders bowed, emphasised his physical state. David's shirt was torn and blood trickled slowly down his cheek from a cut above his eye. Annie did not know it but she presented the most telling evidence of an altercation. Her knees were muddied, she had a glorious bruise on one cheek and her eyes were large pools of shock and fright in a face from which all the blood had drained.

David put an arm firmly around her shoulders. 'Julian tried to kill Annie,' he said matter-of-factly.

There was no response from the man who stood accused. His silence rang like a confession. The Inspector, a fat man but light on his feet like a dancer, moved to whip out the handcuffs attached to his belt and deftly encircle Julian's wrists.

He said to Corporal Fong, 'Get him cleaned up, make sure the police doctor sees him, put him in a cell and then wait for me - I'll decide what we are charging him with later.'

They all watched Julian being led away. He got into the back seat of the car, Corporal Fong slipped in next to him and they drove away.

Stephen said, his bewilderment plain, 'I don't understand.'

David put up a hand to stop him. 'All explanations in a minute. Let us get cleaned up. I need a drink and then we'll talk.'

Stephen nodded his acquiescence and the Inspector said sheepishly, 'I'm afraid I drank one of the gins on the table.'

Annie managed a small smile, 'Go ahead and have the other,' she whispered, her throat sore from the choking, 'I'll get some more.'

They reconvened in twenty minutes. Annie had managed to have a hot shower. The steaming water beating down on her face and the gentle scent of lavender soap did much to soothe her troubled spirit. She dressed in a pair of shorts and t-shirt, tied back her damp hair and went to find David, whom she had directed to the spare room. He had showered and put on his trousers but was looking at his torn and muddy shirt with some reluctance when she walked in. She cleared her throat and he looked up from his disgusted contemplation of his shirt. He did not smile immediately but looked at her searchingly. He saw that there was some colour back in her cheeks and her hands and gaze were steady. He walked over to her and put out a hand to touch the bruised cheek. She looked at him for a moment, and then she kissed him on the cheek.

He said casually, 'I love you, you know.'

'I know,' she said and walked out of the room. He looked after her in exasperation.

The others were waiting for them in the living room. Annie fetched a six-pack of beer and the first aid box from the kitchen and then joined them. David appeared, wearing a t-shirt that was two sizes too small for him. He had been rummaging in the drawers. Annie handed him a beer. He took it gratefully and waved away the first aid box, making it clear that he thought the medicinal properties of alcohol were superior to any external ointment. Annie handed out the remaining drinks, and then curled up on the sofa.

'Where shall we begin?' David asked.

'Why don't you tell us what happened here, as I have a man in custody now,' said the Inspector, taking charge of proceedings.

Annie said, 'I came home from work. I had arranged to meet David here. Julian turned up a short while later.'

David cut in to say, 'I'm sorry I was late. I couldn't get a taxi.'

She turned back to the other two and continued her narrative, 'Anyway, Julian wanted to talk.'

She paused, knowing that there was going to be anger and disbelief that she had kept quiet about the insider dealing for so long. 'I should tell you that I had a call from a client in Malaysia a couple of days ago, accusing someone in the Singapore office of insider dealing.'

She noticed the Inspector and Stephen exchange a look but dismissed it. She felt David stiffen by her side.

'Tan Sri Ibrahim also told me that he had spoken to Mark the evening he died and told him of his suspicions.'

David almost yelled at her, 'Mark knew? But that could have been why he called the meeting!'

Annie nodded, 'I thought of that. I knew that you would all suspect Julian, and perhaps me, of the murder as well…so I didn't say anything at first.'

Stephen asked doubtfully, 'You were afraid of being accused of the murder?'

David said, biting off each word, 'Don't be naïve, Stephen. She was protecting Julian.'

Annie knew that his anger was motivated partly by fear of what might have happened to her.

She continued her tale, chin sticking out, 'Julian turned up here…I think he heard me arrange to meet David. He must have assumed I was going to let the cat out of the bag. He came here to persuade me not to tell.'

She paused, remembering the form the persuasion had taken in the end. David leaned over to give her a quick hug.

Annie smiled at him and said, 'We went for a walk to the old cemetery at the back,' she gestured in its general direction. 'Julian confessed that he had been insider dealing. He offered me half the money.' She still could not believe that he had so misjudged her as to try to bribe her. 'I was really angry, so I told him Rahul had an alibi.'

There was a disbelieving snort from David. She had to acknowledge that this had been a misjudgment.

Stephen interjected, the bewilderment in his tone matching the expression on his face, 'Rahul had an alibi?'

The Inspector said calmly, reminding everyone in the room that he was a police officer, 'Yes, he did, a young man was with him that evening. He preferred to lie about it at first for reasons we are all aware of.'

He continued, his tone deliberate, 'I decided to keep Rahul's innocence a secret, to see what the murderer might do if he thought we all believed Rahul had died a guilty man.'

Stephen subsided back into his armchair, his bushy brows forming a thick, black line that showed his displeasure at being lied to.

Annie took up her tale again, 'Julian attacked me and David turned up in the nick of time.'

Stephen asked, 'How did David know where you'd gone?'

David looked embarrassed. He said, 'I couldn't get a taxi. I was running late. I finally got one …we were coming up the road here when I saw Julian and Annie walking along. I got out and followed them. We got as far as the cemetery and I lost them. It was getting dark and the place is overgrown, full of trees and shadows. I wasn't sure what to do. I was just going to come back here when I heard Annie scream.'

The lines on his face deepened.

Annie was still puzzled, 'But why did you follow us?'

David blushed.

He cleared his throat, took a deep breath and confessed, 'I was worried about you. When I got here, I saw you wandering off with Julian. I thought that there was something between you. I decided to follow you and see for myself.'

Annie looked at his red face, mortified at having to confess to such juvenile behaviour, and started to laugh. Stephen's rumbling laughter and the Inspector's hearty guffaw joined in, all enjoying the discomfiture of this usually confident man. David glared at them but was forced to concede that the story had its funny side. He began to laugh too.

Stephen was the first to recover. 'I guess this means Julian killed Mark?'

They all looked at each other.

Annie said in a small voice, 'I don't think so.'

She could sense David beginning to grow angry again, assuming that she was protecting Julian despite what he had tried to do to her.

She continued, to pre-empt whatever he was going to say, 'He confessed to the insider dealing. But he was still insisting that he didn't kill Mark. He had nothing to lose in telling me the truth at that point. I don't think he did it.'

The Inspector nodded. 'It would be a convenient solution, but I'm not making that mistake again.'

David scowled but did not say anything. Annie hurriedly, albeit temporarily, changed the subject.

'But why are you two here anyway?'

The Inspector and Stephen exchanged a glance.

She said, 'You knew about the insider dealing.'

'Yes, we just found out. I was leaving the Inspector's office when I received a call from Tan Sri Ibrahim. He had only just heard that Mark had been murdered,' said Stephen.

Annie guessed that the Inspector had decided to confront her with the story first before turning his attention to the prime suspect, Julian.

'Why were you at the station?' she asked Stephen.

He said, 'The anonymous letters were from Sarah Thompson. She made up the allegations in the letters. I thought the Inspector needed to know that.'

David asked, 'But how did you find out? Did she tell you?'

Stephen shook his big, jowly head, 'Er…my wife found out.'

The Inspector said, 'It was just as well Stephen told me. We have placed Maria near the building on the evening of the murder. One of the C.C.T.V cameras caught a glimpse of her. I have to say, Maria is top of my list of suspects right now. After all, whether true or not, Mark was worried about the allegations. So her meal ticket *was* threatened.'

There was a pause while they all digested the information.

David said, 'If we could just place her at the hospital as well.'

Annie said, 'What do you mean?'

The Inspector rubbed a hand over his face.

Annie saw his expression and her eyes widened with horror. She whispered, 'Oh no!'

David said quietly, 'I'm so sorry. But we think Rahul was killed too.'

Annie stammered, 'B…but how…why?'

The Inspector answered her, 'Pillow over the face.'

A tear rolled down her cheek, stinging the bruise. She wiped it away with the back of her hand.

Stephen said, 'I need another drink.'

Annie rose to her feet dutifully and fetched him a neat whisky. She put the coffee machine on to make some coffee for the rest of them and rejoined the group in the living room. As she walked in, she caught sight of her briefcase and exclaimed in shock.

They all turned round and the Inspector snapped,

'What is it?'

Annie could not believe she had forgotten the letter. There had been so much going on, so much unpleasantness to divulge and digest, it had gone clean out of her mind. And now she stood staring at her bag as if it were a spitting cobra. With trembling fingers, she reached for the bag, opened the clasp and slipped the photocopy out. She handed it to David without another word.

He read it and grew still. He said, 'How did you get this?'

Stephen interrupted impatiently, 'What is it, for God's sake?'

David handed the paper to the Inspector and Stephen crowded round him to see its contents. The Inspector nodded his head; many things were clearer now.

Stephen said, 'I don't believe it,' but his tone suggested he believed it all too well.

David asked again, 'Where did you get it?'

They all turned to Annie and she said in a small voice, 'My secretary found it at the printer. She made a copy and gave it to me.' She looked at their shocked faces and said, 'I asked David to meet me here to tell him. I told my secretary to keep her mouth shut. But so much happened that…that I forgot I had it!'

The Inspector turned his attention back to the letter again and read it aloud. It was headed 'Resignation Letter' and addressed to the 'Partners, Singapore Office'. It read, 'I hereby tender my resignation from the partnership of Hutchinson & Rice with immediate effect. Before I go, I would like to inform the remaining partners of an episode of which I am deeply ashamed. Approximately six months ago, my elevation to the partnership was under consideration. I had understood from office rumours that Reggie Peters was the fiercest opponent of my promotion. I decided to confront him to ask him about his opposition, as I did not understand its roots. He told me that he did not feel I was a lawyer of sufficient quality to join the partnership. Perhaps he was right.

In any event, he said it was within my power to change his mind. I asked him what he meant and he made it clear that he would support my partnership application in exchange for sexual favours. I am ashamed to admit that I agreed to his terms and we commenced a sexual relationship. In due course, I was elevated to the partnership with his support. I tried to end the relationship thereafter but he refused saying that he would reveal what had happened if I did. He insisted that I would come out of it with my reputation severely damaged but he was senior enough and rich enough to weather the storm. I was concerned that he was right.

Subsequently Mark was killed and I wondered whether Mark had somehow found out about us and Reggie had killed him to keep our secret. I was also very afraid that that motive applied to me as well. It seems now that Rahul Gandhi murdered Mark; I am not sure why. I need no longer fear being accused of murder. I find that my reputation and career mean less to me now than when I agreed to Reggie Peters' terms. I plan to leave practice. I believe it is important that he be prevented from abusing his position again, if indeed this is the first time.
Yours Sincerely,
Lim Ai Leen'

Stephen asked, 'It's addressed to the partners, why hasn't she delivered it?'
David said, 'Perhaps she changed her mind.'
Annie added, 'She won't know we have a copy. My secretary put the original back as she found it.'
Inspector Singh nodded his head approvingly at this cunning.
He said, 'Do these allegations sound plausible?'
The other three considered his question.

Annie was the first to slowly nod. 'I believe it,' she said.

Stephen too wagged his head in agreement. 'I do too, I'm afraid.'

They turned to David. He said slowly, 'I don't know these people as well as you do, but it does fit with some of the outstanding peculiarities of this case.' He ticked them off one by one on his fingers, 'Their original animosity, Reggie changing his mind about her partnership, their sudden 'friendship', the united front they were trying to put up, both had the same secret to keep after all. Ai Leen must have been extremely afraid after the murder.'

Stephen said, 'What a sorry mess!'

Annie knew what he meant. She could not understand Ai Leen's decision to agree to Reggie's terms. She was less surprised that Reggie had proposed them. She could not help feeling sullied, tainted by their sordid agreement. But at the same time, she felt extremely sorry for Ai Leen - that she had wanted something so badly and then discovered after she had paid the price that it was not worth the asking. How had she lived this past fortnight believing Reggie to be the murderer? Her relief that it was Rahul must have been intense. At least she was not holding a secret that someone else was prepared to kill to preserve. But she had been wrong. Rahul had an alibi. Did that make Reggie the killer? She uttered this last thought out loud.

The Inspector said, 'There are loose ends. How would Mark Thompson have found out about the two of them?'

Stephen said, 'He could have seen them together, overheard them…we might never know exactly. My money is on Reggie…he's a complete bastard.'

David was thoughtful, 'No disagreement there…but I would have thought a coward also.'

Inspector Singh looked at him sharply but said nothing.

Annie exclaimed in frustration, 'But there isn't any proof!'

They all turned with one mind to look at the Inspector, the final arbiter on whether it was possible to arrest Reggie.

He shook his head, 'No, there is a motive...but nothing to place him at the scene...either scene! I don't even have enough for an arrest, let alone a prosecution.'

Stephen who had stood up to stretch during this latest conversation kicked at a chair in frustration. Annie started to chew on her fingernail.

It was not long before everyone set off for their respective beds, looking weary but optimistic. David was the last to leave, raising one of his eyebrows questioningly at Annie. She had understood that he was asking if she wanted him to stay. She had been tempted. But in the end, she had shaken her head mutely in refusal. It had been a few days of such extremes - she had run the entire gamut of human emotion, from a deep unhappiness to joy, from black fear to tearful relief. She needed the time alone to come to terms with the events of the day - to measure the effect and impact of each action and reaction. David had understood. In any event, he had not tried to change her mind but walked out into the night with a firm stride, not looking back.

She walked into the house and looked at the detritus of their impromptu session on how to catch a murderer. A half empty wine bottle; a wine glass that had been knocked over; a few cans of beer and a couple of bowls, crumbs and a smattering of salt all that was left of the pistachios and cashews she had put out. An ashtray was full to brimming, the last fag end still smoking - a thin line of white smoke, like a fine pencil drawing, curling towards the ceiling. The Inspector must have smoked half a pack at least, she decided. She stubbed out the cigarette carefully, grimacing in distaste at the dampness round the butt end. She looked again at the mess and wondered whether to have a go at cleaning it up.

If she did nothing, the room was going to smell like a cheap pub in the morning. The odour of rancid smoke would have been absorbed into the very fabric of the curtains and the overturned wine would leave its distinctive sour smell on the carpet.

She decided on the whole, she did not have the strength. Her body was aching. Her exertions to escape from Julian had strained every muscle. Her throat felt sore. Her head was starting to throb as well - a belated reaction to the evening's events. She still could not believe what had happened. She could find no excuse for Julian's attack on her. She had to assume that it had been unpremeditated and brought on by a combination of panic and despair. But it was impossible to take in the enormity of what had happened. Julian had tried to kill her. There was no way around that. At least, finally, there was an end in sight. A third candidate had put himself firmly in the frame. Annie was delighted that the spotlight was now firmly on Reggie, warts and all. Her guilt over Rahul and worry over Julian had relaxed into relief that the culprit was the most expendable member of the firm. Any residue of concern she might have felt over him as an individual and a colleague had been dissipated by his treatment of Ai Leen. It was true that Ai Leen had agreed to his bargain. But ultimate responsibility lay with him. He was the person with the power, the partner waving temptation in the face of someone that had worked hard towards her life's ambition and was about to see it thwarted. Ai Leen's future had fallen into the hands of a man without moral fibre and without conscience. It would be difficult to feel sorry for Reggie if he were apprehended for murder.

-twenty four-

'Whoever intentionally puts any person in fear of any injury to that person or to any other, and thereby dishonestly induces the person so put in fear to deliver to any person any property or valuable security, or anything signed or sealed which may be converted into a valuable security, commits extortion.'
Section 383, Penal Code, Chapter 224

The following morning, Inspector Singh was up bright and early. He trimmed his beard, clipped his moustache with a small pair of nail scissors, brushed his teeth and sat himself down at the breakfast table. His wife placed a large stack of toast and a mug of sweet, milky coffee at his elbow. He said a polite 'thank you' that caused her to look at him curiously. Manners at the breakfast table were out of character. She did not join him for breakfast but instead returned to the kitchen and could be heard pottering away while issuing curt instructions to the maid. The morning paper had been delivered and he read it with interest, apparently absorbed in the reporting. The Inspector was in a good mood. He nodded with approval over an article quoting a Minister as saying that the Government would continue to be tough on crime. He smiled broadly when reading the only moderately humourous funnies. If his wife had noticed his good humour, she would have said tartly that there was a first time for everything. The Inspector was notoriously not a morning person and his wife had learnt over the years to avoid him until his morning dose of sugar and caffeine had reconciled him to a new day.

Inspector Singh's cheer was derived from a single source. He felt in his gut, and it was an ample gut whose instinct he had learnt to trust over the years, that this case was coming to a close. He would be glad to see the back of it. As a man who guarded his independence jealously and employed his own methods to achieve results, he had not enjoyed the constant scrutiny of the press and his superiors.

He pushed back his chair and manoeuvered his girth out from under the dining table. His car and driver were already waiting outside. He shouted a cheerful goodbye to his wife and made his way out of the house. He slipped on his white trainers, still without blemish, and headed jauntily towards his car.

The young policewoman assigned to drive him that week said to him as he wedged himself into the backseat, 'To the office, sir?'

He shook his big head in response to the inquiring gaze in the rearview mirror. 'Oh no!' he said, 'we have other fish to fry this morning.'

•

Annie was surprised to find the sun shining in through the windows. She must have forgotten to turn on the alarm clock the previous night. She turned over to look at the time and groaned. Her body felt stiff and bruised. Her cheek and throat throbbed. It was already ten. She was well and truly late for work. But should she go in at all? She lay back in bed and wondered whether she would be expected or not.

And more importantly, whether she could face being at the office. The impossibility of answering questions about Julian's whereabouts or coming face to face with Reggie indicated that she would be best off at home. On the other hand, she wanted to find out what was to happen next, to discuss matters with David and Stephen. She would feel isolated at home, out of the loop. She eased herself out of bed and headed for the bathroom still debating the question.

One look in the mirror decided the matter for her immediately. The bruise on her cheek had developed into a thing of beauty, ranging in colour from purple to yellow, puffy and swollen in parts. There was no way she was going into the office. She shuddered at the thought of the cross-examination she would face from her secretary, a woman whose persistence and curiosity she had learnt to dread.

•

Julian lay on a thin mattress on a metal bed frame. He was alone. He was surrounded on three sides by white walls, on the fourth, by iron bars. There was a window on one wall, high and barred. A door fitted seamlessly into the iron bars. There was a toilet in a corner and a stack of loo paper by the side of it. Julian had not availed himself of the amenities. The humiliation and lack of privacy weighed heavily on him. He still wore the torn and muddied clothes he had been arrested in the previous evening but a sticking plaster over one brow indicated that he had received medical attention.

He had declined a phone call and legal representation for the time being. He was acutely aware that the person to whom he would have turned in this crisis, was the same one he had tried to kill the previous night, Annie. She believed he had killed Mark. She would have told her story to the police by now. There were no longer any restraints of loyalty to prevent her. He would be branded a murderer. He thought about his catalogue of sins in which insider dealing and attempted murder featured prominently. What did it matter if he was hanged for a sheep as a lamb? Julian understood now how Rahul had come to the decision to kill himself. To escape this pit of black despair - death would be a mercy and a relief. There were no means at hand. He had read that it was possible to fashion a rope out of the limited bedding and hang himself from the ceiling. He knew that such feats were beyond him. He would have to see this out.

•

The unmarked police car bearing Inspector Singh pulled up outside the Thompson apartment complex. His timing was perfect. Maria and the children were walking out of the building. They were carrying rucksacks and wearing caps. She had the children by the hand. Both were chattering away excitedly. It was a scene to delight the heart; a mother taking her kids to the zoo. Inspector Singh rolled down the darkened window and leaned his turbaned head out. She glared at him and turned to walk away.

He said, 'Maria, as it happens, there is something you can do for me.'

•

Ai Leen was at home alone. Her husband had gone to work. She had stayed in bed pleading a headache. He had been his usual considerate self, fetching her some painkillers, making her a cup of hot chocolate and extracting a promise that if she did not feel better in a few hours, she would go to see a doctor but on no account go to work. She watched him dress and leave from deep under the covers and managed not to flinch when he kissed her goodbye. She lay back in bed and stared at the ceiling, unknowingly adopting Julian's posture in a jail cell across town. She felt trapped, unable to decide what to do. Unlike Julian however, her thoughts were not on suicide. Intimidated by Reggie the previous day, she had temporarily given up her plan of sending her resignation letter, with its incendiary details, to the partnership. But she knew she would come about, she was just not sure how. She gripped the bedclothes tightly and repeated the last thought to herself. She would fight for a fresh start.

•

Stephen was not surprised that a number of his lawyers were missing that morning. Annie had left a brief message on his phone explaining that she would not be in and asking him to call her if there were any 'developments'. Ai Leen had not put in an appearance either and her secretary had emailed him to say that she had called in sick. He had not seen Reggie that morning. That was a relief. He was not sure whether he would be able to refrain from letting on what he knew. The Inspector had been emphatic however that no one was to alert Reggie to the fact that he was now chief suspect. Julian languished in jail. Stephen had tried to call the Inspector to find out if Julian had been charged and whether Stephen could see him. He might have tried to murder one of his colleagues but Stephen still had a responsibility for him as head of the office. The Inspector had not yet arrived at work.

There was also Rahul's funeral to arrange. That job too had fallen to him. Rahul's family had been too shell-shocked to do anymore than acquiesce to his various practical suggestions. They were still reeling from the shock of discovering that their only son was gay. The possibility that he might also be a murderer and was now dead could not compete with the humiliation of being the parents of a homosexual man. Rahul might have been a member of the young Bombay elite, a modern, liberal young man comfortable in all the capital cities of the world. But his parents were of an older generation. His mother was in despair, regretting that she had not found him a bride earlier. There had been no shortage of prospects among the circle of young women whose mothers had frequently hinted that they would welcome an alliance with the wealthy lawyer from a good family. She believed he might not have become gay then. His father was not so sanguine about marriage as a cure for homosexuality but was overwhelmed by the shame of the discovery.

Stephen realised that he missed Mark. Together, they had always weathered whatever challenges had faced the office. Now on his own, his colleagues having abandoned any sense of collective purpose to pursue their own interests, he realised for the first time that he truly missed him.

David walked in through the open door. He said, 'Got a minute?'

Stephen nodded, firmly pushing away his melancholy thoughts. He said, 'What's up?'

David gave a quick shake of the head. 'Nothing new. Thought it might be worthwhile having a chat.' He smiled disarmingly, 'To be frank, I'm completely at a loose end. I've no idea where we go from here, don't know where Reggie is, can't get the Inspector on the phone…and Annie hasn't come in.'

Stephen responded to the specific points. 'I can't get the Inspector either. Annie called in sick.'

David nodded, 'Yes, I spoke to her. Apparently, the bruise on her cheek has come up beautifully and she didn't feel up to answering well-meaning questions.'

Stephen looked enquiringly at David's rainbow-hued visage.

David said cheerfully, 'Me? I slipped in the shower!'

•

Reggie Peters walked out of the meeting he had been chairing at the client's offices. It had lasted a couple of hours and achieved nothing, the various lenders and the insolvent

Indonesian company unable to do more than trade insults. Reggie was philosophical. He charged by the hour and this particular debt restructuring had been a real cash cow so far. Eventually, it would dawn on the banks that their various bits of security were worthless. It had always been window dressing anyway. The banks had lent money on the basis that the company owners were golf playing buddies of ex-President Suharto. They had hoped to be subsidiary beneficiaries of his patronage. Now the old man was pleading dementia to avoid facing trial for corruption while languishing under house arrest in Jakarta. His friends were no longer able to raise cheap loans from state banks to invest in some new monopolistic venture. There was basically no money to be had - except to pay the lawyers. Reggie demanded a hefty deposit towards his fees and that his bills be settled monthly. He smiled ironically. The firm was making as much money from this venture as they had done structuring the loans in the first place. Sometimes it felt good to be a lawyer.

Reggie switched on his mobile and it beeped urgently indicating missed calls. There were three, all from the same number, one that he did not recognise. He was on the verge of returning the calls and then thought better of it. It could wait till he was back at the office. He stepped out of the building. Immediately beads of sweat popped out along his upper lip and his shirt started to cling to his back. He dabbed a handkerchief on his brow and squinted at the sun. It was almost lunchtime and he was only a couple of blocks from Raffles Tower. He decided to walk. He had not gone five hundred yards before he was starting to regret his decision. Reggie was not a fit man and he was starting to turn a mottled red, the colour of cooked lobster. His fine sandy hair was damp against his scalp, the creeping baldness more noticeable. He had worn a suit to the meeting and although he had loosened his tie and was carrying the jacket, the scratchy wool made his legs and crotch itch.

Reggie wondered whether to duck into a nearby Starbuck's to give himself some respite. His phone ringing pre-empted the decision. Reggie ducked into the air-conditioned lobby of the nearest building and recovered his phone from the inside pocket of his jacket. He saw at a glance that it was the same person who had been trying to reach him earlier. He answered the call.

•

David was still in Stephen's office. They had started to discuss possible tactics in earnest but without success. It was impossible to know what to do. Should they reveal to Ai Leen that they knew about the draft resignation letter? Should they confront Reggie with their suspicions? Julian was another problem. David reluctantly agreed that, in the cold light of day, he was struggling to see Julian in the role of Mark's killer. But his attack on Annie had been unforgivable. He was not inclined to Stephen's view that it had been a result of the extreme pressure Julian was under. The men had almost lost their tempers over the issue. Stephen was inclined to plead leniency with the Inspector, urge Annie to refrain from pressing charges, sack Julian and put him on a plane out of the country. David was adamant that Julian should not get away scot-free. Rahul too was a problem. Until they could finger Reggie, the firm and the world at large still believed that he was the killer of Mark, and not the second victim of a murderer still at large. They owed it to Rahul to clear his name.

The two men fell silent, one staring down at his desk, the other standing and looking out of the window.

Stephen thumped the table hard with the flat of his hand, 'I can't believe we're stuck here doing nothing!' he exclaimed.

David said, 'I'll try the Inspector again,' and reached for his phone.

Stephen said, 'Use this one,' gesturing at the phone

on his desk. 'If you do get him, at least you'll be able to put him on the speaker.'

David slipped his phone into his pocket and returned to the desk. He dialed the number from memory and hit the speaker button. They both listened to the sound of the phone ringing, two quick tones followed by a brief interval and then the two tones again. Just as Stephen leaned over to terminate the call, the gruff voice of the Inspector was audible.

'Inspector Singh,' he uttered in peremptory tones.

Stephen nodded to David who said, 'Inspector, David Sheringham here. With Stephen Thwaites. We've been trying to reach you this morning.'

The Inspector said with a cackle, 'Well, well! You know I'm a very busy man.'

Stephen rolled his eyes at David but said in his polite booming tones, 'Of course, Inspector. We were just anxious to know the best way to proceed to get to the bottom of this matter.'

Again, the policeman cackled like an old witch, and said, 'Nothing for you to worry about. It's all under control.'

David asked cautiously, 'What do you mean, Inspector?'

His response was evasive. He said, 'What is that expression you use, it's not over till the fat lady sings? Well, the fat lady sings tonight.'

Stephen said, 'But Inspector, what…' The monotonous tone of a phone gone dead was audible through the room.

The Inspector had hung up.

•

Ai Leen had finally dragged herself out of bed, showered and dressed and was now curled up in the sitting room armchair watching a rerun of a chat show on daytime television. It was a dire episode involving the heart-wrenching story of some woman whose feet were so big she could not buy shoes to fit off the rack. The host had tracked down a female basketball player who had just, amidst what appeared to Ai Leen to be unwarranted fanfare, agreed to hand over her old shoes to Bigfoot. Women in the audience clapped enthusiastically and one or two of them were wiping away tears. Ai Leen shook her head. What was the matter with these people?

She realised once again, as if she had needed reminding, that to work was as essential to her as breathing. She could not conceive of a life where she did not have an office to go to and work to lose herself in. It was just as well she had not committed herself to leaving the firm by delivering her resignation letter. There would be other solutions. Another burst of applause greeted the decision of the basketball player to recommend the name of her cobbler to Bigfoot. Ai Leen decided to make herself a cup of coffee and read the newspapers on the Internet instead.

A loud frantic knocking on the front door interrupted her progress to the kitchen. Ai Leen hurried to the entrance wondering who was making such a racket. Probably a meter reader, she thought with irritation. Opening the heavy door a fraction, she saw that it was Reggie. She immediately tried to slam it shut again, but he was too quick. A broad foot wedged the door open and despite her putting her weight into it, he managed to get his shoulder and then his body into the apartment. She fell back, her hand instinctively groping for something to fend him off with. There was nothing that could be used as a weapon. Her hand closed round a bunch of keys.

She said, her voice a scream, 'What do you want? Get out, get out, I tell you!'

Reggie was breathing heavily and his eyes were bloodshot. He put a hand on the door to support himself. She could smell him, dried sweat and the scent of fear.

She repeated, 'What do you want?'

He said, 'I got a call…from Maria,' and trailed off.

He looked at her almost pleadingly.

Ai Leen's body was stiff with tension but she said in a puzzled tone, 'Maria? What did she want?'

'She said that she saw me that night.'

'What night?'

'The night of the murder. She was there…at the office with Mark. She says she saw me there!'

Ai Leen said, 'I don't understand.'

The only sound was Reggie's wheezing, rasping breath. Ai Leen remembered that Reggie was asthmatic.

Reggie said again, enunciating his words, 'Maria claims to have seen me at the office, on the night of the murder. She wants money… or she will go to the police.' He continued almost pleadingly, 'But I wasn't there!'

Ai Leen ignored this latter part as irrelevant and said, 'If she admits to being there, surely that makes her a suspect? She can't go to the police with a story like that. Anyway, it's not my problem.'

Reggie put a hand over his eyes. He looked up at her again and his eyes were full of fear.

He said, 'She knows about us.'

Ai Leen said in a small voice, 'But what about Rahul? The police think Rahul did it.'

Reggie said, 'They won't still think it if they hear her story.'

'How much does she want?'

'A million U.S dollars.'

'When?'

'Tonight.'

A burst of applause from the television in the next room greeted this announcement. Ai Leen released her grip on the keys and said almost to herself, 'That's a lot of shoes.' Reggie was too defeated to question her about her remark.

•

David slipped behind the wheel of the Mercedes

Benz he had just had delivered by a car hire firm to the office. His experience trying to get a taxi the previous day had made him determined not to risk a repeat performance. He had pitched in with a couple of hours of work after his unsatisfactory meeting with Stephen and then given up. The office was short-staffed at present, but he had lost the ability to concentrate. He had called Annie, a little tentatively. But she had been delighted by his suggestion that he drop by and see how she was getting on.

He drove at a moderate pace, getting accustomed to the new car. Despite this, in no time at all he was pulling into the driveway of her home. He leapt out of the car energetically and made his way towards the veranda, noticing as he got there that Annie was lying in her easy chair. He sauntered towards her, amused at her stillness. She was snatching forty winks and had not yet registered his arrival. Suddenly, a cold fist gripped his heart. Was she asleep? He hurried towards her, calling her name. Annie stirred and put up a hand to shade against the sun. A large cat that had been asleep on her stomach, jumped off and stalked away angrily. David stopped running. The tide that had washed his fears away seemed to have taken the bones in his legs with them. Annie raised herself on one elbow and beckoned to him and he walked over slowly.

She asked sleepily, 'What were you yelling about?'

He made a small negative gesture with his head. She put out a hand to him and he pulled her to his feet and gave her a quick hug.

'Tea?' she asked.

David nodded. Annie made two steaming cups of tea and they settled down to sip them. David told Annie about the Inspector's cryptic remarks and they both puzzled over it without success.

She said, 'I get quite nervous wondering what mad plan he has up his sleeve.'

David agreed, 'The fat bastard is capable of anything.

All I can say is that I wouldn't like to be in Reggie's position.'

'Well, as you're unlikely to kill anyone, that seems unlikely.'

Both their thoughts independently and immediately turned to Julian. Whether either would have felt compelled to mention him was not put to the test. This time it was David whose phone rang. He fished the small electronic device out of his pocket and looked at the number blankly. Although he did not know it, it was the same number that Reggie too had failed to recognise some hours earlier that day. He gave his customary shrug and picked up the phone.

Annie heard him say in a surprised tone, 'Maria? What can I do for you?' She scowled and felt her first stirrings of jealousy. 'Now? What is it about?' He continued in a resigned voice, 'Alright! Alright! Of course I'll do it. Don't worry.'

He snapped the phone shut and turned an apologetic face to Annie. Her fingernail found its way to her mouth.

He said, 'That was Maria, she wants to see me. She says it's urgent.'

'I'll bet it is!'

He grinned, amused by her attitude.

'Don't be silly. She sounded really worried over something.' His face became concerned, 'I wonder what's bothering her. She refused to tell me anything over the phone.'

Annie maintained a tight-lipped silence.

'I'll have to go to her, you know. I promised I'd help if she needed anything.'

Annie said in an overly casual voice, 'No, go ahead. I'm sure you're right and it's important.'

'Why don't you come with me?'

•

Ai Leen said in a cold, flat voice, 'We'll have to pay.'

Reggie who had recovered some of his colour said plaintively, 'But I wasn't there!'

She ignored his comment as irrelevant.

Instead she asked, 'How much money can you lay your hands on?'

Reggie shook his head, 'I'm not sure, half a million… at most.'

Ai Leen nodded. 'Alright, I can raise the rest.'

•

Stephen was in a small windowless room, sitting on one of two stainless steel chairs. Julian was slumped in the other. Pale, unshaven, uncombed, wearing grubby clothes - he was a shadow of the young, brash, confident lawyer he had been.

Stephen asked gently, 'How are you holding up?'

Julian did not reply. He buried his face in his hands and his shoulders started to shake. Stephen sat quietly and let the storm of despair wash over his colleague.

Finally, when he thought that the young man was more collected, he said, 'Is there anything I can do for you?'

Julian looked at him; his pale, blue eyes shining with unshed tears.

He said in a whisper, 'Tell Annie I'm sorry. I never meant to hurt her!'

'I'm sure she knows.'

•

Maria opened the front door herself. She was, as always, perfectly turned out - dressed in a pair of designer jeans, a silk shirt and open-toed stilettos. The toenails peeping out from her shoes, the fingernails on the hands that clasped one of David's hands and her lipstick were an identical shade of crimson. Nevertheless, Annie could see that all was not well with her. There was a brittle edge to her greeting and she did not seem discomfited by Annie's presence, a sure sign that Maria had a genuine cause for concern. She led them through the apartment to the sitting room. Except for the hum of the air-conditioning, the place was silent and oppressive. Even footsteps were muffled in the thick carpeting. When Annie asked after the children, she said abruptly that they were staying over at a friend's home that evening and then fell silent. It was only when they were seated and facing her expectantly that she found her voice again.

She said accusingly, 'You said you would help me with the police.'

David cast a quick glance at Annie to see if she knew what Maria was talking about. A minute shake of the head told him that she was as much in the dark as he was.

'Of course we will, Maria. I said that the firm would look after your interests as Mark's widow.'

She threw him a scornful look. 'You talk about it, but you let that man threaten me and you do nothing.'

David let his puzzlement show.

He said, 'I am not sure what you mean, Maria. Who has been threatening you?'

Maria seemed taken aback by his unfeigned ignorance of her predicament. She looked at both of them, her eyes widening.

Annie said, 'We really have no idea what you're talking about, Maria.'

She appeared finally to believe them. She clasped her hands together until her knuckles turned white. She said, 'I thought you could help me, make him change his mind…but you don't even know.'

'We may still be able to help. Just tell us what this is about,' said David.

Maria focused on the floor between her feet.

At last she said, 'The Inspector ask me to help him. When I refuse, he said he would have me deported. I have no choice. I have to think about my children!'

She looked at them, limpid eyes asking for help.

'What did he ask you to do?'

Maria pushed a lock of hair behind one ear, 'He wanted me to make a …a trap. I must call Reggie Peters. Tell him that I saw him at the office the night…the night Mark was killed. He said ask for money.'

Annie had been holding her breath. She released it slowly.

Maria continued plaintively, 'I don't understand! I thought Rahul killed Mark. Now the Inspector says it was Reggie.'

David explained, 'Some new evidence has come up.'

Maria nodded, 'Yes, he said that woman, Ai Leen, who looks at me as if *I* am the slut, she is the slut!'

Maria could not keep an air of smug triumph out of her voice when she mentioned Ai Leen's fall from grace. Annie did not blame her.

She continued, 'The Inspector said Mark knew and so Reggie killed him.' She shrugged dismissively, 'Me, I don't see the problem. She got what she wanted, he got what he wanted…why kill Mark?'

David asked, 'And you agreed to try and blackmail Reggie?'

'Agree? I have done it!'

Annie exclaimed, 'You have called him already?'

Maria scowled at her, 'That's what I said.'

'But what did you say? What did *he* say?' asked David.

Maria was enjoying herself now. She had the undivided attention of her audience.

She said, 'I call him. I ask him for a million dollars or I tell the police he was there that night. He call me a liar. He said if I tell them that, they will know I was there…and the police will think I kill Mark because I am Filipina!'

David nodded at this logic.

'I said that he had a reason to kill Mark, I did not. He pretended he did not know what I was talking about - so I told him that I knew about him and Ai Leen.'

She continued in a frightened tone, 'He threatened me. Asked me how I knew. I said Mark told me. He asked me why I waited so long. I said I was waiting for things to be quiet. But now the police think the Indian did it. And I need money.'

Annie asked, 'Did he agree?'

Maria nodded.

'Yes! Yes, he did. He will come here tonight at eight o'clock. The police will wait for him.'

'But why have you called us?' asked David.

Maria appeared to deflate. The excitement of telling her story, which had propped her up and made her eyes flash, was over.

She said in a small voice, 'I am afraid. He killed Mark. Maybe he will kill me!'

-twenty five-

'Any person who without lawful excuse, the onus of proving which shall be on such person, in any security area carries or has in his possession or under his control —
(a) any firearm without lawful authority therefor; or
(b) any ammunition or explosive without lawful authority therefor,
shall be guilty of an offence under this Part and shall be liable on conviction to be punished with death.'
Section 58, Internal Security Act, Chapter 143

Inspector Singh was pleased with himself. He sat in the staff canteen at the police station headquarters, munching on fried noodles and sipping his Coke. He had just assured his superiors that he had the Thompson matter well in hand and hinted that a solution was within his grasp. He had declined to elaborate on the details, suggesting that there would be time enough for that after the success of what he termed 'operational tactics'. The men in suits had heard and understood this to be a hint that they were better off remaining in ignorance until the matter had reached a successful conclusion. If it did not, then the tactics being employed could be criticised without the embarrassment of prior knowledge. This mutual understanding had worked well in the past, allowing the Inspector the free hand that he insisted on while reserving the right to hang him out to dry if it were necessary. The Inspector was not worried about failure. He was reasonably confident that he had all the angles covered. His main worry had been that Maria would not come up to snuff. But she had, with a little gentle persuasion, put on a performance of a lifetime and it looked like Reggie Peters was well and truly hooked.

The rendezvous was for eight that evening. His men would be in place an hour and a half before. He himself with a small complement of men would be hidden in the house. Maria would be wired for sound. He had been willing to leave a guard with Maria throughout but she had turned him down. She did not want the police in the house until she had made arrangements for the children to leave. He recognised that there was a danger that a man who had already killed two people might not hesitate to go for his hattrick. But he was optimistic that he would be able to intervene in a sufficiently timely manner to prevent more bloodshed. And if by some chance he was wrong, he would have some good eyewitness evidence of the third murder. He knew that Maria was not enthusiastic about the plan. The Inspector, weighing up his options, felt quite comfortable with his decision. He did not shirk from difficult choices where he felt that the overall benefits outweighed the risks.

Maria's immediate audience was more sympathetic. David was genuinely angry that the Inspector had adopted his plan without any consultation with them and bullied Maria into going along.
Annie asked tentatively, 'What should we do, do you think? Ask the Inspector to call the whole thing off?'
David looked thoughtful. 'I'm not sure the die isn't cast,' he said.

'What do you mean?' asked Maria, her eyes darting back and forth between her two visitors, like someone watching a table tennis match in fast forward.

David explained, 'Well, you've already called Reggie...I am not sure we can undo that. If we postpone the appointment, it will make him more dangerous. If we tell him it was a set up, God knows what he will do. One thing is for sure, we'll never get him for the murders!'

Annie was growing angry, 'So, what are you suggesting? That we go ahead with this plan? What's to stop him walking in and killing Maria?'

Maria made a sound somewhere between a squeak and a moan.

David said, 'Don't worry! We won't let that happen.'

A loud knocking at the front door stopped him uttering his next few words. All three reacted with varying degrees of shock and fright. Even David's usual calm was shaken. The noisy knocking reverberated through the house again. Maria looked like a trapped wild animal, crouching and terrified.

Annie pulled herself together and said, 'It must be the police.'

David let a small sigh of relief escape him. 'You're right,' he exclaimed. 'And we can take up this plan with the Inspector.'

Maria had risen to her feet. Now she tottered to the heavy curtains, and shifting them, tried to peer through the crack at her visitors. She leapt backwards, away from the curtains, caught her heels in the heavy pile carpet and fell to the ground. David and Annie rushed to help her. Her eyes were wide with fright. She was scrambling to get up, so afraid that she could not find her balance. David helped her up gently and she grabbed his arm with nails like talons.

She said in a choked whisper, 'It's him!'

'Reggie?'

She nodded blindly, still gripping onto David's arm as

if it was her lifeline.

Annie asked, 'Are you sure?'

Maria nodded again and then said in the same strained undertone, 'She's there too.'

'Who?' asked the others with one voice.

'Ai Leen!'

Annie's mind worked quickly. 'He must be trying to explain himself. He's brought Ai Leen to make it clear that whatever they agreed to between them isn't a motive for murder.'

David nodded slowly, 'At least he can't be planning any violence if he's brought her with him.'

Maria, understandably less easily reassured, hissed, 'Maybe he will kill us all!'

David smiled at her, 'Too many bodies,' he said. 'He won't take the risk.'

Annie said briskly, 'We have to decide what to do. They won't wait much longer.'

A fresh bout of knocking emphasised her words. David's jaw hardened. He looked around the room.

'Where does that door lead?' he asked Maria.

She looked confused but said, 'Another room, Mark's old study.'

David said, 'Ok, here's the plan. You let them in.'

Maria took a step back shaking her head frantically.

He said firmly, 'Listen to me. You have to do this. We must hear what they have to say. He's not here to kill anyone - I'm sure of it. He is too much of a coward. Annie and I will be in there,' he nodded in the direction of the study. 'If he does try anything,' he smiled reassuringly at Maria, 'I'll sort it out!'

Unconvinced by the rhetoric but overwhelmed by the stronger personality, Maria gave a mute nod. She turned to head for the front door. David and Annie let themselves into the study, leaving the door ajar and the lights switched off.

Reggie and Ai Leen walked into the room, following

hard on the heels of Maria. Reggie was sweating. His stentorian breathing could be heard in the adjoining room. Ai Leen looked calm and collected, a well-dressed woman paying a social visit to an acquaintance. She gave no sign that the nature of their errand was unusual. Maria indicated to them that they were to sit down which they both did. Reggie put down the briefcase he had been carrying but Ai Leen kept her capacious handbag on her lap.

Maria said, 'You are early, I do not understand this. Also I do not understand why you bring her,' she nodded scornfully at Ai Leen, her remarks directed at Reggie.

Ai Leen showed no sign that she had heard the contempt in Maria's voice.

Reggie cleared his throat and said, 'I needed a chance to talk to you. I could not bear to wait.'

At the sound of his voice, Annie gave a start. David squeezed her shoulder warningly.

Maria said rudely, 'I have nothing to say to you. I have said it all. Now I want the money.'

'Look Maria, we brought the money.' Reggie gestured to the briefcase at his feet.

'All of it?' asked Maria. 'Then you can go.'

Reggie said, 'But I don't understand. Why are you saying you saw me at the office? I was not there. I did not kill Mark!'

Maria looked at him in disgust. He was not an impressive sight. Overweight, crumpled and afraid.

She said, 'Of course you killed him. To keep your dirty little secret.'

Ai Leen said conversationally, 'Actually, Reggie is right. He didn't kill Mark.'

It took a second for the import of her words to sink in - her tone was so commonplace.

Reggie said thankfully, 'You believe me!'

Maria, more attune to hidden meanings, asked, 'Why do you say that?'

Ai Leen reached into her bag and pulled out a serviceable looking handgun that she waved casually in the direction of the two other people in the room.

'I killed Mark.'

'What?' shouted Reggie.

Ai Leen said evenly, 'I killed Mark. He found out about us. Heard me talking to you on the phone that afternoon apparently. He called the partners' meeting. I came in early to try and reason with him. He refused to be reasonable, so I wrote out a resignation letter on the spot. I went around the desk to show it to him. While he was looking at it, I hit him with the paperweight on his desk. I was not sure he was dead at first. So I kept hitting him until I was sure.'

She rounded on Maria, 'How did you find out about Reggie and me? Did Mark tell you?'

Maria, well briefed, nodded dumbly, never taking her eyes off the gun.

She said in a whisper, 'What are you going to do with that gun?'

In the same conversational tone, Ai Leen said, 'I need a way out. I thought the police were set on Rahul. But if the police find out about my arrangement with him,' she nodded at Reggie, 'there might be doubt. Reggie here may be ungentlemanly enough to suggest it was my idea that I prostitute myself for the partnership.'

Reggie said feebly, 'But it was your idea…'

She looked at him in contempt. 'You're such a big, brave man, aren't you? Look at you, you pathetic bastard! You make me sick.'

She continued in her strangely measured tone. 'I think it was a mistake to kill Mark. I should have brazened it out. Blamed you. Sued the firm for harassment and moved on. But I panicked. Then I had to kill Rahul. And now…and now I have to kill the two of you. The only question is, do I make it look like you killed each other or is murder and suicide a better idea?'

She dug in her handbag again and came out with a smaller version of the first gun.

She said brightly, 'See, I even have a gun for each of you.'

Maria spat her words out. 'You are mad!'

Ai Leen shrugged, 'I don't think so. You've just made things easy for me. Before your blackmail attempt, I was in a tight spot. This bastard was making my life hell. I couldn't kill him…that would shift the spotlight from Rahul. I could not bear any more meetings at the Fullerton… with this…this filth!' The mask was slipping.

Ai Leen shook her head in disbelief. 'I even thought I would have to tell the partnership that he forced me to sleep with him, just to end his hold over me. But you've solved my problems for me.'

'What are you going to do?' asked Reggie in a tired voice. He was almost resigned to his fate. Grateful that there was going to be an end to the horror of the last few weeks.

'Kill you,' she said and lifted the gun.

As she pointed the gun squarely at his chest, David burst out of the side door, accompanied by a frantic yell from Annie. The gun shook in Ai Leen's hand and went off. Reggie fell to his knees, and then keeled over clutching his stomach. Nobody spared him a glance. David dived for Ai Leen's gun hand as she swivelled round to face him. He reached her as the gun went off and knocked it out of her hand. In the next instant, he was on the ground clutching his shoulder. Blood oozed through his fingers. The gun slithered under the couch. Ai Leen made a dive to retrieve it. David tried weakly to regain his feet. Annie, who had been too shocked to move, saw the danger and entered the fray. She launched herself at Ai Leen and knocked her away from her target. But Ai Leen was now fighting like a madwoman. She lashed out at Annie with her feet, catching her sharply on the elbow. Annie clutched her arm and doubled over in pain. Ai Leen tore into her, kicking, scratching and screaming. No one noticed a pounding on the front door. David had reached the couch but now he turned back to go to Annie's aid.

Suddenly, a shot rang through the air and was echoed by a second shot somewhere in the distance. Everyone froze. A tableau of violence. Maria was holding the second gun, pointing it at Ai Leen. Her survival instinct in better shape than the rest, she had remembered it while the rest fought over the first weapon. The sound of heavy feet pounded along the corridor and Inspector Singh burst into the room, gasping for breath. He explained later that he had arrived as planned to take up his position, only to hear shots from within. When there was no response to the pounding on the door, he had shot out the lock, hence the weirdly echoing second shot. He was much inclined to arrest the only person holding a gun, Maria. A brief explanation from David, his face drawn with pain, had set him right.

Medical personnel arrived a few moments later, the Inspector having had the forethought to call for their help when he had first heard gunshots. Reggie was dead, unmourned by those present. David had a clean, if copiously bleeding, shoulder wound, the bullet having passed right through him and embedded itself in the opposite wall. Annie was white faced with pain and a quick examination revealed that Ai Leen's well-aimed kick had broken her elbow. Maria was physically unhurt although the shock of the last hour would take a while to wear off. Ai Leen herself was silent and brooding, flashing those present a venomous look as she was escorted out. She hesitated as she passed Reggie's body and Annie had the feeling she was debating whether to give it a good kick. She desisted and walked out the door.

The Inspector looked sheepish but pleased with the outcome. He had found his man, or woman, albeit after setting a trap for the wrong person and arriving late for the dénouement. He was already debating how to put an acceptable gloss on events in his written report. David was led protesting to an ambulance. Annie rode with him, her arm in a temporary splint. She clutched his good hand with her good hand and was grateful that there were no potholes on Singapore roads.

-twenty six-

'No person shall be deprived of his life or personal liberty save in accordance with law.'
Section 9, Constitution of the Republic of Singapore

Two months later, Annie lay back on a deck chair, sipping a frozen strawberry margarita and watching the sun set, in a mosaic of pink, purple and blues, over the South China Sea. David reclined on the adjacent chair. He was asleep, a half pint of beer next to the limp hand dangling over the side of the chair. It was their third sunset in a row and David had become accustomed to such splendour.

Ai Leen was still in jail awaiting trial. They were expected to testify in the next few months. Annie grinned when she remembered the Inspector's insistence that he had suspicions about Ai Leen all along. David had gone as far as to suggest that he too had wondered in the early days about Ai Leen, but had dismissed her as a possible suspect because of the lack of any motive. When Annie questioned this rash of hindsight, he said that he had based his original suspicion on the record of Mark's last calls. The Inspector had nodded, understanding on his chubby face. Annie had remained puzzled.

'He called her last,' David explained. 'I was sure that he would have called the subject of the partners' meeting first or last. It's human nature to get something over with or avoid it to the last possible moment. And it stood to reason that whoever the meeting was about, that's who killed him. But when no motive turned up, I assumed I was wrong.'

'Whom did he call first?' asked Annie.

'You!'

Annie had resigned from the firm. She had stayed to attend Rahul's funeral and then packed her bags. She found herself unable to contemplate going back to her old life. Stephen had been disappointed but unsurprised and assured her of her place if she ever changed her mind. Julian had also 'resigned'. He had paid over all the money he had made to charity. Annie had refused to co-operate with the Inspector over charging Julian with the attack on herself. Without her evidence, he had agreed to drop the charges as long as Julian would leave the country immediately. Julian had been delighted to catch the next plane home, returning to England a subdued man. David had protested strongly over her decision but when he saw that her mind was made up, agreed. Her thoughts back where they started on the man by her side, she looked at him once more. And then setting the margarita down on the table beside her and settling back in her chair, she too closed her eyes.

•

The black hearse drove slowly towards the cemetery. A single wreath lay against a polished wooden coffin. Corporal Fong, as the only son of the deceased, sat in the hearse next to the coffin. He held a lit joss stick, representing the soul of his father - his responsibility for the final leg of the journey. His father had been as a child in his care; it seemed appropriate that he should be his guardian now.

A small van followed the hearse. It was piled high with essentials that the dead man needed for his journey into the hereafter; a large car made of coloured paper wrapped round a wire frame, a few oversized replica notes, like the fake cheques used to highlight corporate generosity after disaster, all for large sums of money. Corporal Fong had not wanted these trappings of exaggerated wealth. His father had been a simple man and would undoubtedly have preferred a modest departure. His mother, however, had insisted. Now that he was a Sergeant, she said, so rapidly promoted as to be the envy of his peers, his father should have a commensurate status. He had agreed.

His promotion meant less to him than the presence of Inspector Singh in one of the cars in the procession following slowly after the hearse. There had been no words of praise, no nod of appreciation at the end of the Thompson case. He had been re-assigned to another investigation. The Inspector had gone on leave. And then, out of the blue, the letter recommending his promotion had landed on his desk. And now, this final mark of recognition and respect. He mourned the passing of his father. He would burn his burial clothes, wear a black patch on his sleeve for a hundred days, worship an ancestral tablet and miss his father for the rest of his life. But he had the confidence now that his father would have been proud of the man and police officer he had become.

about the author

S Mahadevan Flint lives in Singapore with her husband and two children. She began her career in law in Malaysia and worked at an international law firm in Singapore before resigning to stay at home with her two children.

She has also taught law at the National University of Singapore.

'Partners in Crime' is her first novel.